DOUBLE BLIND

A Mystery Thriller

By Jim Ellis

To Mom, Dad, and Sharon

And all the other families
who helped make me who I am

Chapter 1

I got up to stretch my legs again. My surgically repaired left knee groaned in complaint. I peered through an opening in the drapes and saw the silhouette of pine trees. The sun was still hiding below the horizon, but its light was beginning to arrive. I opened the drapes to reveal a monochromatic view.

Grey and somber. *Perfect.*

"It's morning," I said, mostly to myself.

"You have someplace to be, Hughes?" Hatch grumbled.

"No, nothing like that," I lied.

To be honest, I was getting pretty impatient. My girl, Nina, had vanished over 15 hours ago. I had nothing left to tell the cops. I wanted a couple of hours of sleep. I wanted to start searching. I needed to find Nina.

"Sit down," Ferguson growled.

I paced around the conference room, as I had several times that night. John Hatcher, the resort's Security Chief, followed me around with his eyes. Ferguson, the state cop, continued to read his latest report. Hatch and I both looked like death warmed over, but this guy seemed to be holding up pretty good. Or maybe he just dressed better.

Detective Steve Ferguson thought he was a snappy dresser. His suit was a high grade Armani knock-off. Custom-tailored, dark grey, the tie, fancy red silk, the shirt, pale grey. The problem was, he didn't have the physique for that kind of suit. He was in his mid to late 30's, about 5'-10", but he probably had a few pounds more than my 230, and he wasn't in anything near my kind of physical shape.

The room was all wood—floor, ceilings, walls, furniture. Pine, naturally. Crystal Mountain had been cut deep into the Carolina Woods. Its remote location helped to make it the resort of choice for people with a lot of money and a yearning for serious isolation.

Designed by reclusive computer wizard Max Kaiser, the resort was not only a perfect blend of mountain solitude and creature comfort, but a fine example of an environmentally sound resort. Powered by a combination of solar, wind, and water power, it was winning awards from environmentalists for its awareness and "green" operation.

The room was something of a microcosm of the entire mountain. Sophisticated, but rustic; Modern, yet old-fashioned. Not exactly what you expect from your first impression.

"Do you know anybody who might want to harm Nina Gustafsson?" Ferguson asked.

"I've been telling you all night, no."

"And we haven't believed you all night," he snarled

He stood up, and began pacing himself.

"Here's my problem. I have a resort full of beauty pageant contestants at a remote location full of security--and the only one who brings her own bodyguard gets kidnapped! Why would you be out here if she didn't suspect something?"

"Like I told you, we're old friends. The bodyguard thing was really just window dressing. I was here mostly to keep Nina company."

"You know, I saw you two when you got off the train from Pineville last Saturday," Hatch said. "You didn't seem all that friendly," reminded me.

"Nina wasn't speaking to me when we arrived," I explained. "As a matter of fact, she's been avoiding me for the last few months. She'd only been by once or twice to remind me she wasn't talking to me. Now if that ain't love…" I said with a grin.

Hatch smiled, Ferguson chuckled softly. Most guys have been there.

It had been dead silence from the time I picked Nina up in Dayton until we arrived at Crystal Mountain. Not a word. Maybe a couple of grunts, and once I could have sworn she gave me one of those nice low growls.

At the resort, they unloaded the bags from the train onto a carousel. I spotted mine and picked it up. I saw one of Nina's roll by. She looked at me with a raised eyebrow. I answered by raising my own. She watched me let the next one go by, glaring at me. I gave her my worst 'say cheese' grin. She gestured, I shook my head. She had lost the same argument at the Greensboro airport.

I walked over and stood with her, looking squarely into her almond-shaped, hazel eyes.

"Look, lady, I came here as a bodyguard, not a redcap. You gots to handle yo' own baggage."

Nina's eyes flared for a moment, then she broke out that dazzling smile. I just soaked it in, basking in the sunlight.

"Can I ask a friend for help?"

I looked over both shoulders.

"Sure, if you can find one."

Who was I kidding? Even when she was a skinny little pest of a girl, that smile was her secret weapon. Never could say no to that face.

"Help you folks with your bags?"

One of the legion of resort workers, his first load dropped off, arrived just in time to save my back.

"I hope so," I said, solemnly. "Cleopatra here brought most of the barge with her. You might need reinforcements."

He blinked twice, that same professionally blank smile on his face. Nina began pointing out her bags, which he dutifully piled on his cart. He reached for my single bag.

"That's alright," she said, grinning at me. "Mr. Hughes insists on carrying his own bag."

I looked at the half-dozen piled on the cart. Probably wouldn't have fit anyway. I smiled at Chad or Todd—whatever his name was.

"I'm paranoid," I explained. "Besides, you probably aren't certified to handle explosives."

His smile wavered, just a little unsure, before he moved off.

"I'm still mad at you," she said as we headed for the hotel desk.

"There's a shock," I answered.

"I also still love you, in spite of the fact that you're such an asshole."

"Everybody's got a weakness," I said grinning, glad she finally wanted to talk. "Besides, you know I'm right. Sooner or later, we're going to have to talk to your sister."

"No, we don't. It's over. We're not going together any more. Telling Carla will just upset her."

"Listen, if we don't tell her and she finds out, it's going get really ugly."

"She never has to find out, Trey."

"She'll eventually find out. We've never been any good at keeping secrets from one another."

"OK, when was the last time you saw Nina?" Ferguson asked

"About 11:30 this… yesterday morning. She went to her room after her dance rehearsal. I went out walking."

"Went for a walk, that's pretty convenient."

"Convenient?" I gave him a raised eyebrow.

Ferguson leaned over the table. "Somebody managed to grab this girl while you just happened to be 'conveniently' out of sight. You didn't do a very good job of earning your money… or did you? Maybe you made a few bucks by being 'conveniently' out of the way."

"Then, of course, I had to make sure the cops got called in right away, or I wouldn't be able to get myself caught. Maybe I was wrong about you—maybe you are as stupid as you look."

He reached for me across the desk, but Hatch caught him before he could reach me. I backed up, hands out.

"C'mon guys," Hatch said coolly. "It's getting late, and we're all getting a little touchy."

"Some of us more than others," I grumbled.

I wasn't really looking for a fight, but I was tired, getting pissed. I needed sleep, I wanted Nina.

"Let's go over it again," Ferguson said

"You think it's changed in the last 6 hours or so?" I snarled.

"Start from the beginning," he said.

Chapter 2

"My name is Michael J Hughes, III. My friends call me Trey…"

Start at the Beginning? Sure, why not? Maybe if I went back to the beginning, I *would* be able to figure out what happened to Nina Gustafsson and be able to find her. But where's the beginning. Should I start with Miss Gregory, my first grade teacher, whose obsession with alphabetical order placed Carla Gustafsson (Nina's sister) and I side by side at a double desk? Or should I talk about the bike ride we took that sunny Sunday when Carla and I were 12 and the accident that left her crippled, forever changing all of our lives. Nah, let's start with the day Carla came to me with this ridiculous idea.

I had to stay in Nashville a couple of days for surgery after I got my left knee unhinged playing football in the Music City Bowl. Dr. Buck did arthroscopic surgery repairing the ligaments on the 29th and I flew back to Dayton New Years Eve.

My Roommate, Offensive Tackle Alex "The Wall" Johnson, picked me up at the airport. I had barely got settled in when Carla rang the doorbell.

"What do you want little girl?" Alex said, gruffly.

"Get out of the way, you tub of lard," she said, "I'm here to see Trey." Her snarl was as phony as his growl.

"He's in the living room, reading a book, I think."

"You ought to try that yourself, no-neck."

"I do sometimes, but my mouth gets tired. I'm off to Kroger's, you need anything?"

"No thanks, Alex, I'm fine."

As her chair hummed down the hall, I called over my shoulder. "When are you two going to drop that lame comedy routine?"

"Comedy routine?" she asked innocently

"Funny."

I smiled as she wheeled around the back of the couch.

"Hey, Speedy, how you doing?"

"Trey… how's the leg?"

"Doc says the operation went well. Soft cast," I said, cheerily.

"Great, so you'll be back on your feet in a few weeks."

"Hopefully."

"Did the doctor say you're going to be OK in time for your football camp?"

The NFL scouting combine… the only chance I had to play in the pros.

"He didn't say. I'm not even thinking about it."

"Liar."

The truth was, the doc was hardly optimistic, but it really was a matter of how long it took to heal, and how much pain I could take. Things we couldn't know for weeks yet.

I shrugged. "Seriously, Carla, it's too early to worry. When Doc clears me, I can start running. When that is, I don't know. I really can't think about it until it becomes possible, or not."

"What happens if you don't get back in shape in time?"

"Then I sell used cars or something. How should I know?"

"You don't think they'll draft you anyway?"

"No," I said, flatly.

"But it's possible?"

I shook my head.

Sure, it was possible. It was possible if I was a star at Ohio State or Nebraska or USC. If I had been on ESPN a dozen or so times over the last 4 years, NFL scouts would feel like they knew me. But they were never going to take a chance on some guy from Western Ohio University unless he could prove he had two good knees.

"Wouldn't bet on it," I told her. "If they don't see I'm back to full speed…"

"Somebody will give you a chance."

"Sure." *When pigs fly.*

"If it's that important for you, how can you be so calm about it?"

"Easy. You worry enough for all of us."

"Funny."

"Can we talk about something else?"

"You just don't want to talk to me about this."

"Carla, I don't even want to *think* about this. If and when will be soon enough."

"Oh, come on, Trey, we've known each other for most of our lives. Every time you get hurt, you want to act like nothing happened. I think you just don't want to tell *me* how much it hurts."

She might have some truth there. She had enough to carry around as it was. I suppose I was always a bit sensitive, maybe even protective. On the other hand, Football is a sport of pain. If I started thinking about every hurt, even the major stuff...

"Look, kid, I know you want to share this, but you can't. It's just not worthwhile for me to whine about some injury..."

"When you're going to recover, and I'm stuck in this chair for life?"

"NO! When it doesn't get me any closer to healthy. It's just plain counterproductive, OK? Both my whining and this argument."

I knew I shouldn't have said it like that, but I wouldn't have time to feel sorry for myself if I was going to be ready for the combine at the end of February. If I was ready, I'd have a shot at becoming a pro. If it didn't work out I was still in Grad School until May. Then the summer. Plenty of time to decide what to do next.

We looked at each other for a while—angry, frustrated—we have the same argument every injury. It never gets resolved, but we love each other enough to drop it, eventually.

"You'd tell Nina." She said petulantly

I let her have her favorite last word. Both of them loved to use the other to guilt me into things. It even works, now and then.

OK, almost always.

After what seemed like weeks of uncomfortable silence, she picked up the stereo remote and turned it up a bit.

"Very nice. Who is this?"

"Thelonious Monk on the piano, John Coltrane at sax."

"Got room for me on that couch?"

"Always."

I offered to help, but she shook me off.

"Waltz of the cripples," she grumbled, as she levered herself to full height, then angled her collapse onto the couch.

"Listen," she said, shifting closer, "I just don't want you treating me like I'm delicate or something." She snuggled against me, filling my nose with her scent.

"You've never been anything like delicate. As far as I'm concerned you're always a pain in the ass."

She laughed as I swung her legs across my lap. I'd been rubbing her feet since we were kids. Stimulating circulation. A family thing.

"So, what are you guys doing tonight?" She asked.

"Your boyfriend Alex has a date, I think, why?"

"Nina and I were planning on stopping by."

"Tonight?"

"It's New Years'. I know how you hate to go out, so..."

"So you're going to bring the mountain to Mohammad?"

"Well, Nina's sure to bring hers."

"Nice talk."

"Maybe she'll even bring her new boyfriend."

"Boyfriend?" *Uh oh.*

"She's been going out with somebody, but she won't talk about it. I think she's ashamed of him for some reason. Maybe he's ugly?"

"Maybe."

Maybe it was me, I thought. *We couldn't tell you the truth, because: We love you and didn't want to risk hurting you, or maybe we were just plain cowards*. Nina and I stopped going out before Thanksgiving. It was all over, except for the guilt.

"Little sister is a grown woman, Carla, not only can she see who she wants, but she doesn't have to tell us."

"It isn't like her, though. Nina was never that good at keeping secrets. Usually she would tell one of us…"

She stopped and grinned at me.

"You know, don't you?"

I shook my head. "Oh, no you don't. Even if I knew, it's your *sister's* business. I've been down this road before with both of you."

"Oh, c'mon Trey. Just a little hint?"

"No."

"Asshole."

"Wedding off then?" I said, with a wink.

She wrinkled her nose.

"So what is it you want so badly?"

Her jaw dropped. "Who said I wanted anything?"

"Two of your favorite arguments and we barely got through the opening rounds. I figure you must want something."

"I do need a favor. Just a little one"

"How little?"

She hesitated a second. "It's not for me, it's for Nina."

"Nina?"

"My sister?"

I rolled my eyes. "I know *who* Nina, I was wondering *why* Nina. And by the way, why Nina don't ask her own damn favors?"

"She has to go to this beauty pageant in June."

"Yeah, someplace in prehistoric North Carolina, right?"

"Well, I was supposed to go with her, but I have some tests."

"Who are you trying to kid, school's out by then."

"Medical tests, stupid."

"I thought you had given up on specialists and tests."

"I guess hope springs eternal."

"Okay. So what's the favor?"

"I want you to go with Nina."

"Oh, hell no."

"Come on, Trey, at least you could think about it."

"You're right, darlin', let me think… no."

"You have to."

"No, I don't. She's a big girl. It's not like she needs somebody to hold her hand. Even if she did, there's a couple of dozen of her bimbo friends who would dance naked in the street for a chance to go with her to some beauty contest in Piney Woods, NC."

"Crystal Mountain," she corrected. I shrugged

"I thought the girls were all supposed to have female chaperones. I guarantee I'd look lousy in a dress."

"I checked the American International Beauty Contest rules. All they say is suitable escort. When they opened the contest to married women, their lawyers decided excluding husbands would be a lawsuit waiting to happen."

"I'm not marrying your sister just to keep her company, either."

"I figured you could be her bodyguard."

"Bodyguard?"

"Sure, you're a big tough guy. All you'd have to do is stand around and look pissed off—that's it! That's exactly the expression."

"Why would Sis need a bodyguard? More importantly, why do you need me to go with her?"

"I'd think you'd want to go. I mean this is every guy's fantasy, right. A week in the mountains with dozens of beautiful women?"

"Sure, with Nina around to chase 'em all off. What's really going on, Carla?"

"I just think she'd rather have you with her than any of her silly friends, wouldn't she? I noticed you two haven't been spending a lot of time together lately. It'll be a great chance for you two... I mean you still love her, don't you?"

I tried not to react. Did she know about us? Or maybe she was fishing for a reaction. Then again it could be she was just stating facts. Of course I loved Nina, but did I still *love* her? Carla kept going.

"...I'm not sure I can explain it, I just think... I'd just feel better if you were there, OK? Please, Trey, just promise me you'll at least think about it."

"Wait a minute! Hatch said. "You didn't tell us anything like that before. You never said anything about her warning you."

"I never thought of it as any kind of warning. She was just being mysterious. It was like I said; Carla was trying to convince me to come."

"Did Carla Gustafsson say why she thought you should be here?"

"No."

"But you agreed?"

I shook my head. "Not right away. I said I'd think about it because I wanted to find a way to get Carla to take 'no' for an answer."

"So why did you come?"

"Nina."

"Nina Gustafsson asked you to be her bodyguard?"

"Not exactly." I picked up an empty carafe and shook it. "Can we get some more coffee?"

"Can we stick to the subject?" Ferguson said, impatiently. "Did Nina invite you or not?"

"I signed on to Carla's plan because it was the only way to get Nina to talk to me. She stopped talking to me before Christmas. I thought a week or so in the mountains would give us a chance to make peace."

"I thought," Hatch said, "you were involved with the older sister, Carla? This whole thing was her idea, right?"

"It's a lot more complicated than you think. I've known them both for years."

"But which one... I mean, who are you actually involved with?"

Oh yeah, like I *know.*

"I've known Carla longer, and we're more like two sides of the same coin. We think in sync sometimes—you know, finish each other's sentences—stuff like that. On the other hand Nina…"

"Is better looking," Ferguson grumbled. "Can we get back to today's business? Which one invited you?"

"…Nina's more unpredictable, spontaneous. She makes me get out and do things."

"Great. Now can you answer the goddamned question?"

I grinned at Ferguson. I guess I got his goat again.

"Like I said earlier, Nina and I split up back around Thanksgiving, and she was still trying to avoid me. So I took the girls up on their offer."

"You figured she couldn't get away from you up here?"

I smiled ruefully.

"I figured if we could be in one place long enough, she'd eventually get back to talking to me."

"Did it work?"

"We were talking."

"But you still weren't getting along?"

"We were getting along, I guess, but I wouldn't say all was forgiven."

Chapter 3

A uniformed cop stuck his head in the door.

"Dr. Thomas Gustafsson is on line 2," he said.

Ferguson picked up the receiver. Spoke briefly then handed the phone over.

"He wants to talk to you."

I took a deep breath first.

"Trey, how are you? The police are not giving you trouble, are they?"

"No, I'm fine, Pop. It's just routine."

"You have still not heard from Carla?"

"No. I figure they must be keeping her at the hospital until they get the test results back."

"Hospital! What tests?"

Oh great, like he didn't have enough to worry about.

"I'm sorry, I figured she would have told you. That's why she didn't come with Nina—she was going to have some kind of tests."

"What kind of tests, what hospital?"

"She didn't say. That's why A J was trying to find you earlier. We were hoping she gave you her hospital information."

"Why wouldn't she have told me?"

"Got me."

"Should I come there?"

"I wouldn't rush cross-country just yet. If either of your wayward daughters surface, they will probably call you out there, first. I'm still kind of hoping Nina will turn up on her own."

"But you don't think so?"

"No, sir. She didn't have any reason to go and there isn't much else around here."

"Did you two fight?"

I smiled. "No more than usual."

"OK, if we do not find her tomorrow I'll move up my itinerary."

"OK, Pop. I'll keep in touch."
"You sound tired, son. Get some sleep."
"Thanks, Dad."
He chuckled as he hung up.
"Well," Ferguson said, "I guess that's it for tonight."
"See you tomorrow," Hatch joked.
As I wandered toward my room, I found myself racking my brain. Why wouldn't Carla tell her dad about her tests? What could have happened to Nina? I was going to kill that girl when I see her again. *Either one. Both.* I miss her. I had to search, but I had to sleep. If that girl was just bailing out on this damn pageant I was really going to be pissed.
I unlocked the door and stretched out on top of the bed. Just a little nap.
The phone rang. I must have slept, because I wasn't awake, yet. I picked up the phone.
"Trey." I answered.
"Morning," AJ grunted. "We have a problem. Carla's really missing. I tried her place several times, then tried a few of her friends. I even called Professor G out in Arizona."
"Yeah, I've talked to him already. I figure she's probably still in the hospital waiting on her test results."
"I thought of that, too. I tried every hospital here and down in Cincinnati...she's not in any local hospital. Then I went by her house. Her car's still there."
"Then where is she?"
"Good question."
She might have had to go out of town for her tests, but it would have been nice if she had told somebody. I assumed she had somebody with her, but I couldn't think of anybody she might have asked. Where was she? Louisville, Cleveland, Indianapolis, Minnesota. There were dozens of hospitals around the country doing all kinds of specialized neurological research. I had to figure out some way of narrowing the field.
Maybe her doctor could help. What was his name? Curtis? Cooper?
"Listen, AJ, keep an eye out for her, will you?"
"Sure, still no sign of wife #2?"
"Not yet."
"I'll keep my ear to the ground."

"Thanks, brother."

"Careful, you got enough family already. Later, Trey."

I slammed the phone after he hung up. Why did I let Carla pull this stunt without at least letting me in on the details of her treatment?

On the other hand, what was I going to say to her? I mean she asked me to keep an eye on Nina and I failed miserably. If anything happened to her, how could she ever forgive me? Those two were practically inseparable. How was I ever going to face her again? Maybe Carla's disappearance wasn't so bad. Maybe by the time I tracked her down, I'll have found Nina and know something about why this all happened.

I called Directory Assistance back home.

"I'm looking for a neurologist, maybe a neurosurgeon...on Xenia Road… Collins, Carter, Cole! That's it…"

Dr. Cole's receptionist was really quite unimpressed that I was calling long distance from North Carolina, but did agree to take my number so the doctor could call when he was free.

It was almost 10am. I guess I did get a few hours sleep; it just didn't seem like it. I took a cold shower and was getting dressed to head out for coffee when the doctor called back.

I explained who I was and that I was trying to find Carla.

"I'm sorry, Mr. Hughes, I can't really tell you anything about Ms Gustafsson's treatment. Even if you were a member of the immediate family..."

"Look, Doctor, I'm not asking you to violate any professional ethics. Nor, as much as I'd love to know, what sort of tests or treatment she is currently taking. I just need to get a message to her. Her sister is missing, and we have to find her. I can get her father to call if you're concerned about our relationship. If you're not comfortable giving me information, just give her my number and she can decide for herself to call me."

"The truth is," he responded, "I don't know myself. If she's gone for tests or treatment it wasn't under my authority."

"Did you refer her to anybody?"

"No, but she did ask for some of her records a couple of months ago. I assumed she was planning to consult a new Neurosurgeon."

"I realize you're a busy man, but if you have any idea who might know where to find her I would appreciate your help."

"I'll check with a few colleagues and see if I can help."

"Great. Thanks, doctor."

Something radical. I'll bet Carla is trying some kind of dangerous new treatment to restore the feeling in her legs. The reason she set up this thing with Nina and I was so we wouldn't be there to worry over her or, more likely, talk her out of it. Over the years, she had had several surgeries and countless treatments. All they ever seemed to do was give us false hope.

The only way to find her was going to be figuring out what kind of new idea caught her eye and tracking her down through that.

And if I had any extra time, I guess I should keep looking for Nina.

Chapter 4

I shook my head. If I was going to do anything today, I was going to have to wake up, energize. I hopped into the shower and cranked up the cold water. A few minutes later, fresh clothes on my back, I was heading to the resort's cafe for a large coffee. I allowed myself only an occasional cup when I was in training, but since my football career was over (I couldn't run at the combine—wasn't drafted), I was drinking it by the barrelful.

"Hi there," the hostess said cheerily, "one for breakfast?"

I smiled back as I considered the question. I *was* just thinking a cup of coffee on the run, but maybe a little food wouldn't be a bad idea. I was in a hurry, but to do what? Hatch and his security people had pretty much turned the place upside down searching, then the state cops came in, and were in the process of doing the same thing. If I was going to find her, I had to think of something they missed.

She turned her head slightly, her long hair braid swinging across the middle of her back. I was reminded of Carla and the waist-length hair she had until November. She never explained why she suddenly cut it off after all these years. Maybe it was the stress of law school. Her disappearance was one of several eccentric actions.

The hostess began to look a little nervous, expecting a quicker response. I finally nodded to her. Food wasn't a bad idea, and I needed to think a little, anyway.

As I followed her, I was amazed how much she reminded me of Carla. Like Carla, she was only about 5 feet (in theory), slender, and she also did that little head tilt that I find endearing. Her eyes were a darker brown, but Carla's hair was almost black to her light brown shade.

As I glanced over the menu, I considered a heavy breakfast—sausage, eggs, biscuits and gravy, maybe even hash browns—but I wasn't sure I'd be that hungry. I went with two poached eggs and a bowl of grits. As I rolled a dollop of honey into my bowl, I could almost look across the table and see Nina's nose wrinkle in disgust. She not only wouldn't eat grits, but held a grudge against anyone who would dare to eat them in her presence. I loved them and was willing to fix them some mornings just to torque her.

After breakfast, I got my large coffee and walked over to the tram station. The open courtyard of the resort village was almost devoid of movement. The 'town square' was a well manicured field cris-crossed by concrete paving stamped to resemble cobblestones. The smaller buildings had kind of an old Europe feel, steep gables, wood and stucco facades. The Swiss Alps come to Carolina. The Main complex formed an 'L' on the north and west sides. At the southwest corner was a square wooden gate leading onto a series of trails heading up the mountain. Along the South face, the sleepy little shops were just beginning to bustle with bright-faced shopkeepers checking their displays and sweeping the doorways. The upper floors were residences for the resort workers.

A trio of giggling girls in chic sweatsuits were arm-in-arm leaving *La Boheme,* the French restaurant after breakfast. *Parlez-vous grits?* At the southeast corner, next to the pizzeria, was another set of trails, headed downhill. The Eastern side of the square was given over to the panoramic view down the mountain. Along the eastern corner of the building stood the tram platform.

A uniformed security guard stood near the kiosk at the near end of the platform. His name was Brad, or maybe Bryce.

"Howdy," I said.

"Still looking for your girl," he said, halfway between a statement and a question.

"Still looking."

"You don't suppose she just went to Pineville?" he asked, hopefully.

I shrugged. Her money and credit cards were still in the room. Not much chance she just went shopping.

"I don't understand how she could just disappear," he said. "There's no way off this mountain… I mean, without coming through here. We have men on duty at both ends *and* video surveillance, we should have spotted her. We weren't exactly looking for her until later, but I saw her the other day—no healthy guy is going to miss her, even in a crowd."

He was preaching to the choir on that. Her height, her bronze skin, her auburn hair, that impressive figure, she stopped conversation even among the beauty contestants.

"What about a helicopter?"

"Only places to land are over on top of the Auditorium or in the village square. Even if we didn't see it, we would hear it."

"No clearings in the woods?"

"A few, but it seems awfully risky to try to drop into one. Plus we still should have seen it."

"What about these walking trails?"

"None of them reach that close to town except this one on the northeast side," he indicated the point where the trail began at the end of the building. "But you'd still have to strike off through the brush. The rest all loop or run to the private villas."

"What about the private residences?"

"Not our department. Cops are out checking them, I guess."

I knew Hatch and the resort guys had done a pretty good job of searching the main complex, so it was time to play Daniel Boone.

"Which trails lead to the private homes?"

"Most of them are off that trail down at the western end of the square, but there's at least one private home accessible from each of the main trails."

"You have a trail map?"

"Sure, wouldn't want you lost, too," he said, walking toward the guard kiosk. "You might want to be careful out there. Like I said, cops everywhere and not all of them are going to be friendly."

I smiled. "I'll keep that in mind."

I started with the northeast trail, which meandered down the hill to within shouting distance of the town. As I walked along, I realized I was probably wasting time. I had been walking with Nina yesterday on one of those uphill loops on the west side. The forest was dense enough that if you wandered too far from the trail you could probably get good and lost, but it would take a bloodhound or a Cherokee Indian to find you. Being neither, how was I going to spot signs of someone jumping the trail? I should head back after checking this private home and take the tram to Pineville, see if I can pick up the trail there.

It made more sense to get her off the mountain. The first thing the cops were going to do was turn the place upside down. Getting her into town and out of sight seemed to make sense, but how would you get her down? Like the guy said, security at both ends and video. Somebody would have noticed her.

Video? I wondered if anyone checked with the TV crew. I remember seeing a couple of people shooting pictures for next weekend's TV broadcast. Maybe they shot something useful.

Born and raised in the city, you wouldn't think I'd have any great forest sense, but I knew someone was in the woods behind me to my left. I stopped and turned enough to spot him, but didn't face him directly. I saw him moving right after he snapped a twig. He was a tall, skinny fellow with stringy blond hair. Faded jeans and T-shirt with a lightweight brown camouflage jacket. He held a pair of well-used field glasses to his eyes as he wound through the trees onto the trail. He lowered the glasses and grinned.

I smiled back as he held a finger to his lips, then followed his gaze into the tree.

"*Cyanocitta Cristata,*" he said, emphatically.

"Back home, we call them Blue Jays," I answered. "A female I'd guess by the dull color. They're pretty common back home in Ohio, too."

He held out his hands in mock surrender. He was no bird watcher.

"You got me," he acknowledged. "I'm really out here looking for the missing girl… you a cop?"

"No a friend, Trey Hughes."

"Lonnie Mc Coy," he offered a hand. "Trey?"

"Michael III. Trey is a nickname. I take it you live out here?"

"Mama and I have a place up the hill a piece," he said. "We heard this morning about the missing girl, so I thought I'd take a look around—for what it's worth."

"You don't think they could have gotten her out this way?"

"Got her out? They told us the girl might be lost, wandered off. You think she's been abducted?"

"Trust me; Nina's not the type to wander off into the woods." *Alone at least.*

"Well, even if she did, look around. Ten, fifteen feet off this trail you'd never see her. Besides those resort guys have these trails covered. Here, take these," he said handing me the glasses.

I followed his gesture as he pointed toward the top of a nearby tree. Even without the glasses, I could see the metal arm holding a small security camera out to the edge of an upper limb.

"All the trails have video surveillance?"

"Of course they do. Bunch of nosy damned snoops," he fumed.

"Do they record all these cameras?" I asked, as I used the glasses to follow the wire through the trees as far as I could go. I thought about the walk I took with Nina a couple of days ago. We had made peace and things got kind of cozy. We found a little clearing and one thing led to another… Nina would have been furious if she had found out.

"Does it look like I run their fucking cameras?" Obviously the video cameras on the trail were a sore spot. "Ask them nosy peckerheads up there. I figure they wired the whole mountain just to get dirt on people."

"I'll be damned." The security guy I was talking to hadn't said anything about the video cameras covering the trail. I was going have to find out what else he wasn't telling me.

"If you're thinking they got her off the mountain on foot I suppose they *could* have come this way. C'mon son, I'll show you the end of the trail." Lonnie was probably only in his forties, but it seemed like he was already old in a lot of ways.

I followed him down the hill on foot, fighting two vague feelings. The first was a sense that someone was following us. At first, I was thinking it was the knowledge of the video cameras, but I became more certain as it went along. The second thing was a vague suspicion I had seen Lonnie before.

"You two are from Ohio, huh?" Lonnie asked as we neared the bottom.

"Dayton."

"No foolin'! I worked in Cincinnati for a while."

"We're going to school at Western Ohio." I explained.

He didn't have to point out where the trail to town was. I surprised us both by noticing it.

It was covered in grass and wasn't very wide, but it was clearly worn. The ground was dry, solid. I crouched down, looking for footprints, but between the surface, and the fact that I had no idea what type of shoeprint to look for, it was actually a little silly.

"Just follow it for a couple of hundred yards. It'll run into a trail like this one heading on into town. I hope you find that girl OK. Also stay clear of the cops! Some of them will get pretty ugly if they think you're stealing the credit from them."

"Yeah, thanks Lonnie."

I stood up, turning to speak to him and he had disappeared.

Chapter 5

Lonnie proved to be quite the comedian. The path he showed me was narrow, but well worn enough; he just neglected to mention that the last half of it was almost vertical. Narrow steps notched into the granite face of about a hundred feet of drop. I almost stumbled and went down face first.

Catching myself, I stopped to admire the view. From the top of those stairs, you could see the entire town. Pineville was barely on the map before Kaiser opened his headquarters and they built the resort. At the foot of the ridge was a wooded park with several trails meandering through. Along the far edge of the park was the tram station. A row of very nice houses ran parallel to the face of the ridge across the street from the park. A couple of streets over, a cluster of two and three-story brick buildings circled the Town Square, with its obligatory Confederate on horseback. In the other three directions, on evenly spaced tree-lined streets were more houses. Off toward the southeast corner was the Methodist church. Its steeple the highest point in Pineville. It could have easily been Bellfontaine, or Rossburg, any one of half a dozen wide spots in the road back home in Ohio. And just like those other sleepy little towns, there was also the new town. Along the southern edge of a town unchanged since the mid 19th century, a three-lane ribbon of asphalt rolled from the parking lot at the station southeastward across a little hogback toward the nearby highway. From there the world became your oyster, taking you to Asheville and points East, or across the Smoky Mountains to Knoxville, Tennessee and Interstate 75. I laughed when I saw the red and yellow arches along the road announcing the presence of America's ubiquitous fast food restaurant.

On out toward the south was a brand new town with pre-fab and manufactured houses sliding on down the valley. In the midst of this new town was a huge monolith of glass and steel. Kaiser Electronics dominated the new version of Pineville, surrounded by subdivisions and 7-elevens, and of course, Wal-Mart.

I looked carefully at the steps. Unless you were a cat, or a bighorn sheep, you couldn't risk going down this ridge after dark. It was, however, a pretty easy thing in the daylight and going up the hill would avoid the risk of a near-fatal face plant. It might not be the way somebody took Nina out, but it might be the way the bad guy(s) got up the mountain. I had to walk sidestep down the ridge. The footing was narrow, but pretty certain. The steps obviously predated the resort. Created as an old hunting trail, I suppose, or maybe the path to the local still. Come to think of it, all the mountain paths seemed pretty worn, too. Like the new town, Crystal Mountain was simply tacked on, grafted to existing reality.

Ignoring the new town for a moment, I walked toward the square. I landed at the corner of Police Station and Library and was just about to cross over for the library when Ferguson rounded the corner with the local Police Chief.

"What the hell are you doing here?" He growled.

"Seemed like a good day for a walk," I answered.

"You get any sleep?" he asked, almost as if he cared.

"You mean, while we were talking last night?"

"You're just a funny guy aren't you?" He introduced me to Chief John Longstreet.

"Are you related to the Civil War general?" I asked, as I held out my hand for shaking.

"Maybe. Longstreet Park here is named after one of the founders of the town. I'm related to *him*, but we're not sure he's related to the general."

He was in his mid thirties. Probably a former High School star. A year or two of community college and he becomes a cop. His former popularity helps him climb to the top of the small force. Like Ferguson, he had put on a few pounds since his athletic days. In a small town like this, the fastest thing he would probably have to chase is a donut.

Ferguson glared at me. "We don't need you down here to join the search. We already have enough people on the job. Maybe you'd do better staying near the phone in case she decides to call."

I held up my cell phone and raised my left eyebrow.

"Look, Hughes," he said, as if he was my pal. "I know you're worried about your girlfriend, but we won't be able to find her if we're busy tripping over you. You need to stay out of the way. Leave this to the professionals. I don't want you fouling up my case."

"Why don't you jump off that bridge if we get to it?" I snapped. "I give less than a damn about your case if I get Nina back."

"I have the authority to make your life miserable if you go fucking around in this investigation. I've just seen the jail here. There's plenty of room for you."

"If you want to arrest me for sightseeing, go ahead. I know several lawyers."

"Just stay out of my way." He elbowed past me and stalked down the street.

“Don’t sweat Ferguson,” Longstreet said, cheerily, “He’s full of sound and fury, but he’s a fair man.”

I shrugged. It didn’t really matter. He’d have to either jail me or shoot me to stop me.

“He’s just frustrated to be back here,” he said. “Before he became a hotshot State investigator, Ferguson had my job. He hated it around here and hoped to end up in Charlotte, Raleigh or at least Greensboro. Instead, he gets posted just down the road in Asheville. Now, he gets his first major case, sure to get him some attention, but he ends up back here. Come on inside, I can buy you a cup of lousy coffee.”

I figured he was going to pump me for information. Maybe I could get a little out of him. Either way, making nice with the local police chief can’t be a bad thing.

It wasn’t good, but lousy was a bit too harsh for the coffee. I got a cursory tour, then a comfortable chair in his office.

"You ever consider being a cop?" he asked, smiling

"No," I said, without malice.

He stood up and walked to the map on the wall.

"The way I see it, this is a police chief's nightmare. Everybody has their own agenda. Crystal Mountain is looking to avoid liability. We're the closest law enforcement, and the command post for the search, but since the resort is unincorporated, we have no jurisdiction. The county sheriff has authority, but he knows when to duck. The state police, personified by our friend Ferguson, are ramrodding this thing, but he’s looking to make a name for himself using *my* officers. If we don't find her in 72 hours or we prove she was kidnapped, the FBI takes over and it gets even worse. They're going to treat me like some kind of inept yokel and it's my town! You can see how embarrassing it would be for somebody to find her here, and I'm not involved."

I smiled a bit at him, but said nothing.

Guilt twisted the corner of his mouth. "OK, I suppose I have a bit of ambition as well. Hey, I don't plan to be chief here forever. Solving a case like this and the publicity it'll draw might help me move on, too."

"All the way to Asheville," I said, grinning.

"Yeah, maybe," he chuckled. "Anyway, I don't have any authority outside of town, but it's OK with us here if you run around asking a few questions. I'll be glad to let you know anything about our town. I'm just asking you to let me know if you find anything."

A good deal for him. I was going to be asking questions anyway. He gets an investigator for nothing. I, on the other hand, can only get directions. If anything went wrong, like I was caught or killed, all he had to do was disavow all knowledge.

I didn't care. Nina was all that mattered.

"I do have one question," I said. "Where does a fellow go to rent a car?"

Roger's Recks sat at the corner of progress and tradition. Down Washington Street from the police station, at the corner of the new main road. A Gas station and two-bay garage that might have been there as far back as the thirties. The corner office and asphalt paving were more modern touches. Around the corner, along the main road were about a dozen cars of varying age.

The woman was a short dark-skinned black woman, large, but not fat. She wore a conservative dark blue dress. Her round face seemed ageless. She could have been anywhere from forty to eighty. Without any evidence, I figured her at or past retirement age.

"I'm going to go out on a limb," I said, grinning, "and say you're not Roger?"

"My husband went on to his reward five years ago, praise god. I'm Dinah Williams, how can I help you young man?"

I had never met this woman, but I knew her pretty well. Born and raised here in town, she was a lot like the older women at my church. Polite and patient, she carried an old wisdom beyond schools and books. She had that underlying steel of women from that generation. Never confrontational, but powerful and unyielding nonetheless. Like Grandma… or Rosa Parks.

"Yes ma'am, I understand this is the only place in town to rent a car."

"My husband, rest his soul, always had an old car or two around here for people to use if they needed one. When they built that up on the hill, we added a couple more cars. It's just been growing like a weed since then." Her eyes narrowed. "You're not just here to rent a car, are you? You're here looking for that white girl from the beauty contest."

I glanced at the floor, searching for my jaw.

"It's a small town, honey," she explained. "Everybody knows your business. Sometimes before you do."

I smiled and nodded. "She's a friend of mine,"

The lady shook her head, as if she couldn't quite understand. Miz Dinah grew up in the segregated south, a place and time when white people could be kind, helpful, civil, generous… but never friends. Although neither Nina nor I fit a strict definition of black and white, we were close enough to it for her to be skeptical.

"I was hoping she might have rented a car here. She's a tall girl, about my height, dark red hair..."

"Well she hasn't been through here. We were open from 9 till 7 yesterday and we only rented one car. Two girls, they were… well, I saw them…"

"They were… together?" I acknowledged her

She nodded.

"This is a respectable, god-fearing town; we don't have those kinds of goings-on."

Out in the open, she meant. The biggest difference between here and there is that they close the doors first here.

"What did they look like?" She eyed me severely when I asked.

"One was a little skinny thing with blonde hair the other one was taller, with dark hair cut like a man's and skit up to there."

I nodded. I'd seen them huddled together myself. The blonde was a pageant official; the raven-haired one a contestant from Quebec—friends in low places?

"Which way did they go?"

She frowned at me again. "Knoxville, I guess. Girl bought a Tennessee map. They should be back today." She smiled. "You think they saw your girlfriend?"

"No telling."

"Do you have her picture? We could put it up around town."

Now there's a bright idea. It hadn't occurred to me, of course, but then as soon as we start spreading pictures around, this town will get buried in reporters, satellite trucks, and the usual *accoutrement* of the media frenzy. As soon as that happens, the bad guys would be alerted for sure and they certainly couldn't keep her in Pineville.

"I'm sorry, I don't. But we might be circulating one a bit later. We're trying to keep things quiet for now." I said conspiratorially.

"Well..."

"Michael, Michael Hughes." Somehow my actual first name seemed necessary.

"Michael, I'll pray for the safe return of your friend."

"Thank you, ma'am." Hopefully, she'd pray for me too.

As I opened the door she called out to me, "You be careful, honey, some of these crackers down here still think its 1861."

Chapter 6

There was an official reception for the contestants and contest officials. Cocktails at 5. Assuming the joyriding girlfriends would want to take full advantage of the open bar (never a bad assumption), they would be back with time to spare. Although, if they left Knoxville at Noon, the standard check-out time, it was unlikely they'd be back before 2pm. At the very least, I had an hour and a half to kill. Time to hit the Pineville library.

The Library had probably been built at the end of the 19th century, but it was freshly retrofitted and, not surprisingly, high-tech. Kaiser had supported the library generously in both money and equipment. Many of the books were of recent vintage and the equipment was state-of-the-art. The original building was apparently not enough as signs pointed toward the section of the former Kresgee store now used as the annex. My destination, Periodicals, was on the main floor toward the back. I browsed through the racks for the *New England Journal of Medicine*, but I stopped short. A copy of the June *Ohio* Magazine—Nina's face filling the cover. I closed my eyes, hanging on to that face, reaching out trying to get some sense of her, a feeling, a thought. Some kind of re-connection. We used to do that, sometimes, seem to reach each other across distances, think together. Even an imagined clue would do some good at this point.

I jumped about a foot when the librarian spoke. I asked about the New England Journal and back copies.

"We also have the *Journal of the American Medical Association*, I'll bring that as well."

I sat at a nearby table with the couple of back issues from the rack while the librarian bustled around. I smiled at that old library, dark and closed. When I was a kid, I used to spend part of every Saturday morning in the library. If I closed my eyes I could almost hear the nasal whistle of Mrs. Johnson's breathing. The new building back home was all open space and skylit, almost like reading outdoors. I didn't realize how much I missed the old one, until now.

Mrs. J was also as sneaky as a cat on carpet. She would just scare the goo out of you when you turned around. This one had a squeaky shoe.

"Do you know what you're looking for?" She asked, hopefully.

A needle in a haystack? An honest woman? The love of my life? The truth was, I was just killing time. Without some sort of hint, I wouldn't know where Carla was if I saw it.

I explained I was looking for new treatment ideas for paralysis.

"You might want to check the Internet. There's the Miami Project, they've got a whole list of websites. You also should try the PVA, Paralyzed Veterans of America."

"Yeah, and the EPVA," I said, gruffly. "Thanks." I'd been on this road for ten years now. I knew the websites and journals by heart

It was always a little disturbing for me to research the latest developments in the fight against paralysis. It's only when I'm researching that I really think of Carla as disabled. Because I'm always with her, I never think about what it's like to *be* her. I mean we deal with practical things all the time with the chair or her crutches. Access and limits. But that's just reality.

When I get into the medical journals, I start to feel the pain and the frustration, the loss, the fear. You'd think it would be the opposite—the big picture would make me more detached, clinical.

It's funny what you remember. I can call up the entire day of that accident, if needed, but the indelible details always seem silly. Carla was the tallest back then, almost done growing. My sixth foot of growth was still waiting at Chaminade High. Nina just had to ride Carla's new bike. They were still arguing right up until the crash. We weren't going anywhere, you know, just riding.

The driver ignored the stop sign, never even slowed down. She stank of Bourbon, which didn't seem right—I always thought women got drunk on clear liquor. I just caught a glimpse of that huge car as it missed me, hit Carla square, then bounced up the concrete curb into the mailbox—a federal offense. Nina crashed into the back of the car, spinning out onto the pavement.

I threw my bike at the car, as if that would help. Carla almost seemed to be comfortable, sitting under the oak tree down the block. If her legs hadn't been twisted in the bike frame and blood all over her head, I'm not sure I would have known she was hurt.

I wrapped her head with my shirt and covered her with my new jacket. I had been saving my money from shoveling snow and doing odd jobs to get a really cool Reds jacket that I knew I would never bring myself to wear again. As I started to knock on the door of the corner house, a woman rushed out of the house next door with blankets.

The woman in the car wore this ridiculous pink hat. She just sat there until the police arrived.

Don't blame me, the car bumper said, *I voted for Anderson.*

It never fails. Every time I do this stuff, my damn eyes start watering. Some kind of allergy I guess. The cell phone rattled my leg. I answered in a low voice as I walked out to sit at the top of the cement steps. It was AJ.

"Two things. First, somebody broke into the girls' apartment last night."

"How did you know it was last night? We've been gone since Saturday."

"I looked in yesterday. Everything looked normal."

I made a note to ask him one day how he ended up with his own key to Carla and Nina's, but we had more important issues.

"What were they looking for?"

"They got the TV, Stereo and both computers. They also trashed the place and might have got some small stuff. I was going to call the cops, but figured I'd see what you think."

"No reason not to. You know if Carla was going to be gone for a while, she might have taken her laptop…"

"Right with you, Sherlock. I'll e-mail her right away."

"You said two things."

"What? Oh, you're on Headline News."

"You mean the story."

"I mean pictures. You and Nina grinning and laughing. She was wearing that Blue oriental deal she was showing off last week. Somebody got you on tape before she disappeared."

"Oh, great. It ought to hit the fan now."

"Not necessarily a bad thing. More eyes to look for her."

"Easy for you. You don't have to trip over the reporters, not to mention the *Federales.*"

"Sorry, but you're the one that hired out as a bodyguard."

"Ha, fucking, ha. Next time call with good news, huh?"

"See ya, Trey."

I looked out on the town square. A pair of News satellite trucks had parked on the opposite side. A pair of balding technicians were each rolling out cable so their cameras could have the best angle to put the Old Confederate right behind their own Empty Heads.

Like things weren't complicated enough.

Chapter 7

Ferguson was holding an impromptu press conference in front of the Tram station. A dozen or so intrepid journalists had made it from Knoxville and Asheville already with more on the way. By evening we'd have NBC, CBS, CNN—The whole alphabet soup. And then, of course, the FBI.

There was also huge crowd (for these parts) scattered around the station, some waiting for the next tram, others just curious. Having just dropped off their car, our two girlfriends were in the crowd somewhere.

"...Actually, all we have so far is that Nina Gustafsson has not been seen since yesterday about noon. There are no clear signs of violence, but as I already said, we are keeping our options open."

"Is it true that she was under death threats?" A TV guy asked, his hair dark and perfect.

"We have no knowledge of any threat at all against Miss Gustafsson."

"Isn't it true she brought a bodyguard? Wouldn't she have to have been afraid of something?" A singularly ugly woman. Newspaper or radio.

"The bodyguard is apparently also a family friend," He spotted me and glared. "We think he may have been here simply as a companion." Several made notes to ask the bodyguard later.

"What about the pageant officials? Had they received any threats?" TV reporter, a bit skinny, the same wild and curly red style Nina usually lived in. Fake. The color anyway.

"Not that I know of." He said, way too quickly.

"Could this be a publicity stunt?" A blond fellow. "I mean ratings for Miss America have been terrible. Could this contest be trying to drum up a little attention? I mean, rumor has it this girl has already been replaced."

Ferguson hesitated. "Well… we have to investigate as if there was a crime involved. It's pointless to speculate. But like I said we have no evidence of a crime at this point."

"But it's possible?"

"Like I said, we have no hard evidence of a crime, yet."

That son of a bitch! I surely wasn't going to let him get away with that.

"Isn't it true her money and ID were found in her room?" I asked from the spectators.

That caused a commotion, but the only reporter who saw me when I spoke was our little redhead. Ferguson glared furiously.

"Like I said, we haven't ruled out any possibilities."

"Why are they refusing to let us up the mountain?" Perfect Hair asked. "They can't keep us out forever."

A chorus of voices assented to that demand. Ferguson held up both hands.

"We're as frustrated as you are, folks. The Tram is out of commission. Unfortunately, it is the only way to the resort, so everyone is stuck here until it's repaired."

Several voices asked for details.

"The problem is that it's stuck mid-way, so it's been difficult to get a repair crew down to work on it."

As he continued to make excuses for the closing of the tramway, I was making a mental note to rope Ferguson into a poker game if I ran short of cash. He kept letting this little guilty smile cross his face as he spoke. Besides I had learned a couple of things the resort people might not have told him but he should have noticed. At the resort end there is not only a spare engine, but also a small electric rail cart. He actually referred to the engine as an old diesel, when there were signs all over the place explaining what biomass fuel was and how he resort's garbage helps to run the tramway.

He also wasn't fooling me with the 'I'm stuck here too' routine he was trying to suggest to the folks. Earlier in the morning I heard a couple of helicopters thumping overhead. If anything happened up top, Ferguson would be the first one there. Then, maybe it was just the flushed and sweaty face that gave him away.

In any case, his excuses were treated with the skepticism they deserved.

"Who are you?" Our little redhead was checking me out. "How do you know what the police found in the girl's room?"

"Hey, it's a small town. Everybody knows your business, sometimes before you do." Catchy phrase that. "Who are you?"

"Lee Holt, CNN Fashion News."

"Fashion news?"

She huffed. Not a new question, I'd assume.

"We were here for a special report on the Pageant...."

"I'm Michael." I shook her tiny hand. "Don't look now," I continued, "but you seem to have lost your camera crew."

"My cameraman's at the top of the hill. He's been here since Sunday. I was just coming in today and got stuck here at the bottom of the hill. That's what's so frustrating. All I can do is ask questions for background. No pictures. I take it you're not from around here, Mike?"

"What makes you think that?"

"Your accent… or lack of it."

"Maybe I'm like Sidney Poitier."

"The actor?"

"When he came here from the Bahamas, he decided he wanted to speak a more elegant form of the language, so he imitated radio and TV announcers until he lost his island accent."

"You're kidding."

"No, he really did that." It was always one of my dad's favorite stories.

"You seem to know a lot about this case. Are you with the police?"

"No."

Ferguson stormed over, grabbing my arm.

"What the hell do you think you're doing, Hughes? Give me one reason why I shouldn't haul your sorry ass straight to jail."

I pulled my arm free. "You got nothing to charge me with? There's no conclusive evidence of a crime, right? If you drag me off to jail in front of this lady from CNN, she'll report that there was definitely a crime here. In no time the feds will be here and you'll be on the sidelines like the rest of us."

We stared-down for a long minute. His scowl trying to trump my grin.

"Hughes? You're the bodyguard? I thought you were a cop."

"Impersonating an officer?" Ferguson said with a wicked grin.

I yawned.

"Listen, I'm just trying to keep you from screwing up this case."

"So there is a case?" Lee asked.

"Look, off the record, we're trying to keep the other contestants from panicking," Ferguson said. We just don't need a lot of hysteria at this point. The truth is, we don't really have much to go on yet."

"But you'd tell us if you did?" She asked.

"Well..."

"That's what I figured."

The silence grew uncomfortably from there. Ferguson looked like he was going explode, but he didn't want to feed the press. Our intrepid reporter wanted details, but neither of us intended to give her any, and I had nothing to say to either of them. I wanted to walk away, but they would have followed me.

Lee's cell phone finally broke the deadlock.

"I have a local station setting me up to do a live report for the network. Can I ask you some questions later?"

"Sure, you can ask," I said, grinning. "I'm not going to promise any answers."

I watched her closely as she walked away to do her report. Her legs were really skinny, but otherwise she was well formed.

"What am I going to do with you?" Ferguson complained. "I warn you about getting in the way, then I turn around and find you playing Meet The Press."

"Hey, you were the one holding the press conference."

"We had to tell them something."

"Especially since you're trying to black out the mountain."

He reacted violently, then tried to play it off. "What do you mean black out?"

"When you update the press, you might want to remember the trains run on organic matter, not diesel. You also might mention the other way up the hill."

"What? What other way up the hill?"

"People lived on the mountain before they built the resort. You're telling me they never found their way to town?"

"Well, I guess there might be a footpath or two, but I wouldn't have any idea where they might be." He seemed to be getting worse at this game.

"Is it true about them sending a replacement for Nina?"

Ferguson shrugged. "I heard that rumor just when you did."

"Have you talked to the pageant folks...asked if anybody made a ransom demand?"

"Do you think I'm an idiot?" He paused long enough to tempt me. "Of course we did. They haven't heard a thing."

"But you're not monitoring their communication, phone, faxes, anything like that."

You could almost see corn sprouting from the furrows in his brow. "Why would we do that? It's a dead end."

"I was just thinking. Nina didn't officially have to be here until 3:30 today. Why are they scrambling to substitute for a person who doesn't even have to be here yet?"

"They're just being cautious. This pageant is hoping to get off the ground here. Missing contestants would make things difficult."

I shook my head. Then walked into the station. I noticed an empty bench over near one of the two women I was looking for that morning.

“No ransom note?”

“Nope,” he answered,

"Listen, if this is a kidnapping for money," I argued, “they'd have to go to the pageant. Law of the Deepest Pockets."

"What about Dr. Gustafsson? I mean he's pretty well off, isn't he?"

"Pop's not an MD; he's a professor of History at Northern Arizona University. We're all in school on scholarships and loans. They'd have to go to the pageant."

Ferguson shook his head.

"But there are other reasons for kidnapping someone."

Yeah, rape, torture, murder—I had to keep hoping it was about money or some kind of symbolic thing. To think of Nina hurt or dead wasn't going to help me any.

"With more than one kidnapper the motive is usually money."

"What makes you so sure there's more than one?"

I smiled enigmatically. Not because I had a clue how many kidnappers, but because I knew Ferguson was going to have to get out there and to prove me right or wrong. Even if I was wrong, we'd have a point to start. If we eliminated one possible motive, we might learn more about why and therefore whom.

Then I caught myself with a genuine smile. It was the sort of thing Carla would do. Make a flat statement based on no evidence, then dare you to prove her wrong. She wasn't wrong that often.

"So what's next?" I asked him.

"I keep investigating. You stay the hell out of the way before you get hurt."

Sound advice, but we both knew I wasn't going to take it.

Chapter 8

I watched Ferguson leave. He stopped at the door to speak to a tall blond guy with a crew cut. I had finally rated a tail.

I walked over to the dark haired woman back from her trip to Knoxville, who was carefully avoiding eye contact with her former traveling partner. They were like this the last time I saw them up at the resort—trying to avoid tipping off any observers.

She glared at me with that classic 'Don't even think about it' attitude. Of course, walls were meant to be climbed, right?

"Hi there." Nothing like those original and sophisticated opening lines.

"Hello," she replied without any politeness.

Sitting on the bench next to her, I looked across and smiled at her older, blond companion. Both women were staring knives at me.

"There's another way up there you know?"

My seatmate's eyes widened. Maybe I wasn't a plague after all.

"There's a path through the park over there," I continued. "If they don't get the trains running in about 25 minutes, and they won't, meet me at the picnic shelter over there."

I stood and leaned over to her left ear. "Feel free to bring your friend."

As her jaw dropped, I walked out the door and headed down the highway. The tall fellow casually detached himself from the wall and began walking in the same direction. He was blending into the scenery, completely invisible. I was very careful not to embarrass him by giving him a friendly wave.

The Pineville Cafe sat directly across the square from the library. It was pretty unimpressive. Longer than it was wide, a couple of tables sat in the front window, rolling back into a row of booths along the left-hand wall and a counter facing the grill along the opposite.

The aisle continued past a pair of cramped restrooms dead ending at the wall. The open door on the right side just past the counter led to a storage area and hopefully, the back door.

My faithful follower waited outside. Impossible to be inconspicuous in a group of six. I walked to the far end of the counter and sat quietly. Behind the counter, a woman in her late 50's, 5'-7", long grey hair tied in a braid down her back, was chatting with a pair of local Romeos about her age.

I felt a little nervous. I kept thinking about riots in the 60's over black folks sitting at a lunch counter in North Carolina. Every eye in the place was watching me. They weren't staring… exactly, but there wasn't any doubt that, as a stranger, I was the center of attention. I doubt even the new resort had made any great change at the Pineville Cafe.

"You're not from around here," a voice said

The guy farthest from me at the counter was a short stocky type. Almost White hair in what was once a crew cut, his hair ironically abandoning him at just about the same time his hairstyle recovered its popularity. His ruddy complexion was more probably due to manual labor outdoors than a love of alcohol.

The woman smacked him softly with a dish towel.

"Come on, Walt. You know him. He's the young fellow who was with the girl that disappeared."

"Am I wearing a sign, or something?" I asked.

"You're a TV star," she said, indicating the television in the corner over the door. "You've been on about 4 times already."

I wasn't sure if I should enjoy this new found popularity or be embarrassed by it. The attention I always got from football was always game related. Some people recognized me, but I managed to keep a pretty low profile personal life. For one thing, I was a linebacker. All that Big Man on Campus stuff went to the QB's and Running backs. The guys who scored touchdowns. Besides, I was a local guy. I had family, friends, I wasn't out being the football star in the clubs and such. This new attention was bigger and a lot more personal, and I was uncomfortable.

I shook my head.

"Any luck?" Walt asked.

"No."

I looked down and saw the menu on the counter. I looked up at her.

"What can I get you hon?"

"Can I get a grilled cheese and a coffee to go?"

"Sure thing. Sure you don't want fries?"

"No, ma'am, just the sandwich."

She drew a styrofoam cup from the stack, filled it, then placed it in front of me.

"Cream or sugar hon?"

"Just sugar, please."

I stirred my coffee in silence as she began to fuss at the grill. I wondered why I chose grilled cheese. I loved them as a kid, but I was no great connoisseur of them now. I was always a carnivore. Body fat consideration put me more into poultry or fish, but cheese was never an option.

Maybe it was because it was one of our last memories of Aunt Lani, the girls' mother. She was tired of us pestering her all the time, so she showed us how--you know, how to work the stove, don't burn the bread, don't burn yourself, stuff like that. She's always been in the kitchen with me, much more than my own mom. Watching her pirouette gracefully, humming a tune, her beautiful black hair with just one little streak of grey hanging almost to her waist.

It seemed she was sick the next day, dead in the blink of an eye. Maybe I ordered the sandwich because I needed to feel her presence. With me, I guess each major crisis is inexorably tied to the first.

"I suppose the cops have been all over that mountain with a fine-toothed comb," Walter said, trying to jump start the conversation.

"I suppose so."

"Walter," The lady said, shaking her spatula, "you stop pestering that boy."

"You can't call him a boy, Roberta, it's an insult. Ain't you heard of Political Correctness?"

"Very funny. You just stop pestering him."

Walter looked hurt. "I'm just trying to help out, offer my expertise."

"What kind of expertise?" I asked to be polite.

"20 years. Marines. Drill Instructor at Parris Island. You learn a lot about people there."

"I suppose so. My dad's a major in the Air Force. Stationed in Germany. So where do you suppose these people are Sergeant?"

The man sitting next to him spoke up. He was maybe the age of the other two, but he seemed older. He was almost invisible next to his buddy, and his careworn and wizened face and arms gave the impression, that he had been shrunk, his dark complexion made him seem even more like a raisin.

"If I were running this operation, I'd be out of town in a heartbeat. I'd never even stop to eat," he said, emphatically. "It's too small a town to let myself get seen in."

"I don't know, Tom," Roberta said over her shoulder as she folded the sandwich into a unit. "They could pass themselves off as tourists."

"Oh, please. Our young friend is the first tourist we've seen in town for the last what? Two, three weeks—and he's only here looking for his girlfriend."

"Nobody comes to town?"

"The only people who leave that mountain are either headed out of town or over to Kaiser."

"What if you were from here? Where would you hide a girl?"

"There are a couple of places around, we'd be glad to check for you."

"I'll say," Walt joined in. "This is about the biggest thing… oh, sorry son, I don't mean…"

I held up my hand. It *was* kind of exciting, when I didn't think about Nina and whether she was OK.

Roberta put the small bag with my sandwich in front of me.

"That's three twenty five, Hon."

I handed her a five.

"They mean well," she said, nodding to the guys, "and they know this town better than anybody. If your friend is here we'll find her."

I needed all the help I could get, it wasn't like I had a clue, but I was worried about sending out the Sunshine Boys to play detective.

"We don't know what we're up against out there," I reminded them. "You guys keep your heads down."

"Don't worry about us," she said. "We all fought in the war."

"Desert Storm?"

She patted my cheek. "Bless you."

I wrote my cell number on a slip. "If you guys hear or see anything let me know. Or call the cops--that's what they're there for."

"Don't worry, son," Tom said, "If she's here in town, she's as good as back."

I grabbed my cup and bag and headed into the back room. No one said a word. Sure enough there was a back door.

I walked down the alley, munching the sandwich. It was possible they'd find something. It was possible I'd find something. Somebody needed to find something.

"This is crazy, Collette. We're out here in the woods to meet some psycho?"

The blond woman was older than I had first guessed when I saw her a couple of days ago. Good makeup and distance having fooled many a man. I now figured her for the shady side of 40. If Collette was even 25, I'd eat my shoe, maybe both of them.

"He's not exactly a psycho." *Not exactly?* "He's that missing girl's bodyguard, and he said he knew a way up the mountain."

"Listen to yourself, Collette. The only girl he knows here has been kidnapped and god knows what else. For all we know he's got her carved into little pieces and is out looking for fresh meat."

"There's something about him, Joanie. I trust him."

"Well, I don't like it."

"You don't have to," I said, as I stepped out from behind a tree.

They both jumped pretty good. I turned on my charming smile; Joanie pulled a can of pepper spray.

"Stay away from us," she said, angrily.

"Whatever you say." I answered.

“What do you want?”

“I figured we’d all get up the hill faster by walking.”

“We’ll wait for the train.”

“Suit yourself.” I started toward the trail up the hill.

I didn't feel like explaining myself, and I figured wouldn't have to. Before I got up the hill, Curiosity would overwhelm their paranoia and they'd come to me.

Chapter 9

The two women followed me up the steps, then along the narrow trail to the main one, conversing in anxious whispers. After a few yards on the main trail, Collette had walked up and tapped my arm.

"Hey, how you know about us?" She asked.

Her English, like Pop Gustafsson's, picked up heavier accent when nervous or distracted.

"Somebody saw you when you rented your car."

"What do you want from us?" Joanie demanded.

I shrugged. "I thought I'd do you a favor by getting you back to the top of the mountain."

"Out of the goodness of your heart? I'm touched, but I don't believe it."

"I did have a couple of questions," I said.

"About what?" Collette answered.

"What kind of questions?" JoAnne asked

"You two came down the mountain yesterday afternoon, did either of you see anything unusual?"

"That's it? No, of course not. We've heard about the disappearance. If we'd seen your girlfriend we'd have let somebody know, but we didn't."

"Collette?"

"What?" She was startled. "No, I didn't see her either."

"Nothing unusual?"

"No, I don't think so."

"Well, it was worth a shot."

"What made you think we saw her?" Joanie asked.

"She had to have been taken down the hill sometime yesterday afternoon. Since you were there, I thought it was possible you saw something."

"She's like, seven feet tall, how could anybody miss her?" Collette asked.

"That is the question, isn't it? How could they sneak her down the mountain without being noticed?"

"What about a wheelchair?" Joanie asked.

"There was a woman in a chair?" *Carla?*

"No," Collette said. "It was some ninety year old *ancien*… a how you say… geezer."

I looked at Joan. She had softened her face. Eased up on the tension. Without that professionally miserable expression fashion models tend to use, she wasn't too bad looking.

After mulling over the real question, she shook her head. "I don't know…I guess it *could* have been her, but it looked like an old man. I mean he was wearing a hat and kind of bundled up, but it wasn't… well, to be honest, we didn't have any real reason to look that closely."

They had a good point. Still, it was one of the few possible ways to get her down the hill without drawing attention. Almost impossible to gage height from the chair, throw on a hat, dark glasses, maybe even a fake beard…

"This wheelchair-bound person… he wasn't traveling alone."

"There was a nurse, kind of average, I guess. Dark hair. Very professional."

"Much starch," Collette added, "you know, old fashioned white uniform and everything. I think it was awfully formal."

"Just the two of them?"

"Yes. In hindsight, they did kind of stay at the far end of the train. I just figured it was self -consciousness. They didn't really talk to any of us."

"How did they leave?"

"Leave? How should I know? Jesus, if we knew it was important, we would have been sure to keep track of them, forgive us for not following around some old guy in a wheelchair hoping he's your missing girl."

"They got in a van, I think." Collette said

"What kind of van?"

"I don't know—a *van* van."

"It was light colored." Joanie said. “I think.”

"Did it have a lift?"

They looked at each other, shrugged in unison. If it was a specialized van, it would be easier to track, but there would only be a limited number of possibilities anyway.

"Does this help? I mean, how do you know if you're on the right track?" Joanie asked.

My turn to shrug. I wasn't on any track. I was just poking around, pretending to investigate. So far the only thing I had accomplished was getting under Ferguson's skin. Maybe he was right, leave things to the cops. On the other hand, I couldn't just stand by and wait.

"What about the camera?" Collette asked.

"Camera?"

"There was a TV man filming when we got to the station at the bottom. Maybe he got pictures of your van."

"Maybe he did. Any idea who he was?"

"I think he was the guy at the reception thing a couple of days ago. You were there weren't you?"

They obviously hadn't seen Headline news. I was there, but I didn't remember any TV guy. Of course, it was my job to keep an eye on Nina, and in the outfit she was wearing, I didn't have to be asked twice. Logic suggested he was the same guy Lee Holt left up top. If that was true, it would be a good idea to find him before the Train started running again. If not, he was sure to show up at tonight's soiree.

The woman at the desk bore an unmistakable resemblance to her grandmother. Miz Dinah's source of information became obvious. I asked Rose Williams about Lee's room number. She raised an eyebrow, but decided to bend (or break) the rules about giving out room numbers.

"I'm curious about another thing," I continued, "Would you know if anybody up here uses a wheelchair? I have a friend who uses one and I was wondering about access problems, transportation, stuff like that."

"Well we don't have anybody that I know of, but the resort was very careful about maintaining access. Our airport shuttles have chair lifts and things like that."

"So no one has been here recently using a chair? I heard someone was on the tram yesterday heading down."

She shook her head emphatically.

"Not that I know of. Of course, guests don't have to tell us about having disabilities, or maybe somebody came up to shop or eat in one of the restaurants."

Or maybe the chair was just a blind. Seemed unlikely any body would bring their own, though.

"Do you have any wheelchairs available here?"

She was a little perplexed for a moment, then she blinked.

"We have first aid equipment, and a trained EMT nurse on call. I know we also have some ambulance equipment, you know, stretchers and stuff, but I don't know why they'd have a wheelchair."

"I was just thinking somebody might need help getting down on the train without something as dramatic as a stretcher."

"Oh, I see what you mean. Our Safety and Security force would probably know about wheelchairs. You should talk to Mr. Hatcher."

Video Surveillance, wheelchairs, maybe even a ransom note. I really should talk with Mr. Hatcher.

Lee Holt was occupying room 317. I was assuming her cameraman was booked in close proximity. 315 and 319 were on either side. I made sure not to think about this guy not being in the room, having a room elsewhere in the hotel, or any other calculation of the odds involved.

The woman in 315 was about sixty and kind of irate. If I wasn't gone in 10 seconds, she was going to call security. I apologized for knocking at the wrong door. It wouldn't have helped if I told her I should talk to Mr. Hatcher anyway.

319 was empty. It *was* worth a shot, but even if he was at the door, how would I know it was him? Surely a wild goose chase.

Just for grins, I tried the room across the hall, 316. Maybe they were booked in numerical proximity.

"Bout time," he was grumbling as he opened the door.

No doubt he recognized me. He stepped toward me with frightened aggression, kind of like a star back leading a sweep. Running toward you hoping you'd back down and save him some bruises.

"Hey, you can't stop that tape. It was news, and besides the pageant people approved."

I smiled. He thought I was worrying about his shot of Nina and I at the party the other night.

"You got paid for that, right?" I asked him.

"Yeah…" He answered, very warily. "I guess so… I mean, I don't have any of it yet."

"So, I guess you could say you owe me."

Now his ears shot up.

"I'm not here about those pictures," I told him, "I need your help."

His bravado returned.

"Why should I help you?"

"Because I'm still being friendly."

"You don't scare me." *Oh, yes I did.*

"I want to see the video you shot at the train stations yesterday."

"Who said I shot anything?"

He smiled. I smiled back.

"If I had seen the girl, I would have told somebody. What, you think I got the kidnapping on tape? That only happens in the movies, son."

"I ain't your son. And I still want to see that tape."

"What happens if I don't?"

"I tell the cops what you have on tape, and they confiscate every piece of tape you got. On the other hand, if we find the stuff we're looking for, we just duplicate that and hand it over."

He shook his head. "I wouldn't have to do that. I'm a journalist. Protected by the First Amendment."

"You're a long way from any courtrooms up here, dude."

He scratched his chin, speculatively.

"What's in it for me?"

"Hey you got the pictures—keep selling them. You're the only game in town for the next couple of hours or so."

"I want an exclusive interview with the family."

"I'll see what I can do, but I'm not guaranteeing anything."

"Not good enough."

"Maybe I have one other thing." I told him about my suspicions, that the Pageant may have received a ransom demand.

He was skeptical. "Where's your proof?"

"That's where you come in. You're the journalist, protected by the First Amendment."

We went to the resort's video center. Jay, our photographer, found what we were looking for in no time. He had shot about 3 minutes worth of random shots from different angles. Along with JoAnne and Collette, there were 4 guys in suits--probably Kaiser executives. One of the beauty contestants from New Jersey, I think, and our wheelchair with nurse.

"Flashback from the 50's," Jay said as we saw a closer shot of the girl in the nurse's uniform, fussing over her patient.

It *was* painfully old fashioned, and I thought rather poor fitting. I suspected it was borrowed, but I was assuming it was all phony anyway. I needed evidence. Something that somebody else would believe.

His last few shots were of the Nurse and driver loading the wheelchair into the van. As I had suspected, it was equipped with a chair lift, which should make it easy to trace.

"Let me see that last shot again."

"License number?"

"Not the license, but that." I pointed at the screen.

"On the door… Oh, I get it, a fleet number."

"Yep." I scratched them down on a piece of scrap paper. "Now go back to that shot of the nurse."

"Did you see something?"

"Just double checking. I wondered what she's doing."

It took three passes, the last one in slow motion to see what I really needed to see.

"Can you enlarge this picture?"

"You mean zoom in? Sure."

He punched a couple of buttons.

"See this joystick, twist it to zoom in or out."

I focused in on the activity in the shot. The nurse was replacing the dark glasses on her patient. For a brief second you could see part of the "mystery man's" face.

Those hazel eyes were practically a neon sign.

"Nice eyes," Jay said.

"The rest of her isn't bad either."

Chapter 10

Hatch stood out like a frog in a punch bowl, looking officious in a brown sport coat with the resort logo. I, on the other hand, was *tres suave* in a charcoal grey double-breasted suit. Carla picked it out. I was never a big fan of doubles, but having no real passion for fashion, I tend to defer to the girls when I go to buy clothes.

The ballroom was quickly filling as I came in. I smiled and winked at my hiking companions, already sampling the *hors d'ourves.* Both were careful not to race over and greet me.

"I heard you were stuck at the bottom of the hill," Hatch said.

I smiled enigmatically. "You mean the trains still aren't running?"

I dared him to tell me they were watching me. Or, that the trains were being held up.

"I hear you're missing a wheelchair," I said.

"Wheelchair?"

"They probably drugged Nina, bundled her into a wheelchair and rolled her right onto the train, no questions asked."

"What?" His exclamation was loud enough to draw stares from a few of the assembled pageanteers. "What the hell are you talking about?" You could hear the steam whistling from his ears.

"We got it on tape," I explained. "Nina was accompanied by a woman with dark hair in a nurse's uniform."

"How did you get a tape?"

"Just a matter of knowing the right people."

"The right people!" he exploded. He looked at his growing audience for a second, then violently gestured toward the door with his head. I followed cheerfully.

He made his way around a corner before blowing a gasket.

"Who's been talking to you? I want to know where you've been getting access to *my* security equipment. "

"Oh, it wasn't on one of your surveillance cameras," I said, nonchalantly. "CNN caught the unloading at the Pineville tram station."

Hatch shook his head then scowled. "Why are you telling me? You should be telling all of this to Ferguson. If they're down in Pineville they're out of my jurisdiction."

"I figure you should tell him,"

"Me?"

"Sure, you're the security chief."

His eyes narrowed, his face tightened into a sardonic half-smile.

"C'mon, spill it."

"I just don't think Ferguson will believe anything if I tell him. He can't just ignore you."

I paused. "There are, also, a couple of things I need to know from you."

Hatch rolled his bottom lip over his top and shook his head.

"What could it hurt," I said, soothingly, "to at least hear what I want to know?"

He rolled his eyes a little.

"Look, this isn't a strict *quid pro quo*. I mean, I'm not forcing you to answer any questions. If you don't tell me somebody else will.

"Question #1: Is there a new Ms. Ohio on her way here?"

"Look, that's the pageant people's call. I had..."

"I'm not looking to place blame, I just need to know facts. Did they call in a replacement for Nina?"

"Yeah, she should be here tonight."

"Tonight? That means they called her yesterday?"

Hatch shrugged honestly. Didn't know, wouldn't tell, didn't matter—pick one.

"Question #2: Did the pageant receive a ransom demand?"

His jaw dropped, then he snapped his mouth shut. He thought for a moment then tried to smile. "Hey, it's not like they'd tell me." His voice took on the phony overtones of a 60's DJ and you could almost hear him debate throwing a 'pal' or 'buddy' on the end of his sentence. He was a worse liar than Ferguson.

"I figured it might have been just a rumor," I said, sarcastically, walking off.

Hatch frowned a bit as we began to head back to the ballroom.

"What makes you so sure it's our wheelchair?"

"Man shows up with his own wheelchair, somebody notices, right? People would try to help and perhaps remember him. If, on the other hand, he has a dizzy spell or something, he'd get one of yours--completely disposable and untraceable if he doesn't leave prints."

"Any idea where they went after they got to the bottom?"

"Not yet, they loaded her into an accessible van, probably a rental."

"Light grey van with Blue?"

"Yeah?"

"Kaiser Electronics."

I should have known. All those Kaiser guys, in and out all the time. They had to have local transportation.

"Tom Chesney, he's a vice president," Hatch was explaining. "His son, Bradley, has Cerebral Palsy. Mr. Kaiser insisted they have an access van available for the boy."

"So everybody in Pineville knows about this van."

"Sure, but it would almost have to be somebody at Kaiser to get it out of the complex."

Still it meant the kidnappers were from here, or got local help, so why Nina? She hadn't been here long enough to make any enemies. If somebody local knew she was coming, did that mean the resort people did, too? Or was it possible it was random? They got her from her room, which meant they must have been watching. Did that mean someone in security had something to do with it? Should I trust Hatch?

I made sure Hatch was well in front of me when I re-entered the ballroom. No use being a frog by association. Between the contestants and their companions, pageant officials, corporate sponsors, and various other somebodies, a couple of hundred were expected for the cocktail party. Only about half of the group was on hand, though. The others were either stuck at the bottom of the hill, or waiting for someone who was.

Of course my luck was that one of the people I really hoped could be stuck was not only there but seeking me out. The head of the Ohio delegation was heading toward me at full sail, cheeks puffing, waves of chiffon and flesh rippling along in the wake. I didn't think she came to say howdy.

"No, no, no," she puffed. "You shouldn't be here. You are no longer part of our delegation."

She grabbed my right arm, trying to turn me around. I shook my head.

"If you don't leave I'll have you forcibly removed," she threatened.

"Look Mrs. Jenkins…"

"Jackson!"

"Mrs. Jackson, I have no intention of leaving this party. I can either mingle and talk with these people and maybe ask a few quiet questions, or I can ruin the whole thing by brawling and busting the place up while being forcibly removed."

She huffed angrily.

"I also have a couple of questions for you," I continued.

"I don't have to answer your questions."

"So don't answer. When did you call for a replacement for Nina?"

She spoke soothingly, like I was an angry child.

"Mr. Brunson asked us to call Mary Jean, just in case. If your friend comes back she can still participate. We just want to make sure the pageant ran smoothly."

"Who's Brunson?"

Apparently, everybody knows Mark Brunson (I've got to do something about my memory lapses). He was the Pageant's director and creator for that matter. He was a significant partner in the resort, and he was flying the girl down here in his private jet.

"When did he call you, yesterday?"

"About 5pm, I guess, why?"

No reason, just that the pageant was replacing her at almost the same time I found her missing.

"So if Brunson flew her in, where is she?"

"She's probably just arriving. The trains have been out of service."

"So I've heard."

A new clutch of people arrived. Mrs. Jackson swept off to meet them, waves rippling behind.

For the next few minutes I mingled with the contestants and officials. I think I was actually more famous among the girls than the B-list actor the pageant hired as host. They were full of sympathy for Nina and concern, mostly for themselves, but had nothing significant to add.

"You owe me an interview," Lee said from behind me.

I was actually glad to see her again. She would at least know who's who, and maybe even a little more.

"No I don't," I said, without turning.

"You promised." She took my arm.

"I said you could ask, I never promised to answer."

"We did you a favor."

"Which I already agreed to return."

"Oh, I get it… you or the family."

"Something like that. First we should talk to Brunson."

"Mark Brunson?"

"See, I had never heard of him, either," I said, grinning.

She shook her head.

"What are we talking to him about?"

"The ransom note he got yesterday."

"They said there wasn't a ransom note."

"*They* lied."

"Can you prove it?"

"Doubtful."

"Then why cause trouble?"

"I have to know the truth. Besides I'll have enough leverage to get back out again… courtesy of CNN."

Chapter 11

Lee wisely decided not to come with me, but she pointed Brunson out. Then she went and joined Jay at his camera position. You have to step back to see both Quixote and the windmill.

The man in question was only an inch or so taller than me but almost comically skinny. He had medium length blond hair and one of those pointed goatees like the Three Musketeers used to wear. Even in a social setting like this, he was followed by a pair of efficient assistants, ready to take a note, answer a call from Shanghai, or agree wholeheartedly with him on demand. Also nearby was his bodyguard. Now, this guy made AJ look undernourished. He was about 6'8", and well over three bills. He seemed pleasant enough – who'd cross him?

Tailing the entourage was our old friend Ferguson. No knock off this time, today the Armani was genuine. If I had to sling somebody across the buffet, I'd found my boy.

Brunson had no trouble recognizing me. Must be the sign I'm wearing these days. He introduced himself, the assistants (Coles and Barnes) security (James) and of course you know Sergeant Ferguson. He even seemed willing to talk.

"…of course if there's anything we can do for you…"

"Would you tell me what was in the note?"

I even remembered to keep smiling, maintaining the illusion of friendly conversation.

"Note?" He answered, with surprise. *Him*, I'm not inviting to the poker game. Even knowing better, I was tempted to believe him. Ms. Coles, although pretty good, was still qualified to play.

"The ransom note you got yesterday." The big guy was just starting to crowd me. Ferguson began to circle around the other side. A perfect trap. Right where I wanted them.

"I'm afraid you're mistaken, Trey… can I call you Trey? I heard those rumors myself, but they are just conjecture."

"Now I know why you don't want to admit it publicly. I think I might have handled it the same way you did, if I didn't know the victim. It might even have worked. I just need to know a couple of details."

"You have to believe me, I have no idea…"

"Can the corn," I finally said, in my best Bogart. "Did the note mention her by name?"

"I don't know anything about a note." He was getting just a bit frustrated. He had the charm turned up full blast and it just wasn't working.

"I'm just guessing they didn't make any arrangements for the drop yet, either."

Ferguson squawked behind me. The room got a little darker as the big guy got close enough to block my light. The rest of the room started to crowd in as well. I spotted my cameraman moving to get a better angle.

"I'm not sure we should be discussing this here, Trey," Brunson said, feeling the pressure himself.

"Discussing what? We're just having a friendly chat about a note that never existed. Why the entire thing is completely hypocritical… (medium pause) Sorry, I think I meant hypothetical."

Brunson's face darkened. "Hypothetical or not, we should discuss this later."

"Later isn't a luxury we actually have. I think your ransom note is a smoke screen. They might take your money, I know *I* would, but they have no intention of returning Nina."

"Smoke screen?" Ferguson squawked. "I'll give you a smoke screen. I've warned you to stay out of this investigation. I'm running you in this time."

I never took my eyes off Brunson. He was still puzzling over my last statement.

“What investigation, Ferguson?” I tossed over my shoulder. “All I've seen you do so far is threaten me and show off your wardrobe. The point is, Mark, your people got the ransom note before we reported her missing, which means somebody knew who they were kidnapping. As Slick here, said yesterday, why pick on somebody with extra security?”

I leaned closer to Brunson.

"This is an inside job. Somebody involved with the resort, or your pageant, is working with these kidnappers. It had to be someone who could get into Nina's room or get her to let him in."

I could see the man's brain kick into gear as I explained how she was kidnapped and taken down the hill.

"Here and now isn't the place to discuss this," he said. "Perhaps tomorrow morning?"

"Tomorrow?"

"First thing. You've made a point, but I would have to confer with my board of directors before I could discuss any correspondence."

"I thought you were the board of directors. Who's pulling the strings here? Are you worried about the pageant or Nina?"

It was a silly question. Brunson was a successful money guy, profit and loss. The pageant affected his bottom line. Nina was just another face in the crowd. Even if he was dating her, he would just take the next one in line. This wasn't to say he wouldn't pay the ransom. The money would be bait for a trap and if he got her back he'd be a hero. If they didn't, he'd probably get the money back another way. The publicity would do him good as well.

The bigger question was: who's in charge? Max Kaiser, wherever he was, owned Kaiser Electronics, which controlled the town, a chunk of the resort, and owned the van used to kidnap Nina. Brunson owned the pageant and the other chunk of the resort. Did Kaiser own part of the pageant? Was Brunson tied to Kaiser Electronics?

Could Kaiser be involved? Could Brunson? I knew a computer jock who could hunt through the financial reports and holding companies and get me an accurate picture, but Spike Cavanaugh was worse than a pain in the ass. It was going to be tough for me to deal with him—even for Nina. It was also possible he wouldn't help. For the time being, nothing like the straight approach.

"Does Max Kaiser have a piece of the Pageant?"

Brunson frowned. "I will not discuss this here. Tomorrow we can discuss this letter and anything else."

"Very hypothetical of you," I said, sarcastically. "But how do we know tomorrow won't be too late."

He turned and began to walk away. The big man stepped in front of me as Ferguson grabbed my left arm.

"You're under arrest, *slick*," he said, "obstruction of justice, withholding evidence, and hopefully, resisting arrest."

I considered messing up his suit until the big guy put a hand on my shoulder. Maybe going quietly was a good idea, after all.

As I was being marched out of the ballroom, I saw Jay, my cameraman give me a thumbs up. Hatch looked a bit perplexed. Mrs. Jackson sported a superior smile.

One of the last faces I saw was a tall skinny guy with wire-rimmed glasses, his long blond hair tied in a ponytail. A casual observer might have guessed he was an artist or film director or something similar. He fit in perfectly and looked splendid in his tuxedo. I'm glad he left those pathetic field glasses at home.

Chapter 12

As the train rolled downhill, Ferguson asked questions about the van, and how I knew about the note. I sat on my *Miranda* rights and said nothing. He went from wanting to cut a deal to threatening lethal injection. The big man sat at the other end of the car. Apparently he didn't want to play. Neither did I. He didn't get off the train, his job just to make sure I got off the mountain. The walk to the police station was uneventful.

Chief Longstreet was still on duty. "Suddenly I feel underdressed," he said to Ferguson who immediately launched into a laundry list of charges and profanity. The chief looked at me. I shrugged.

"That Carmen Miranda was a wonderful girl," I said, casually.

"Get him out of here," Ferguson roared. "We'll see if he's still a smartass after a night in jail."

The cells were old and grungy, but unoccupied by human or vermin (as far as I could tell). I had been there only about an hour when a young officer came for me.

"He's gone," Longstreet told me, when I got to his office. "I can't turn you loose, but I can at least let you out of the cells."

As I had suspected, the Police chief was not really going to be a great deal of help when something really hit the fan, but I was sure he'd be glad to take all the help from me he could get.

"What if I made a run for it," I asked, half-joking.

"I shoot you," he said, half-serious.

I nodded.

"You must have really ruffled some feathers up there."

"Important people hate to be called liars, especially when they're actually lying at the time. Mark Brunson?"

Longstreet shook his head.

"Some slick New York guy. Owns some of the resort, but no reason for me to have checked him out."

"The fact that I both insulted the rich guy and found a clue, Ferguson decided I needed to rest, so he put the arm on me."

"Without you ruffling his fancy silk suit?" He said, grinning.

"The suit came with its own bodyguard."

"Huh?"

"Hard to explain. You had to have been there."

"Probably just as well. That suit must have cost him an Armani leg."

"He probably worked his tailor to the bone," I parried. "You find yourself wondering how he affords those fancy duds, don't you?"

His smile died as we stared at each other. I didn't really expect him to answer. A good cop keeps his mouth shut. Badmouthing brother officers is just plain unlucky.

"You said you found a clue?" he finally prompted.

I told him what I had learned about the method used to smuggle her down the mountain.

"So you think she's here in town?"

"If she is, they'll want to move her fairly soon. The search was bound to end up here as soon as they were done up on the mountain. I think that's what the ransom note was really about, stalling for time."

"I thought there wasn't a note?"

I smiled. "That's just what the pageant folks wanted us all to think."

"That would explain what the Feds are doing—a ransom drop."

"The Feds are here?"

Longstreet grinned. "Four, led by a real ice queen, right out of a Wagnerian Opera. They blasted in here, flashed badges, announced themselves and took off like they had a hot lead. That's why I'm still here, thinking they'd probably be back."

The light finally went on. That's why they were so anxious to get me out of the picture. They didn't want me screwing up their ransom drop. I was going to spend the rest of the night hoping I was wrong, they were right, and Nina would be back.

"That couch is most likely more comfortable than one of the jail cots if you want to sleep up here." It was then I realized I was yawning. It had been a long day and sleep was definitely tempting. I think I would have curled up right then if Lee hadn't arrived with just what I really needed—food. I could have kissed her.

She blew into the room without even acknowledging the police chief, already in full conversation, or was that diatribe?

"I was going to get a couple of burgers, figuring the locals might not feed you in your cell," she said. "I went to the cafe across the square, and I found myself surrounded by the Pineville branch of your fan club. They insisted on sending a feast: Chicken, Mashed potatoes, greens—they even sent you a pecan pie."

She looked me over severely. "And shouldn't you be downstairs looking through bars?"

"It's a dry town," Longstreet joked. "No bars."

She fixed him with a glare. "So they put the comedy club in here?"

He smiled at me. "Not bad."

I did the introductions. As I turned my attention to the food, Lee was upbraiding the chief on reasons why I couldn't be held. He explained to me and the wall that he was merely the jailer for Ferguson and the state. He had no vested interest, or charges from his jurisdiction, this was why Trey wasn't being held downstairs. Lee eventually ran out of gas.

"So, did you show him the tape?" I asked.

"I didn't get a chance. Brunson got into a chopper almost as soon as you started downhill."

I shrugged. "Guess I'll be here tonight after all."

"You knew you were going to be arrested?" Longstreet asked.

"I knew it was possible. So I arranged a little get out of jail card."

"We taped the conversation between Trey and Brunson," Lee explained. "Trey was trying to get him to admit there was a ransom note. He didn't exactly admit it, but he implied it was possible."

"Since they had insisted there was never a note, he's going to have to keep that tape quiet," I said.

"That's awfully good stuff. Aren't you tempted to use the tape anyway?" Longstreet asked.

"Not really, Trey owes me an exclusive."

"Sorry, no jailhouse interviews," I said. She was going to get me sooner or later. I voted later.

"Is he a good TV actor?"

"He has a great voice," Lee said, "and he's very photogenic. He really looks good in handcuffs. All those biceps."

"Hey now," I admonished around a fried chicken leg.

"Which reminds me, Trey," she continued "I had a question about something you said early in that conversation. You said you knew what they did when they got the note and you would have done the same thing?"

"Sure, the first thing they did was replace Nina. To the pageant, her value as a kidnap victim was equal to her status as a contestant. By bringing in a replacement, they insure the contest goes on. With their leverage gone, the kidnappers would, most likely, cut their losses."

"You mean they'd turn her loose?"

"Or get rid of her."

Her eyes widened. "You mean kill her?"

"That's why it only sounds like a good idea if you don't know the hostage. Killing the victim is a constant danger whether you pay or not."

"But doesn't that scare you?" She asked.

I walked to the window. Thinking about what scared me wasn't helping me find Nina. Of course, that was almost all I *was* thinking. Everybody kept trying to get me to think the unthinkable or worse. I had to find her, alive and well. I couldn't bring myself to think about alternatives.

The old General was lit up in the square. Poor guy fought almost 150 years ago, risking his life, just to eventually become a backdrop for the TV news.

"Trey?" I felt the hand on my bicep. I turned and looked at Lee. I guess I'd been standing there for quite a while.

"It was a damn stupid question. I'm sorry."

"No. It's OK."

"What's she like?"

"Nina? I guess the first thing is that I still can't believe she would do something like this. It seems so totally out of character.

"I thought you were convinced she was kidnapped?"

"No, no, no. I mean this pageant. Nina was never interested in superficial judgments and external appearances. She's a real person."

Lee didn't say anything, but I felt a bit guilty. If I had learned anything watching these contestants for the last few days, it was that not all fit a stereotype.

"I'm not suggesting the others aren't real. I just think most of these women feel the need to compete or, want some kind of validation of their beauty. Nina never seemed to even care about her looks until this thing."

"You mean she always seemed to take her looks for granted?"

"She was always beautiful. Not in this kind of shallow visual sense, but where it counts. This obsession with looks and fashion is all new to me."

I felt tears on my face.

"You really miss her."

"We've been almost family since we were kids. I can't think about…"

I stopped talking. It wasn't like I was making sense anyway.

"So, what's your next move?" she said after the silence. "You should be out in the morning."

"I don't know. We'll have to see what the morning brings."

She was still holding my arm. I could smell her perfume. We locked eyes and looked at each other carefully, mapping each other's face… reading, questioning, searching. I felt that short drop in my stomach. Another time I might have already kissed her, but I was still fighting…

Suddenly, a commotion outside broke the spell. The Feds were back. Just in time.

Chapter 13

I saw what Chief Longstreet meant about the FBI team leader, Susan Nansen. She was only a little above average height, but her posture and long elegant neck made her seem taller. White-blonde hair and pale blue eyes made her seem more suited to Norse mythology than North Carolina.

She walked into Longstreet's office, regarding Lee with an eyebrow. Then folded herself carefully into the chair in front of his desk. I went and sat on the couch to her left, along the common wall. She swiveled 90 degrees to face me.

"I understand you've been a bit of trouble," she said without preamble.

"I'm looking for Nina."

"Your public outburst may have endangered your friend."

"Why? Because they didn't take the ransom?"

Her eyes narrowed.

"If they had taken the bait," I explained, "you'd still be following them. Since you came back empty-handed..."

"They called and canceled the drop," she said, "almost as if they knew something?"

I nodded. More proof of an inside man.

"You seemed to know quite a bit about things tonight. Any idea who might have tipped them off?"

"Nope."

"I heard you were going to play professional football before your injury."

"We'll never know, now."

"Your girlfriend was on scholarship?"

I speculated for a moment. What was she driving at?

"Must be tough, financially," she continued.

"Sometimes. Starving and student are often synonymous. What's your point?"

"Just curious. You're the one who reported her missing, right?"

"Right." I then told her some of what I had discovered.

"Who told you about this guy in the wheelchair?"

"Someone who was on the train. What difference does it make? We have it on tape."

"How do we know the tape was shot when you said?'

"Ask the guy who shot it." I was starting to get a little hot. She was fishing for something.

"Wouldn't he lie if he was getting enough money?"

"I suppose. A lot of people might, if they were getting enough money and thought nobody would get hurt. Do you think he's lying? What purpose would that serve?"

"Maybe to dupe us into believing she was kidnapped."

"As opposed to…"

"A publicity stunt. Or maybe a con."

"Nina wouldn't do that." I said, angrily.

She shook her head just a little. I was the poor deluded boyfriend, or a fellow conspirator trying to keep the truth from coming out. Or maybe...

"You two were close?"

"Very."

"No fights, disagreements, arguments?"

"Sure, plenty."

She seemed a bit surprised. Expecting me to deny it, I guess.

"Anything recent?"

"We've had one running since before Christmas."

"About what?"

"Us." I saw her eyes focus. I was moving up the suspect list. "We argued about splitting up. I was against it, she was… ambivalent."

"She was going to leave you. How did you feel about that?"

I shrugged. "We were still going to be friends, no matter what."

She frowned skeptically. I don't blame her. I wasn't as certain as I pretended to be about that. It's my worst fear.

"You weren't hurt?"

"I didn't say that. Besides, it wasn't a done deal."

"She was going to leave you, you were angry."

I shook my head.

"You need to make up your mind, either we staged a phony kidnapping, or I did her in. Pick one."

"I hear you know your way around town pretty good."

"You heard wrong."

"People delivering dinner to jail? Sounds like you have a lot of friends."

I smiled slowly. That fried chicken was excellent. "It's the quality not the quantity."

"You know what I think? I think you have a hand in all this. You keep conveniently finding things that no one else seems to."

"That's easy. I've been asking questions while the rest of you were waiting for the mythical ransom drop. You said they called and canceled?"

"Yes. Do you have a cell phone?"

"Not on me. They emptied my pockets when they took me into custody. Did you think I used it to call and cancel the ransom drop? Why would I set up a ransom, then challenge the idea of paying it, then cancel the payoff."

"Sometimes criminals do that kind of stuff, cleverly deflecting suspicion from themselves."

She got up and began pacing.

"You don't believe that," I said. "Your problem is, that everywhere you turn there's a new wrinkle. If she was kidnapped for money why didn't they take it? None of this is adding up."

"I don't know… there's also you."

"Me?"

"Everywhere we turn there's you in this investigation. You report her missing; you find this wheelchair video which you claim the missing girl is in. You know all about the ransom note and had the means to make the phone call. Perhaps you staged the whole thing."

"What about the video tape?"

"Could have been done anytime. Plus we only have your word that it's her."

"Why would I do it?"

"Money. You were hoping to make a score to make up for the football money you lost when you go injured. Then you fouled up the ransom to double-cross your partner, or partners. Or were you the one who got crossed?"

"You're barking up the wrong tree. A couple of weekends ago, I got an MBA from Western Ohio, and have already had a couple of interviews with Fortune 500 companies. I'm set to make a living even if I don't play in the NFL. Maybe you should consider the idea that the ransom was a delaying tactic. A sure way to get you all in one place."

"Seems pretty risky, why would you do that?"

"I *wouldn't*, but it would make it the ideal time to move the prisoner."

"Move her? Move her where?"

"Knoxville, or maybe Asheville. They might have bought a day with all this ransom foolishness, but this town is way too small to keep anyone hidden for long. Now, let me ask you a question: How much did they want?"

"What?"

"The ransom. How much?"

"I'm not at liberty to say."

"Over half a million?"

"I really can't tell you," she said, shaking her head.

I shrugged. The couch I was sitting on was starting to reach out for me again.

Special Agent Nansen was giving me the 'don't leave town' speech as I faded out.

To sleep, perchance to dream.

Only to have Ferguson and Longstreet come slamming into the office arguing. I know it was the Chief's office, so he had every right, but I found myself thinking that I would have gotten a lot more sleep down in the cells.

The object of their argument was a high school class ring; 14-karat gold band with a ruby in the setting. Inscribed in the band was a single word. *Crash.*

"It's Nina's," I agreed.

The nickname had come from her days as a basketball player in high school. Her height made her a natural, but she had learned to play with me and some of the boys, who all played like, well, football players. All fouls were called by the 'get up' rule. If the guy you decked was conscious it was—'Get up fool, you ain't dead.' As the years went on, her game became less… dangerous, but her nickname stuck, with her team, anyway.

She quit after her freshman year at Western. No explanation.

My new friends, Tom and Walter, had found the ring while checking out an abandoned laundromat on the far north end of town. The ring was in one of a pair of socks she had managed to toss into an open clothes dryer. They came to the station to consult with me, but ended up with Longstreet. Ferguson arrived a bit later. Was the evidence a matter for the town where it was located, or the state, who had the principal crime? They returned to the station still bickering over who was in charge of the scene.

Their jurisdictional dispute was finally solved when the FBI trumped them both, but by then, neither Tom nor Walter seemed eager to cooperate. They said where they found the artifact, but were unwilling to tell what prompted their search of the place. They wanted to meet with me. Nansen threatened them, but as Lee pointed out, throwing civic-minded Vietnam vets into jail was a bad move.

It was finally agreed that they could speak to me with Nansen in the room.

They had been out searching, but had stopped at the Cafe for coffee when they ran into another regular, a fellow named Levi (Catholic, not Jewish, they told me). He reminded them about the building, then went on to mention that his dog had been behaving differently the last day or two as they took their daily walk past it. Levi had dismissed it as squirrels or maybe raccoons denning in, or along, the building.

"When we checked the place," Tom said, "we found both the lights and water were on for the building and the back door unlocked —sort of."

"You broke in?" Nansen asked.

"The padlock was busted off, so it was just a matter of jimmying the door lock."

Walter produced a long, thin switchblade. "Misspent youth. That's how I ended up in the army."

"Anyway, the door seemed to indicate somebody came in recently, but the place seemed unnaturally clean and neat. So we poked around and found that ring."

"Why the dryer?" Nansen asked.

"If she just dropped it on the floor," I pointed out, "her captors might notice it. She needed someplace available but not necessarily obvious."

"I guess that's it until the crime lab guys are done with the building. We'll talk tomorrow."

"Go home guys, get some sleep. And thanks. Meet you tomorrow morning at the Cafe."

"You seem awfully confident you're getting out in the morning." Nansen said

I smiled. "You got nothing to hold me on."

Chapter 14

I woke under Ferguson's angry glare.

"You're free to go," he grumbled, leaving no impression it was his idea. "Pick up your effects when you leave." He spun and left.

"Good morning to you, too," I rumbled. I swung my feet off the couch, toes reaching for my shoes. I was tying the laces when Mark Brunson came in.

"Morning." My cheerful greeting startled him a bit. He expected a more hostile response.

"Ah, good morning." He was stumbling, unused to small talk. "It wasn't my idea to put you in jail."

I shrugged.

"As far as our decision to replace Nina Gustafsson, we had to do what was best for the pageant. We've got a lot riding on this, not just the publicity for Crystal Mountain, but we're kind of operating on the edge here. I've put a lot on the line here and without further national sponsorship or a long-term TV deal, our contest, the AIBC organization, might not have a future. A lot of local charities and sponsors, not to mention the women involved, are all counting on us. I know none of that matters to you, or your friend, but I wanted you to know we weren't just counting dollar bills. We always had every intention of paying the ransom. We just needed to cover both bases."

"How much did they ask for?"

"Four Hundred thousand."

"Your money?"

He nodded. "Borrowed it against Calypso Holdings, my company. An emergency provision."

"Does Max Kaiser have a stake in this pageant?"

"He's one of our board members, and he's a co-owner of the resort which has about 10 percent… But no, he doesn't have any stake of his own. Surely you don't suspect one of the richest men in the world...."

"Have you met him?"

"Voice on the phone and signatures. Nobody's seen him for 20 years or so. A far as I know, you could be him."

I shook my head. "Wouldn't want the pay cut," I joked.

Brunson chuckled. "Whoever he is, he has a good flair for making money. This resort is going to pay off seven to ten years ahead of schedule. I need more ventures like that."

"Did you ever meet Nina?"

"I saw her the other night, at the reception Kaiser threw. She's a very pretty girl, but we never had any contact at all."

"Kaiser threw that party?"

"Kaiser Electronics."

We sat and looked at each other.

"Do you know any of the other contestants personally?"

"What do you mean?" He asked nervously.

"Have you had contact with any of the girls?"

He hesitated.

"OK, I know one of the girls—oh, not the way you're thinking. The Ms. Michigan, Callie McPherson… I went to school with her dad. I've known her since birth. But I never exerted any influence—she got here on her own, and I'm not helping her in any way."

He half smiled. "You think I would have done it differently if it was her, don't you?"

I shrugged. I was thinking it should have been this Callie, or anybody closer to him than Nina.

"Anyway," he said, "we'll see what happens if they try again."

"Yeah."

Lee was waiting at the main desk when I signed for my personal effects. We were leaving when Hatch showed up. He handed me a Manila envelope.

"These were in your room, I figured to give it a check before Ferguson or the feds tore it apart." Inside there was a copy of the ransom note, the fax detailing last night's ransom drop, and a Nurse's report on the disappearance of her office's wheelchair.

My jaw dropped.

"I hadn't seen any of these either, except for the wheelchair report which didn't make sense until you explained the scam last night."

"But how did they end up in my room?"

Hatch smiled slowly. Lee raised an eyebrow. Nobody seemed to believe I didn't know my secret source of information. My secret was safe, I guess, especially from me.

"Anyway, I just wanted to tell you if you need anything from my people, you just let me know, OK."

"Thanks, Hatch," I said offering my hand. He shook, then headed off down the street.

"So, where to?" Lee asked.

I pointed across the Town Square. "Breakfast."

As we walked around the Square, I phoned home and spoke to AJ.

"Professor G is going to be there in the afternoon. Between 2 and 3 pm, he said."

"I'll try to meet him. Anything else new?" I asked.

"Cavanaugh."

Oh, great. Just what I'd been trying to avoid.

"What did he want?"

"Called wanting to help. I told him about Carla."

AJ sounded slightly worried. I didn't blame him. Cavanaugh was a computer whiz who could find anything and would annoy you to tears explaining how he did it. He could be helpful, as well as obnoxious and demanding; but at this point, it was a done deal. Might as well take the chance. Faint heart never won fair lady and all that.

"When you hear from him again. Tell him I need all he can get on Max Kaiser and Mark Brunson. Finances, personal, anything that might help."

"I'll let him know."

The Cafe, almost full, broke into applause as we entered. My brief stint in jail had apparently made me a local hero. Folks not only came out to meet me, they came to help. I learned from a few people that Ferguson was not very popular during his tenure as police chief. After doing my politician bit, I took my usual spot in the back.

"You're good for my business," Roberta said cheerfully. "Can you get thrown in jail every day?"

I laughed. "Only if you make sure I get back out." It was busy enough to have husband Frank at the grill, and a sullen (15-year-old) granddaughter, Nancy, helping around the floor.

Lee wanted a mushroom omelet, no cheese and dry toast. The camera adds 10 pounds, they say. I went with bacon, eggs, and grits.

"I hate grits," she grumbled.

"Good. You're not getting any of these."

"Ever since I moved to Atlanta, people have been trying to get me to try them."

"Did you?"

"Huh?"

"Did you try them?"

"They look disgusting," she said. Answer and explanation, I guess.

Tom walked in and made a beeline for us.

"Walter's not going to be here. His little granddaughter took a bad turn; they had to go to the hospital over in Knoxville."

"I understand."

"Not much we can do now, here, either, is there?"

"Same as before, eyes and ears open. It's possible they could come back, but it seems likely they're gone for good. We still have to know who, though, and I can almost guarantee he has ties to the area. Who ever did this knew all about the routine and the personnel up there and the best way to get around them."

"But he could have learned all that on the mountain as a tourist, couldn't he?"

"Sure, except for the laundromat. Somebody had to know it was there, and more importantly, somebody had to get the power and water turned on."

"Point taken."

"Tom, what do you know about a local character named Lonnie?"

"Lonnie McCoy? Local character might be a good description. He's a nice enough fellow, but he's a little crooked in the head. I'm never sure if he's a bit slow or…"

"I met him. He seems a bit vague, but I don't think slow is his problem."

"I can tell you I wouldn't be the least surprised," he said. "That mother of his is enough to take anybody around the bend.

"There isn't a lot of doubt about her. Widow Maitland, as she wanted to be called, married some rich man from up north, Cleveland, Chicago or somewhere like that. When he died, she got a truckload of money. She also had some kind of breakdown about 10 years ago right before she came back here. She lived in town for a little while, but couldn't stand it. Sheriff's had to go up and get her several times. Running around naked, half-naked, shooting at everything that moves...

"Doctors over in Asheville have tried to have her put away several times, but she's got good lawyers, not to mention the money. She's had several live-in nurses up there to try to keep her 'regulated'. It doesn't help that she brews hooch up there and that she's one of her own best customers. As for Lonnie, he doesn't seem to do much, except try to keep his Ma out of trouble. You said you met him?"

"Yeah, yesterday."

"He normally avoids strangers like the plague. What was he doing?"

"Helping search up on the mountain."

"Well, I just wouldn't get too involved with him. He's pretty unpredictable."

"I'll keep that in mind."

Chapter 15

"Brunson implied the pageant was running on a shoestring," I told Lee. "Any idea how long or thin the string is?"

"Haven't heard a thing about it. I have an interview this morning with one of the pageant officials, JoAnne McCullough. I'll see what I can find out."

I didn't think it would do Lee much good to mention she knew me.

"What about the girls? Have you heard any rumors about Brunson having a thing with any of them?"

"He'd better not," Roberta said, sliding my breakfast into place. Lee and I exchanged surprised looks.

"Don't you ever read *People*? Brunson and his wife are going through a really ugly divorce. She's managed to tie up all his assets until it's all settled. All he needs is to get caught in the sack with some 20-year old nymphet. He'd probably end up with nothing but a used outhouse."

"I remember, now," Lee said. "His wife was some kind of actress wasn't she?"

"If you want to call it acting."

"Oh, that's right, she's an adult film star."

"Adult, ha. More like arrested development. Bunch of damn perverts."

"As I recall..." Tom interjected.

"Oh, shut up, Tom." She said with serious venom.

Tom leaned in as Roberta moved down the counter.

"Nothing worse than a reformed anything." He grinned at me. "Bert had a blue period of her own, if you know what I mean. Coming out of the army, rumor had it she was a jiggle dancer down San Diego."

I closed my eyes, trying to avoid mental pictures.

Lee continued. "There was a rumor about Miss Nevada and some big shot—could have been Brunson. But you know how rumors are?"

"Yeah, but I also know women love to discuss their sexual exploits. I just find myself wondering if somebody wanted to squeeze Brunson, why wouldn't they pick a girl he knew personally."

"What makes you so sure he didn't know...?" She stopped, looking guiltily.

"Look, I'm sorry, Trey, but boyfriend or not, you have to admit it's possible they knew each other."

I realized I was frowning. It wasn't just that I love Nina and she loves me. I just couldn't see any practical, or even impractical ways the two of them could have been in one place long enough to make any magic.

As far as I knew, she hadn't left home in over a year, and Brunson probably thinks Dayton is a beach in Florida.

"I guess it's because I can't see how those two could get together." I finally said

"Look, you're probably right, I just think we should be open to possibilities."

I had no good response to that. I concentrated on the food.

We ate in the quiet murmur of other ongoing conversation.

The buzz died when The FBI stalked in. They might as well have been wearing uniforms. On a toasty warm Carolina spring morning, they wore navy blue coats, starched white shirts (perfectly buttoned), Ties and Ray-bans. Heads held high, Faces rock stolid.

The only concession to Nansen's gender was a navy skirt that stopped almost at her knees. It was a shame. The beginning of the story was pretty good. I would have liked to have read a longer tale.

The two junior agents, one of whom was tall enough for contrast, stayed a step behind like good little puppies. They had already located me before entering and were heading unerringly toward us.

I could feel Lee tensing up on that side. She clearly took a strong dislike to Nansen. It would be a good fight. Nansen had size and reach, but Lee had a real Tasmanian Devil kind of thing in her eyes.

Tom sat, mouth open. No doubt hearing the trumpets of *die Niebelungs*. The boys stopped about halfway. Nansen stopped at the empty chair on Tom's other side.

"Quite the town meeting," She said with a hint of sarcasm.

"They heard you were coming," I said, with a straight face.

She flicked her head toward the grill. "So what's good here?"

"Anything to go," Lee said, almost under her breath.

After the awkward silence, I stood up and peeled a $10 from my wallet. I nudged Tom slightly so we could nod in farewell.

Lee stood and stared defiantly around me at her.

"Hey, your money's no good here," Roberta said.

"Better take it," I said, over my shoulder. "You wouldn't want any Federal hassles."

Lee and I parted at the tram station.

"Where are you going," she asked.

"To find some wheels." I smiled enigmatically.

Chapter 16

From the ground, the Kaiser Electronics compound looked more like a prison than an industrial complex. A pair of 15-foot high perimeter fences topped by razor wire. A couple of the outside gates were open but the inside perimeter was opened and closed only on demand, even with a pair of guards at each gate.

As I came near the gate, I could see a young kid in a red ball cap struggling with the pair of guards. One held him in a half-nelson type hold with one arm pinned behind his back. He was clearly taller than the boy, whose feet were swinging off the ground. The other guard was waving his baton. Although the kid was still struggling, the guards seemed to have things under control. The baton man turned away, then swung around full speed, smashing the stick across the kid's knee.

I winced. That blow was just the kind of thing to do pretty good damage. Then he jabbed the stick into the kid's midsection once, twice, three times before his buddy let him collapse to the ground.

A two-handed ax chop aimed for his head, crashed into his right shoulder when the young man ducked accidentally.

"Hey!" I shouted.

It might have been an actual fight in the beginning, but trying to bust the skull of some kid retching on the ground…

The guy with the stick was starting to kick the kid as his partner turned to face me. I got to within about seven or eight yards of the scuffle before the big guy reached for his baton.

"I don't know guys," I said, loudly. I was going to continue with something like: 'He looks pretty down to me', but the guard charged me. He had the stick raised high, expecting me to freeze in fear, I suppose. I took two quick jab steps and launched my self into his middle. It was a tackle Coach K would have been very proud of. I caught him right in the solar plexus, taking the wind out of him. His baton crashed to the ground as my momentum slammed him into the concrete. I side-rolled off him to my feet as the other guard came in swinging.

I parried his baton swing with the forearm block Master Cho taught me in Junior High (you really don't forget those things), then gave him the classic Joe Louis uppercut. His feet seemed to leave the ground as he dropped to the deck.

I picked up his stick then stepped over to help the young man. The big guy was rolling around trying to breathe, but the little guy hadn't moved—I assumed he hit his head when he fell. I got the beating victim to his feet, gingerly.

"You OK?'

"I'm gettin' there," he drawled.

The smaller guard reached down toward his right ankle. I thought he had twisted it for a split-second.

The little chromed pistol must have been in an ankle holster. It didn't look that intimidating, but it fired bullets and I was way too close for it not to do damage. I raised my hands very slowly.

"Easy there, Ace," I said, "no need to go off half cocked."

I smiled friendly, but he didn't seem to care. He kept the gun trained on me as he eyed the two of us. I don't think he really was supposed to be armed, but he was also the complaint department just then.

"Drop the gun," commanded the voice from behind me. The little gun strayed from me for just a moment.

The fellow over my shoulder was wearing a blue golf shirt, khaki pants, and an Atlanta Braves cap. If it wasn't for those Ray-bans, he could have been any dude on the street. I was suddenly tempted to kiss Sue Nansen.

"FBI," he said, for emphasis. "Drop it."

He dropped it.

"What kept you?" I asked, as if we had planned this.

"That was a damn fool thing to do. Jumping into a fight like that. Saving your ass was not part of my assignment."

"Sorry. Guess I couldn't just stand by."

"Me, neither." He pulled a cell phone from his pocket.

I stepped over and reached down to help the bigger guard. He hesitated for a moment, but took the assistance.

By the time the cops arrived, the rest of Kaiser's security was already there. About half a dozen arrived from opposing directions in cars. The rest came to the inside gate. No one reached for a gun, but they did bring a couple of snarling dogs. Having us surrounded and out numbered, they stood in smaller groups, chatting, leaving the three of us feeling like the 7th Cavalry. Kaiser's head of Security, David Patton, was not really pleased, but was slightly intimidated by my new FBI friend, Chris Daniels.

Patton squawked about private property, disruption of business, and government abuse of power. It was just plain assault, Daniels countered, and all he wanted were the two guards. The little guard, one Jason Thompson, argued that our beating victim started the scuffle. I pointed out that once he was down, it should have been possible to just restrain him.

Apparently, the youngster had come in looking for a job application and was a little reluctant to be turned away. According to the guards, the kid got belligerent, the little guy, Thompson, pushed back, then it got out of hand. Looked to me more like a good old fashioned beat down.

Longstreet arrived with another Pineville officer and Agent Nansen.

"I should have known you'd be in the middle of it," the Police Chief said to me with a grin. "You have a real flair for annoying people."

"If it's worth doing, it's worth doing well."

Before an extra car arrived to transport our combatants back to the station, Ferguson arrived with several press vehicles.

"Oh, great," Longstreet grumbled, "Film at 11."

"Make him useful, have him transport the security pair, you take the young guy. You're out sooner."

"Not a bad idea, who are you riding with."

"I'm staying. I have a few questions."

"They don't seem real hot on visitors today."

"Your point?"

"I'll stay," Nansen said. "Keep him out of trouble."

I smiled. My sister, Marcia, used to get the same assignment. Didn't work back then either.

By the time the passengers were ready to go, a couple of major suits arrived. Karl Werner was the company president. Tom Chesney was VP for operations.

"This is an outrage," Werner bellowed. "You can't just swoop in here..."

"Actually, I can," Longstreet said. We have these two for assault, assault with a deadly weapon, might even get attempted murder on Shorty. You people are just lucky he didn't shoot anybody."

Werner went on for a while. Apparently his lawyers had lawyers and they were going to sue Pineville, the state of North Carolina, and most of the rest of North America. Longstreet listened politely up to a point.

"I could run you in, too, if it would make you feel better."

Werner huffed, and puffed, but finally lapsed into outraged silence.

In the meantime, I was asking Tom Chesney about the Motor Pool. Specifically, the access van that might have been in town a couple of days ago. The driver might have seen something to do with the kidnapping.

"I'm sure you're wrong, detective....?"

"I'm not a detective; I'm a friend of the victim. Trey Hughes."

"Trey? Oh, of course. Mr. Kaiser has taken quite an interest in your case. He has asked that we extend you any courtesy."

That didn't make much sense. Why would Kaiser offer to help? Me, personally? I never met the man, or had I? I guess the advantage of being a recluse is that you can also be anonymous.

"I'll be glad to check, but no one has driven that van since last Thursday when I took my son to the Hospital in Asheville."

Agent Nansen and I got the grand tour of the motor pool with mixed results. The keys were kept locked during off-hours. Chesney had a key, along with Werner, Kaiser (I'd assume), and Connie Bennett, the CFO. The mileage logs fit Chesney's version, never moved since last week. On the other hand, the visual inspection showed the same van I saw in the video.

"Would you mind if a crime scene unit went over the van?" I asked.

Nansen's jaw dropped. I no had authority to call a crime scene team, but as I explained later, he couldn't know that.

"Actually, I can't authorize that—only Mr. Werner or Mr. Kaiser, I'd guess. It's a matter of privacy, you understand. Certainly if you had a warrant..."

"What happened to full cooperation?"

"Sorry."

"Can I borrow it?"

Chesney smiled. "I don't think I can authorize that either. Nothing personal."

"Thanks anyway, I guess."

Chapter 17

I choose to walk back into the old town, hoping my feet might jar loose an idea. Sue Nansen dismissed the cop car waiting for us and joined me.

"So, is he covering up, or does he really not know?" I asked her.

She looked at me skeptically, then smiled.

"You're sure that's the van?"

Access vans are as rare as French sports cars. The possibilities of people just picking one out of thin air identical to the one I saw on tape was pretty unlikely. The idea of someone deliberately disguising another van to look like the Kaiser van was also preposterous.

"I'm sure. The question is: Who doctored the paperwork? I don't think it was Chesney. He seemed pretty straightforward."

"I agree. He seemed genuinely unsure about letting us search the van. If he knew what it was used for he would have been more clearly defensive."

I nodded agreement.

"I didn't take a real close look at the mileage logs," I said, "because I didn't want to tip anybody off. Think we can get the FBI to take a closer look at those records? Just to be sure, that kind of thing."

"I thought you wanted the crime lab to go over the van?"

"I don't think they'd ever get it in one piece if it came to that. I'm a bit concerned about Vandals."

"Fourth century, or modern day?"

"Modern. In fact tonight."

Her mouth opened. "You're not suggesting..."

I shook my head. "Our van driver was probably out there today, and I think it might have given him an idea. I can hear them now: 'Vandals, maybe friends of the kid who got beat up this morning, broke into the compound and trashed the motor pool including our very expensive access van'."

My leg rang. It was Pop Gustafsson.

"I am on the shuttle bus from the Knoxville airport. They say I should be there in about 90 minutes."

"Great, Pop. See you then."

"Anyway," I jumped back on track, "I was thinking if the night was going to be kind of slow, somebody should keep an eye on it. Perhaps you could spare one of your three musketeers…"

Her nostrils flared. Apparently FBI agents were far to valuable to stake out vans.

"OK…maybe the Pineville cops, or even better, Ferguson," I suggested.

"You don't like him much," she said, laughing.

"No. I think because he reminds me of some of guys my dad used to deal with in the Air Force. Never going to get anywhere until they learn a little respect for others. Dad used to call them small men."

"Plus he threw you in jail."

"Not exactly Dale Carnegie, is he?"

"I'm thinking of throwing you two into a locked room."

I shrugged.

Before I could make a snide remark, the phone rang again.

It took a second to recognize the squawk at the other end.

"Max fucking Kaiser! You want information on fucking Max Kaiser?" Brian Cavanaugh screamed. "How can you not know Max Kaiser? He's a legend! A god!"

"Not in my church. While you're at it, Brian, see if you can find a picture of him too, he seems to be a recluse."

"I know *that.* How does he fit into this thing?"

"No idea yet. He really might not. There's no way of knowing until you send me the information."

"Do you have any idea how much stuff I have about Max Kaiser? Born: Asheville, North Carolina. B S Electrical Engineering: University of North Carolina, Master's in Physics Massachusetts Institute…"

"Cavanaugh, just send it."

"I'll have to FedEx it. Do you have any idea how much they charge?"

"That's OK, Cavanaugh, I'll pay for it."

"Please… Nobody I know actually *pays* for FedEx."

"Then what are we arguing about?"

"If you had a laptop with you, or even a decent cell phone instead of that 1990's dinosaur..."

"I left it at home."

"How can you go anywhere without your laptop? That's why it's called a *portable* computer..."

The Cavanaugh headache was building. No matter where and when, he always managed to get sidetracked and find something to rant about that would leave my head pounding. He rattled off a litany of electronic devices I could (but didn't) have with me that he could use to send the info within scant seconds. All of which he could have obtained by completely illegal means for pennies on the retail dollar.

Knowing what I didn't have wasn't going to help him with this immediate problem.

"Cavanaugh," I said, when I finally managed to shoehorn in a sentence. "Let me know if Kaiser and Mark Brunson have any joint ventures other than Crystal Mountain resort."

"Who the hell is Mark Brunson?"

"He's a legend, a God. Just look him up, huh?"

As I sat waiting at the station for Pop, the tall cop who shadowed me yesterday made himself invisible over by the little newsstand. The tram landed at the bottom disgorging Lee Holt, Jay Morrow and several others.

"You lied to me," she said, grinning.

"Which lie? There have been so many."

"You pretended you didn't know JoAnne McCullough."

"No, I just didn't tell you."

"Exactly."

"She's one of your van witnesses. She told me."

I shrugged very slowly.

"She's an eyewitness! She has to go to the police."

"And tell them what? She saw a person in a wheelchair put into a van? We've got all that on videotape."

"I can't interview videotape."

"Now we get to it. You want her on camera. Why didn't you ask her?"

"She refused. But if you...."

"If I what? If I asked her personally, told her it was important? Tricked or duped her into talking with you..."

"Seems kind of sordid when you put it that way."

"So it should."

She smiled resignedly. "I would have tried a different approach if I'd known, that's all."

She toured the room with her eyes.

"Are you on your way up? Or waiting for me?" She batted her eyelashes in comic exaggeration.

"Neither. I'm waiting for Nina's dad."

"He's here?"

"Soon."

"Can I wait and meet him?"

"No," I answered rhetorically.

Pop looked exhausted. Of course if you were missing your family, sleep would be a difficult thing, too.

"You look like hell, Trey," he said with concern. "Have you slept?"

"Like you, not much."

"Is there any news? I tried to call last night, but could not reach you."

Pop was born and grew up in Norway, coming here as a college student. His English had grown increasingly American over the years. It was only at stressful times when his inflection got heavy.

"It's a long story."

I quickly filled him in on the progress, or lack thereof so far, and introduced him to Lee and Jay.

"They are idiots, buffoons—locking you in jail."

"Yes, sir, but they are struggling with the same questions. Who did this? And why Nina? They have to go with trends and possibilities because they don't know any of us. They needed me out of the way and there you are."

He nodded. "So, you are not too much the worst for wear, eh?"

"Nah, little sore arm from this morning's fight, but I'm OK."

"Have you heard from your family? Your father, Your sister?" Just making small talk.

"Talked to Germany last week. The Major is retiring in November."

"Your father, retiring? No! Then he is coming home?"

"No. Actually, he's already agreed to work for General Motors in Amsterdam. Birgit is already looking for a place for them. Kat wants to finish High School in America, so if I can find a job..."

"She will stay with you?" I caught a hint of surprise.

"Well, Marsha and Tom have their hands full with baby Michelle. Katerina turns 17 in February, so it's not like she's going to be helpless."

"I'm sure you'll take excellent care of your stepsister," he said, confidently.

Of course I hadn't done such a hot job with 20-year-old Nina.

Chapter 18

Once I got Pop booked into the resort hotel, I took him back down the hill. The FBI asked him a few cursory questions. I gave him a tour of the town. Then Lee joined us at the Café for dinner and a strategy session.

We sat at one of the tables in the front window so the cop tailing me would take comfort in knowing I wasn't out making trouble.

There wasn't really that much to strategize about. I had no idea what to do next, except keep an eye on that van. We turned back to the questions of who and why.

"If they kidnapped her for money," I challenged the panel, "why cancel the ransom drop?"

"They were unable to come?" Pop said.

"You don't suppose they lost her?" Lee joked. Suddenly, her eyes lit up.

"Maybe it was a test run!" She said.

"Test of what?" I asked.

"They needed to see if somebody would pay the money. Like you said, the deepest pockets were Brunson's, who, as we now know, has all his assets tied up. They needed to know if he could still get money."

"But who kidnaps on spec? 'We're grabbing a girl at random to see if somebody's willing to pay the ransom.' It doesn't make sense. Even if you did, the deed's done now. It's no more risky for them to actually *collect* the ransom than it was to stage a dry run. A second attempt just adds more risk."

"Unless the ransom was an afterthought," Pop said. "It's almost like the kidnapping and ransom are separate things."

"Exactly!" I said. "That's why it hasn't made sense. We have two crimes. And possibly two criminals. One for Kidnapping, the other, Extortion—or maybe Grand Larceny."

"Try this" Lee suggested. "Brunson, with all his cash tied up, gets a note that one of his contestants has been kidnapped. The note makes mention of a ransom but no when or where. By the next morning, he or one of his faithful retainers hatches a brilliant scam. A ransom demand is one thing that can unfreeze assets or get emergency quantities of cash from a bank or insurance company."

"OK, but why the dry run?" Pop asked. "Like Trey said, 'In for a penny, in for a pound'."

"Test the level of his resources," I said. "Find out just how much the system would let him take. Two to one the next demand is for more money, and they'll make the drop."

"But how do we prove it?" Lee asked.

"I don't know. Don't think we can."

"Why would the real kidnappers demand ransom without, well… setting up an actual ransom?" Pop asked.

"To disguise their true intention."

"Which is…?" He asked.

I rubbed my eyes.

"I have no idea…yet."

The food was just in front of us when my cell phone "rang".

"I'm just about to eat, Cavanaugh, what is it?"

"It was so obvious I almost never even thought of it. I've been running searches of police departments, fire departments, private ambulances, car rentals, and every other fucking thing I could think of… then it hit me… Insurance! The only way this thing would work is with some kind of fucking insurance. Hacking insurance companies are so easy!"

"Cavanaugh..."

"They share everything with each other—stuff they're not even supposed to know. I mean why would an insurance company need to know your blood type."

"Brian?"

"I think I could write a book just on the illegal information companies trade back and forth.

"CAVANAUGH," I roared, startling the rest of the Café. "Was there *any* minor point to this?"

"Sure. It was easy. All I had to do was punch in the name, and poof here she is."

"She who?'

"I found her!"

"You found Nina?"

"No, Carla. I figured it would be easier to find Carla because she wasn't hiding—at least not in the 'cover your tracks' sense of hiding…"

"Cavanaugh! Where… is… Carla?"

"Oh, yeah… She's at some place called the Cole Neurophysiology Center. I've got a search in for the location…"

I hung up the phone. I already knew where it was.

"Did I hear you say you found Carla?" Pop asked.

They both leaned closer over the table.

"Yeah, I did. She's in Knoxville, at University of Tennessee Medical Center."

"As in 'just over the mountains' Knoxville?" Lee asked.

"Just over the mountains. All this time. I really *am* going to kill her."

Chapter 19

We got to Roger's just as Miz Dinah was closing. She handed me the keys to a '98 Buick—no credit cards, no application. It always pays to know the owner.

I couldn't tell you how fast I was going, but I peeled something in the neighborhood of 30 minutes off a trip that normally took nearly 2 hours. Pop and I didn't speak the whole trip. We were both pondering the same question: How to tell Carla we (more accurately, I) managed to lose her sister.

It was about 8:10 when we got to the Hospital.

"I'm sorry, sir. Visiting hours are over," the efficient receptionist told us. "You'll have to come back tomorrow."

I leaned over the desk. "This is Doctor Thomas Gustafsson." I paused, as if she should recognize the name. "He just flew in from Phoenix to check on his daughter's condition. Because of his busy schedule, coming back in the morning is very problematic. Surely, he could just check on her for a moment."

"That's impossible."

"Can he at least consult with her attending physician? Certainly it would ease his mind."

She argued for a bit, but finally agreed to call up to Carla's floor.

"Trey, I am not a medical doctor."

"I know, but you *are* Dr. Gustafsson, you *do* want to see your daughter or at least know how she's doing. You can lead a horse to water but he's responsible for his own assumptions."

He shook his head. His agitation probably looked to the girl like the impatience of an important man used to getting his own way.

"Go to the Fourth Floor, Dr. Chamberlain will meet you there."

We walked around the wall to the elevators, Pop's leather shoes echoing off the soulless floor.

I hate Hospitals.

All those cold, florescent, empty, linoleum hallways. All of them painted in non-color. Neutral, I guess they'd call it. In deference to the school colors, the University of Tennessee hospital made use of Burnt Orange. Instead of adding color, the orange seemed to be neutralized by the already dead walls. Like the fake wood paneling on those Metal hospital beds, the color on the walls added irony, not life.

Hospital rooms are neutral, the food is neutral, even the people, no matter how compassionate, end up neutral, as well. Some are neutral by choice, avoiding the emotional damage that inevitably comes with the job. For others, the emotional losses force them to surrender to neutrality.

All hospitals feel the same. Anger, fear, pain, and despair, with just enough joy to make the rest worse.

And they all smell the same: The metallic clang of blood, the ammonia and methane assault of body excretions. Sweat, disinfectant and death.

Pop put his hand on my shoulder as we boarded the elevator. I smiled at him. I wasn't exactly looking forward to doing this, but it had to be done.

Dr. Chamberlain was a short, kind of square woman. She was the assistant to Michael Van Der Saar who actually devised the treatment.

"Dr. Gustafsson, your daughter agreed to participate in a double blind study to determine the effectiveness of a combined treatment program."

A double blind study, I later learned, is one where neither the doctor not the patient knows whether he's getting the real treatment or just being told he's being treated (the placebo effect). In a blind study, the Doctor knows who's getting the drug and who's getting sugar pills.

The advantage of double blind is that the doctor can evaluate the results without the temptation of knowing how it affects his original assumptions about the treatment.

In this case, she was explaining, they had two treatments they were testing: a drug therapy, and an electrostimulus device. The test group was divided into three. One got the drugs, one got the device, and the third got both.

The drug was apparently the latest in a series of drugs designed to stimulate reconnection of nerve tissue. Some of these drug treatments have been able to stimulate growth and re-connect but never enough to handle major (trunk or spinal) injuries.

The drug treatment was really nothing out of the ordinary. The real breakthrough, according to Van Der Saar, was his electronic nerve booster. This electronic device was the element they were hanging all their hopes on.

Think of the nervous system as a huge set of electrical wires. Repairing individual nerves is possible because it is just like fixing a single wire. Spinal injures are more like cutting a telephone cable. It's impossible to repair because you can't match the wires within the bundle.

That's why the study required patients with nerve damage due to physical trauma instead of degenerative condition or disease. The idea was that these clamped or cut nerve areas had all the right signals, but they were not strong enough to get through the damaging blockage. Van Der Saar's magic device was a battery- powered microchip device that worked as an electrical amplifier.

"As you know, Dr. Gustafsson, your daughter is suffering from damage to the trunk nerves in both legs. We started drug therapy a few weeks ago. We did the surgery this afternoon, so she's still very heavily sedated. She should be able to get back to her normal routine as soon as she is released in a week or so."

"A week?" I asked, surprised.

"Just because it's experimental. Most similar procedures would have people back in their own homes within 48 hours."

"Hello, Alex." Pop said.

If there was a bigger shock than seeing AJ at University of Tennessee Medical Center, I don't want it. *How did he get there before us?*

"Hey, Doc," he said cheerily. "When did you guys get here? I was going to call you tonight."

"But how did...."

"Carla sent an e-mail. I tried to call you, but I guess you were out searching for her sister, so I came down myself. She told me she was going to be in and out for most of today… How did you do, any luck?"

I shook my head.

"Well, we found one sister anyway," he said.

"Her sister was here this afternoon," Dr. Chamberlain said.

"Nina was *here*?"

"Her sister? Oh, no doubt. The resemblance was unmistakable."

"Resemblance?" The only obvious resemblance between those two was in action, not looks.

"Are you sure she claimed to be Nina Gustafsson?" I asked.

"She just said she was the patient's sister. Is something wrong?"

"Doc," AJ said, "Carla's sister is almost 6 feet tall, red hair, and eyes you couldn't miss on a bet."

"She's also been missing for 3 days," I added.

"No, this girl was about 5-foot-3, long dark hair, pretty..."

"Sounds like the nurse that just kicked me out of Carla's room," AJ said.

The description also fit the "nurse" who kidnapped Nina.

"Where is Carla's room? Around the corner?" I was already on the move.

"Yeah, at the end… Trey?"

I heard the crash before I turned the corner. I lowered my head and sprinted down the hall. As I reached the nurses' station about halfway down, several nurses stepped out to investigate the noise. I tried to keep both momentum and balance weaving through the pylons, but I caught a hip and staggered a little.

Several of the girls were wearing burnt orange surgical scrubs as was the one that came out of the room near the end of the hall. She had a black satchel in one hand while the other obscured most of her face. Even with the bag, she beat me to the exit.

As I hit the door, I saw the 'alarm will sound' device, but I didn't hear the alarm. As I entered the stairwell, the girl, near the bottom of the first flight downward, turned and swung the satchel by its strap, like an Olympic hammer thrower, launching it at me. The bag caught my knee and forced me to stumble at the top of the stairs. By the time I got going again, she was nearly a full floor below me.

On the second floor landing, she had ditched the burnt orange shirt. As I leapt down the last flight, I saw her stepping out the door in a black tank and spandex pants thing. Might have even been a one piece, I later told the cops. My foot caught in her orange scrub pants as I saw her hopping into a brown Ford Taurus. They flew out of the quiet zone leaving a good sized patch of rubber. I didn't catch the plate number.

Chapter 20

I trudged back up the stairs, empty-handed. As I got to the third floor, I saw red dots. *Blood.* The blood trail continued up toward the room. The satchel thrown at me, as I had guessed, was the computer bag I had given Carla for Christmas. I doubt the bag, or the computer, was designed with that sort of abuse in mind.

I was following the blood back toward Carla's room when I heard them call Code Blue. When I got there, the little doctor was shoving Alex out the door—no mean feat.

"She just stopped breathing," Alex said to me. "She seemed to be trying to speak, then started struggling for breath."

"They think she's been poisoned," Pop said

"But... what about the blood?"

"Apparently, The phony nurse's. Carla must have got in a pretty good shot. I'm guessing she got her nose broken."

"Good." There was plenty left over for me to break.

A nurse slowly drove us back down to the hall, just past the nurse's station to a lounge. Assuring us they would do what they could, she left the three of us dying in the night.

"Why is it so hot in here," Pop complained.

It's a hospital, the temperature is never right.

"Don't sweat it, Pop," I answered. It'll be cold by morning."

I sat in a chair and closed my eyes. It was going to be another longest night of my life. A night on the edge of forever.

"Children aren't allowed in the ICU." The nurse seemed kindly enough but resolute.

Then why is Carla in there? I stood my 12-year-old ground. Somebody had to be with Carla. Pop (Dr. Tom in those days) was still downstairs while they patched up Nina (Squirt). Dad was on maneuvers with his Squadron—Lackland Air Force Base, San Antonio, Texas. We had made the mistake of going down for a few days that previous summer. Summer in Texas might not be hell, but it can get work as its stunt double. My mother was trailing Pop and Nina at full flood. She hated Carla and Nina, but she was drunk and had an audience. So she was devastated.

Every two minutes. Just like Old Faithful.

"Why not?" I challenged the nurse.

"There are, well… a lot of… wires and things."

"IV tubes, Monitor leads, Oxygen hoses… that kind of stuff?" I had learned something about hospitals when Lani died.

She was treating me like a child and I was furious. I wanted to cry, to scream, but I knew I couldn't. They made that rule about kids because they were afraid we would make a lot of noise, or get hysterical. I just wanted to make sure Carla didn't wake up alone. I was keeping my promise to her mother, or trying to. I would be quiet as a mouse, but I wasn't leaving.

"We're just afraid it might be a little upsetting for you."

She was going to be in Intensive Care until her intracranial pressure stabilized. After that she would get her legs fixed and she'd be back together again.

"I'm not going to get sick or nothing… anything," I corrected myself. "I was with her when she got hit by the car. If that didn't make me scared…"

"Honey, it's the hospital rules. Besides, you have to be immediate family."

"I am family."

She giggled momentarily, but cut it off when She realized I was dead serious.

My eyes were burning, but I wasn't going to cry. They weren't going to run me off because I was a hysterical kid. I couldn't swallow, but I wasn't going to cry. I closed my eyes. I felt a couple of tears sneak out. *Traitors!* I fought the rest back, opening my eyes again. Angry, defiant—I wasn't crying! I refused to acknowledge any tears. No wiping, no sniffling.

The nurse was rolling a single tear down her own cheek. I could see others welling up at her eyelids. She used the back of her carefully folded left thumb to catch the tear. She sniffed quietly, then sighed heavily.

"What the hell," she muttered, caressing my cheek while she wiped another tear from my eye with her trailing thumb. "If I didn't see you, I couldn't stop you."

She lost a couple more tears as she broke into a wide grin. I smiled back, but turned away kind of quick. It wouldn't have taken much to have both of us flooding the place.

In the half hour before Pop got there, both nurses and a doctor had been in to check on Carla. Not one of them smiled, blinked, or gave any indication I was in the room.

She seemed so tiny and lost on that bed. I held her hand and finally did cry a little. I felt guilty. I hadn't seen any cars moving when I crossed the street. I know the driver ignored the stop sign, but I did not remember even *seeing* that car when I crossed.

I should have done something. I had promised the girls' mother I would look out for them, now they were both in the hospital and I had no idea what happened.

"Your mother is worried about you."

I probably jumped a little, then turned and shrugged. It was possible she cared, I supposed, but the concerned mother act was for the benefit of her audience.

"How's the pest?" I asked Dr. Tom.

"She's going to be OK. She broke her wrist and hurt her ribs pretty bad. Are you sure you weren't hurt?"

I shook my head. Not even a skinned knee. It wasn't fair—I was there too. I should have a scar.

"The police officers and paramedics said you did a great job of getting help and taking care of…" his voice caught. *Great, more tears all around.* "…the girls and everything. He also said you were blaming yourself a little."

"I should have seen it, done something. I promised."

"The woman ran a stop sign Trey—you couldn't guess that. I know you promised Lani you would take care of the girls, but there's only so much any of us can do. All she'd want is for you to do what you can. You did a great job. Your dad is very proud of you. We all are."

He was right, I did everything I could. So why did I... do I feel guilty?

If there is a trick to surviving these nightmares, it isn't to keep reassuring yourselves, or wondering what they're doing. Pacing the floor and worrying and jumping at every noise won't help either. Unless you're a doctor, seeking out updates every few minutes isn't helpful. The best way you can help is staying out of the way. I would say pray, but that seems obvious. The trick is to find a way of getting away. Close your eyes and concentrate on the silence or the background noise. Relax, try to sleep. Save your emotions for the end—You don't want to bankrupt the tear bank.

While I'm at it, the guilts and playing 'what if' is even worse. We all have to live with ourselves, what makes you so special?

You can talk about every question except *the big one*. Be quietly optimistic, or just quiet.

As veterans of the long night, Pop and I watched Alex pace the room. We both wanted to stop him. To explain the futility of agitating yourself—but neither of us knew words he would believe anyway. Talking to him would probably only agitate him more. All we could do is set a quiet example for him.

Dr. Chamberlain walked into the room.

"Her heart stopped briefly, but we got it going again. She's still having a lot of trouble breathing. We've got her on a respirator, and we're going to move her to Critical Care, just as a precaution."

Great. My favorite part of the hospital.

"Do you know what the poison was?" I asked.

"We found traces in the syringe. We think it's curare."

"Curare?" AJ asked.

"An organic poison used by South American natives," I said. "Mild doses cause temporary paralysis. Full doses shut down the entire nervous system. Some doctors actually use it in controlled doses as a local anesthetic."

"That's very good," Chamberlain said. I could not have explained it better myself.

"Thanks, I read a lot." Actually it was an 8th grade science project.

"You ever consider medicine as a career."

I smiled as I shook my head.

"Is she going to be all right?" Pop asked.

"Too early to tell. If we're right about the curare, the effect will begin to decline in the next several hours. The problem is, we don't have much data on nervous systems that are already damaged. If she gets through the night, we'll know a lot more."

"Thanks, Doc." I walked out with her to ask one more question.

"If she had died, Doc, and you hadn't known about the needle or the nurse, what would have been the verdict--natural causes?"

She nodded emphatically. "Absolutely. Allergic reaction, post-op complications, maybe reaction from our experimental compound. No way would they have suspected this was poison. And it wouldn't have shown up in the standard post-mortem."

They moved her up two floors.

When silence becomes unbearable you start talking. At first you talk about everything you can think of except, of course…

Then when everything else gets talked out that's all you do talk about. What they said, what they did, how they talked. *When was the last time…*

"Carla called me about a week ago," Pop said, casually. "I was dining with… a colleague and wasn't home. She said it was kind of important but never got back to me. Maybe to tell me she was coming here."

I shook my head. "She would have left a message."

I paused for a bit. "So tell me about this 'colleague'."

He reddened slightly. "Why would you want to know about…"

"Well if it was the usual colleague, you would have just named him or her. Since you're treating it like a government secret, I figure the professor's got a lady."

"Whether I have her, or she has me, is yet to be decided," he grinned. "I do know it's become rather serious. We're considering getting married."

"About time," I said emphatically. "I think it's great! Do the girls know?"

"I…" Very long pause. "No."

"Scared?"

"Concerned, I suppose." *Scared.*

"When this is over, we'll all have dinner and meet the lady. The girls will be fine—after they get over the shock."

"I just feel… I don't know. I guess I'm afraid they'll believe… Trey, I'm not trying to replace their mother."

"Listen, Pop, Lani wouldn't want you to be missing out on life just because something happened to her. Neither would either of her daughters, and I'll remind them if I have to."

"Thanks, Trey."

Chapter 21

"You really are trouble you know?" Sue Nansen said, grinning. "Every time I turn around, you're either at the hospital or putting someone in it."

"You just caught me on a good day."

Nansen and Chris Daniels arrived after the Knoxville police had been in and taken a report and Carla's damaged laptop to see if they could learn anything useful. They also left a guard against further attempts.

The local investigation hadn't seemed very thorough, but one of the uniforms let slip that the FBI had already put their bid in. All the K-ville cops were supposed to do is keep us all in one piece until they got here.

Whoever might have been working on behalf of the state of Tennessee must have seen how the wind was blowing and stayed in his hole.

Van Der Saar arrived right after the Knoxville cops. He seemed to think we had something to do with what happened.

"Who are you people? What are you doing? Do you have any inkling how many years of research you've ruined? It has taken us years to find the candidates we needed for a proper double blind study. To introduce an outside neurological agent—It not only invalidates her results, but risks the validity of the entire experiment.

"I cannot believe this! Where's our security? I don't know how you people...."

AJ stepped directly in front of him and grabbed the front of his shirt, if not his entire chest.

"Listen, Doc. I'm sure you're a bit disappointed about your little research project, but to be honest, we don't give a damn. Just make sure Carla's OK."

"Easy AJ," I said, "we don't want to break the doctor."

He released him. “Sorry, doc, I’m just a little worried about Carla.”

The doctor nodded, glad to be back on terra firma, unbroken. He looked at the three of us then nodded again.

“You’re right, of course, her health is certainly more important than my research. It’s just so frustrating to think that all this work might prove useless.”

“Did the lab results come in yet?” I asked.

“Laura might know. I’ll see if she has anything new.”

He moved pretty quick getting out of there.

AJ shook his head.

“Shouldn’t have done that,” He said morosely.

“You just beat me to it.”

Dr. Chamberlain came in with good news. Carla was starting to breathe weakly on her own. She would make it. It was still too early to speculate on long-term effects, but it looked like she was going to recover.

Then, as the sky lit itself in pre-dawn grey, the Feds arrived—by helicopter, of course. Pop had just gone downstairs for a spot of breakfast.

“How are things here?” She asked. “You guys get any rest?”

“Not a bit.” I gestured toward AJ, who had nodded off in the corner of the waiting room. She smiled.

“We’re doing OK, I suppose. Pop and I are veterans at this sort of thing. I assume you already talked to the doctor, right?”

She nodded.

“So you know the longer she hangs on, the better her chances.”

“You were right about someone trying to destroy that van. They torched it tonight.”

“And you, of course, apprehended them”

Nansen’s face turned dark. “Now, whatever gave you the idea that we were actually trying to arrest criminals?”

“You mean they outran Ferguson?”

“He would have to have *seen* them, wouldn’t he? It gets worse. Tom Chesney was shot. By the perps, we presume, but why was he there at all?”

“I don’t know, maybe he decided it was possible somebody was using the van and tried to catch them at it.” I said.

“What changed his mind? He seemed pretty adamant yesterday.”

“I don’t know. He checked the mileage log, right? Maybe he saw an entry that just didn’t look right. After we left, he double-checked and realized it wasn’t an honest mistake or a typo, it was proof of what we were saying.”

“Why didn’t he just call us?”

“Company loyalty. If he called the police, they’d disrupt everything. If he could give you the actual thief/joyrider he would save both his fellow executives and Kaiser a lot of hassle. Where was he shot?”

“Twice, in the back. Does it matter?”

“Probably not. I just wondered if he knew who shot him.”

She frowned. “You think they shot him because he recognized them.”

“All they had to do was recognize *him.* The odds are really good that at least one of the conspirators has some tie to Kaiser.”

She shook her head. “Oh, come on, anybody could have grabbed that van.”

“Sure, but there would have been discrepancies on the mileage log. The van might have been out in the open, but the log was safely locked in the Kaiser offices.”

“Good point, I hadn’t thought of that.”

“Don’t worry, I won’t tell.”

She laughed. Then her eyes widened.

"Hey, Trey," AJ said.

For a guy the size of a small country, AJ could be disturbingly quiet.

“I’m going outside for some air.”

Knowing it was daylight again, I was thinking I wouldn’t mind a little fresh air myself.

“Good idea, I think I’ll go with you.”

AJ looked at Nansen.

“Sure,” she said, “we’re all done. Don’t leave the country.”

She broke into a huge grin. I smiled back, just a little. It wasn’t that funny.

Chapter 22

The red-orange sky of dawn was just beginning to get its daily case of the blues. We walked down to the street and began circling the block. The cool morning air was doing me plenty of good, but AJ was still pretty agitated.

“Listen, Trey, I got to tell you something.”

"Sure, go ahead."

"I just wanted to let you know… I mean, I wasn't going behind your back, I just…"

"Could we slow down and try this in English? What are you babbling about?"

"It’s just… OK, I've been going over to Carla's."

"Yeah, I know. You mentioned the key the other day."

"Well, I know you two are, or were… you know… something. Anyway I wanted you to know she's just been helping me study."

"Study?"

"Yeah, we just been studying. Maybe out for a beer or a burger afterward, but it's all like, you know, buddies. Nothing's going on. I just thought you might want to know.

Poor Alex had been holding it in for months. Torturing himself. Feeling like he was stepping into my territory with Carla. I could see his dilemma. Carla and I had been together so long, we tended to act a bit like a married couple, doing everything—talking, playing, laughing, even fighting with the casual intimacy of people who know each other very well.

Years before, when we began high school, we tried to be the romantic couple, but we both found it a little uncomfortable. My sister, Marsh, who I used to talk a little with about girl things, said it was because we couldn’t let go of what we already were to become the new thing we weren’t even sure we wanted. I sometimes wondered if I was a little intimidated by the chair. Every time it seems like I hesitate to do anything with her, I always have that vague doubt.

In the end, although I will always love Carla, we were not a couple. I was never jealous of any guy she went with—but I had to admit, I was a little relieved to know she wasn't going with AJ. It would have just been awkward, that's all. He was my friend, she was my friend. Like he said, we used to be… well… something.

"Studying for what?" I asked trying not to sound relieved

"Law school entrance exam. The LSAT."

"Law school?"

"Yeah," he was actually embarrassed. "Wheels thinks I can get some minority scholarships and stuff—make it work."

"A lawyer? AJ, we've roomed together four years...you ain't said shit about being a lawyer." We had talked a lot about dreams, goals, and the future. Why hadn't he mentioned this kind of thing to me before?

"I always figured it was a waste. I mean a guy like me. Can you imagine me rumbling around like Godzilla in a courtroom? I never really wanted to talk about it. But then I kept talking with Carla and I just couldn't quite explain to her why I couldn't do it, you know what I mean."

I nodded. It was tough to make up excuses around Carla.

"After a while longer, I got to believing maybe I could do it. Now, I guess I'm set to give it a shot."

"How long have you wanted to do this?"

"As long as I can remember. I used to watch all those TV lawyer shows—Perry Mason, Matlock... I knew they weren't always that realistic, but I liked the idea of somebody standing up for people making sure they got a fair chance.

"When I was in high school, Mama and I went to Washington on vacation. I talked her into letting us go to the Supreme Court. It was so dull Mama actually fell asleep, but I was fascinated. I just kept looking at the judges in their robes and listened, and listened. The arguments were nowhere near as entertaining as you and Carla or you and Nina, but they were more… I don't know… important, I guess."

"So why didn't you ever mention it?"

"I guess I figured you'd laugh. Big ol' lineman like me trying to fit in with a bunch of smart lawyers."

I was a bit of surprised. Although not the best student, AJ was certainly a smart enough fellow. I had never known him to be self-conscious about his size, either.

"I think you're just the kind of lawyer we need these days. A genuine good guy who cares about what happens to his clients. I think you're just a little frightened to find out that that you can actually get what you always wanted. That kind of thing can be a little intimidating."

He took a deep breath. "That's what Carla keeps saying."

"So she's right for once," I said, laughing.

We walked a little further then I turned to him again.

"Law school?"

"Yeah." he smiled a little guiltily

"I guess that means I'll never be able to trust you again."

When we got back, Sue Nansen was arguing with Pop. In a quiet hospital, voices carry pretty well.

"I am absolutely certain. If I knew something I would have told you already. My daughters are grown women who do not have to share the intimate details of their lives with me."

"Come on! Somebody kidnaps one daughter, tries to kill the other, and it's all just coincidence? Don't you have any idea who this woman could be?"

"No. I am sorry, I do not know any reason why anyone would want to harm either of my daughters."

"Who would the girls confide in, share secrets with?"

"Each other, mostly. Perhaps Trey. Besides that, I know of no one."

"Do you think Trey might be holding out on us?"

I startled her. "Maybe you should ask him that again when I'm not in the room?"

"It would not matter," he said. "I know Trey would move heaven and earth to help either one of the girls. If he is not telling you something it is because he does not trust you."

"Is that it Trey, you don't trust us?"

I shook my head. "I have nothing to tell. Whatever these two got themselves into, they made sure to keep me out of it."

"No old enemies, Dr. Gustafsson?"

"I teach history," he said, incredulously, "No one would kill my daughter over a C-plus."

Nansen shrugged a bit. Unlikely, sure, but nothing criminal seems impossible any more. She seemed convinced one of us knew.

"What about your wife?'

"Leilani died when the girls were young."

"Natural causes?"

"Yes," we chorused. She turned to me.

"I was there when she died." I explained.

"Cancer," Pop said.

"Nobody with a grudge?"

We both shook our heads.

Chris Daniels broke the deadlock. He came in and whispered into Nansen's ear. She hopped up.

"We got a break. They caught one of the accomplices, maybe even a suspect."

"You should go, Trey," Pop said. "We'll keep you informed from here."

I shook my head, emphatically. I didn't want to leave Carla.

"I think you should," Nansen said. "It might be someone you can recognize, which would help us." She smiled softly. "Give you a ride in the copter?"

I really didn't care about how big a break it was, I wanted to stay with Carla. I argued with Pop for a few minutes, but I ended up climbing on the helicopter. I felt a tear working down my cheek. Damn allergies.

Chapter 23

This "big" break turned out to be ransom note #2. Rose Williams was holding it when John Hatcher checked in at the front desk. He reported the finding to Ferguson who promptly arrested the girl as a conspirator. We found him sitting at the desk in Chief Longstreet's office looking smug. The police chief looked skeptical, Hatch furious.

"You can't honestly think..." Hatch was arguing.

"She was holding the ransom note." Ferguson said

"She also told me it was the ransom note, blockhead. I'm telling you this girl wouldn't get herself involved in this thing."

"Hey, I'm *from* here. I know her grandparents and all, but that doesn't change the facts. How would she end up holding the note if she was innocent?"

"Because, like she said, somebody left it in the fax machine."

"Did anybody check the fax records? See where the last couple of faxes might have gone?" Longstreet asked.

Both shook their heads. "Even if it proves there was a fax it doesn't mean she wasn't the one who sent it." Ferguson said.

"Don't you think it's a bit thin to arrest anybody on, anyway?" I just couldn't resist.

He scowled. "Interesting you should pipe up, since you're involved with this ransom note, too. You've got problems of your own. "

"Oh, how's that? You plan on arresting me...again?"

"They want you to deliver the ransom," Hatch said.

No answer for that. A logical choice, I suppose. "When?"

"Not until tonight. The drop's in Asheville this time."

"This time? Where was it last time?" I asked.

"Cherokee reservation," Nansen said.

"I thought they ran all the Cherokees out of this part of the country? Something called the Trail of Tears?"

"There's still a small patch of them left," Hatch said.

A dramatic change in location, from wilderness to the closest thing to big city they could find.

"We sure these are the same people?" I asked Sue Nansen.

"Far as we know," she said.

She didn't seem terribly convinced by her own answer. You could actually *hear* the shrug.

"Do they want more money?"

Sue nodded. "Half a million this time."

Didn't seem like enough for Nina—then again, it was more than I could ever get together.

"Why the change in location?" I asked us all.

"Afraid of being scalped? How the hell should I know?" Ferguson said.

Seemed like a strange thing to change. If they had a place scouted out, why switch?

"So, what about Rose?"

"You got something going with her?" Ferguson said. I just grinned at him

"We don't think she's involved," Nansen said for the FBI.

"I don't see it." Hatcher said.

"You really need more evidence than you've got," Longstreet agreed.

Ferguson glared around the room. He tapped a pencil furiously on the desk for about half a minute. Finally, he snapped it.

"Oh, all right, damn it. But I'm having her watched.

"Lowery!" He bellowed. The tall fellow who was following me stuck his head in the door. Ferguson gave him his instructions and he left—to disappear into the background like a shadow again. I was tempted to warn Rose not to wave at him.

"You don't have to do this ransom drop if you don't want to," Nansen said

I thought of Nina. And Carla. *Yes, I did.*

"Better watch it," I said. "People are going to start thinking you care, darlin'."

Her eyes flashed, but she smiled.

"There's just all this extra paperwork if civilians get their empty heads blown off."

"Keep my head low and powder dry?"

"That's it."

A uniform stuck his head in the door.

"Press is here."

Ferguson tried to look nonchalant, I guess, but the others saw through him as well.

"You called 'em," Longstreet said, "you get rid of them."

I turned to Agent Nansen. She shook her head slowly.

"Hardly worth coming back for," she said quietly. "You want to go back to Knoxville?"

Yeah. I wanted to go back as much as I didn't want to leave in the first place, but it looked like Carla was going to be OK and her dad was with her. Nina was still missing, and if we were counting on cementhead over there...

"No, I've got a package of stuff coming from back home waiting for me up the hill…"

Ferguson stopped in his tracks, then reached for the door.

"Hold it, Ferguson." I told him, "Maybe I *don't* have to go up?"

His face looked like *War and Peace*. It would take weeks to read all that guilt.

"Well…" he stammered

"Stealing a man's mail," I said, ironically

"A federal offense," Nansen chimed in.

"I wasn't stealing it," he said, defensively

"You just decided to be a nice guy and save me a trip?"

"It was at the desk when we arrested the girl. We took it in as evidence."

"Evidence of what? An affair with the FedEx guy? Just admit it, you got nosy and read my mail."

"I didn't read it!" He bellowed angrily. Then muttered, "I didn't have time."

Chief Longstreet opened the door and spoke to one of the deputies, who came back quickly with the sealed FedEx box.

"It's still sealed," Ferguson pointed out. "Just like I said."

I collected the box, smiling gently, then left the office. I crossed paths with Dinah Williams on the jailhouse steps.

"She should be out in a little bit," I said

She smiled broadly and patted my cheek, unable to speak. She shed a tear, I matched her.

As she went past me up the steps, I felt a hand on my opposite shoulder.

"I feel like I owe you breakfast," Sue Nansen said.

"At least."

She fell in step with me as we crossed the town square.

Cavanaugh had outdone himself on Max Kaiser. Everything from his birth certificate to his academic transcript. The partnership agreement for his first venture, K&S systems, The corporate filing for Kaiser Electronics, Patents, news articles, and a single picture from MIT. Four bright-faced young men in their 20's in an electronics lab. Although identified as Max Kaiser, Mitch Sugai, Vince diRosa and Tom Chesney, there was no indication which was which. The fellow with the slight oriental cast to his eyes was Sugai, I assumed. Then, I recognized Chesney, now in stable condition in an Asheville hospital, leaving me with a 50/50 on Max Kaiser.

I turned my attention to a large manila envelope marked *personal and private*.

"Son of a bitch!"

"What?" Sue asked. "What is it?"

"My e-mail."

"E-mail?"

I couldn't believe it. I was going to strangle him.

"That little son of a... hacked my e-mail."

"You mean as in..."

"He sent me printed copies of my e-mail."

"That's illegal."

Illegal, *hell, it was personal.* It wasn't that he might not have meant well. He knew I didn't have access to my computer; maybe he thought something useful might be in there. It was just knowing that Brian Cavanaugh could stick his nose into my private messages whenever he felt justified. The least he could have done was ask. Of course, I would have said no and threatened him with grievous bodily harm.

Nancy, our sullen teen-aged waitress slammed my breakfast plate on the table at my right elbow. I took a second to watch her glare at Sue before she walked away.

I cooled down a little, realizing I was being a hypocrite. I was using Cavanaugh to hunt through other people's private files—I guess I was, as Shakespeare said, hoist upon my own petard.

I shook my head violently, then began to read through the e-mails. Weekly note from stepsister Kat, some spam, girl I used to date (lunch next week? —not a chance!), Hello, a note from Carla.

Need to talk to you about family matter when you get back.
C

So glad she didn't waste words on details. She did attach a file to the note, though. I rooted to the bottom of the pile. I felt like I was staring at it for weeks, not quite believing what I was seeing.

"Something interesting?" Sue asked.

"Sort of," I answered. "I'm not sure I understand why, but Carla sent me a copy of, I guess, her birth certificate."

I handed her the document.

"Keilani Malani. You're sure this is Carla?"

"That's her birthday. I just always assumed she was born in Dayton like the rest of us."

"Could both girls have been adopted?"

I shrugged. None of us ever had a hint, as far as I know. No surprise Carla would want to talk about *this*. I mean, we all assume both our parents are… our *parents* until somebody tells us different. Although she was still Lani's daughter, the blank on her birth certificate suggested that Pop was not her father. Maybe that explains why she hadn't talked to him, why she might have been reluctant to tell him about her treatment plans. Those two were guaranteed a few awkward moments in the future.

"Why wouldn't he have told her?" Sue asked.

"Pop? He was her dad, why confuse the issue when she's little. When she gets older, and her mother dies, you become her only family. How do you just break the only family tie she has like that?"

"But she needed to know."

"Did she? What does she gain by knowing? Now she feels like she doesn't have any family. He'll feel like he lost her, too."

"But what about her real family? What about the truth?"

"The truth seems perfect in theory, but it's as mythical as this 'real family'. Nina and Pop are her family. All the official documents in the world can't change that."

I'm not saying it would have been a bad thing to have told her, but I could understand how it could be impossible for Pop to do that. The last thing he would have wanted was to alienate her. It would have killed him to lose her—even temporarily.

"I just don't see it." Sue said.

I couldn't *see* it either, but I'd known them both for so long I could feel the fear, doubt and pain. From both sides.

Chapter 24

"Well, well, doesn't this look cozy?"

I turned and grinned at Lee Holt. She sat next to Sue Nansen and looked at her, daring her to say something.

"Just in time," I said. "The Feds are buying breakfast."

Sue's eyes and mouth widened, then she gathered herself.

"Sure," she said, eyes blazing at me.

"Guess I could go for a free lunch," Lee said, laughing. "How's your girlfriend?"

"Carla? She looks like she's going to recover."

"Good. Looks like you've got quite a bit of information there. Are you on to something?"

"Like I'd tell you? Just some background on Max Kaiser, Brunson and maybe something about Tom Chesney."

"The guy who got shot? What's his role?"

"I don't know. It's just a possibility. He's been with Max Kaiser from the beginning."

Her eyes widened when she saw the photograph.

"Kaiser's one these four?"

"The guy on the far right is Chesney. The left is probably Sugai."

"So Kaiser really does exist… or he did." Lee leaned over the table. "What if that's the big deal? The reason he's such a recluse is because there isn't a Max Kaiser anymore."

"Kind of like Howard Hughes dying in the 50's and an actor taking his place?" Sue said.

"This official from the FBI?" I asked, eyebrow raised.

"No, my college roommate had all kinds of conspiracy theories and the Howard Hughes thing was one of them. Before my time with the FBI."

"I'm not saying he's dead," Lee said, "It's just a possibility. These other guys were probably shareholders and confidants to Kaiser. No one would question their authority, so they run the company like usual and live off Kaiser's name. For all we know he might be off in Barbados or something."

"But what would that have to do with Nina?" I asked.

"It might explain why Kaiser Electronics would be covering up so enthusiastically," Lee said

"She has a point there," Sue said.

I was studying the picture.

"Why wouldn't Chesney be the President of the company if he's Kaiser's best buddy…" I started speculating until I saw what I hadn't seen.

It was the haircut that had fooled me the first time I looked. I knew which of the four was Max Kaiser and he was very much alive.

I walked to the payphone in the back and called Kaiser Electronics. I got nowhere trying to get Kaiser himself, but I eventually got to Tom Chesney's secretary—I mean his administrative assistant.

"I need to get a message to Max Kaiser," I said.

"I'm sorry, Mr. Kaiser doesn't take phone calls."

"Just give him the message, huh? He gets to decide whether he needs to deal with me or not."

"I'm afraid..."

"Tell Kaiser the Blue Jays are in season and I'll meet him at the usual place."

"The… what?"

I repeated the message.

"I don't understand."

"You don't need to. Uncle Max will know."

"Who are you?"

"*He'll* know who I am, that's what counts."

I went back to the table and picked up the picture.

"Where are you going?" Lee asked.

"I have a meeting." I said

"With who, Max Kaiser?" Sue joked

I grinned back. "No with Howard Hughes… or maybe it's Elvis… Don't worry I'll be back soon."

Lee pouted. "Fine, don't tell us."

I headed toward the door.

"What should I do with all this stuff?"

"You're a trained journalist, snoop. Let me know if you find anything useful."

For privacy, Max had camouflaged the junction of the path to his house and the main walking trail with a combination of local vegetation and astroturf. Once you got in about ten, fifteen yards, the path was clear as crystal. As a visitor, running up and knocking on the door would have been a bit aggressive. Instead, I sat at the base of an oak and waited.

He looked the same as he did a couple of days ago.

"You come here alone?"

"Nobody would have believed me, Max, or would you rather I call you Lonnie?"

"Maximillian Napoleon, I answer to either. Come on up to the house, it's a lot easier on your butt than that tree stump."

I'm not sure what I was expecting. Maybe something from one of those '30's movies, logs caulked with mud, laundry pot out front, still out back, mud floor—somethin' outta Li'l Abner. I knew better but....

It was built out of wood, but from there, any similarity with that log cabin of my imagination was strictly coincidence. It was a good-sized 2-story house with a long front portal with steps and railings. The closest thing to a cooking pot was the satellite dish along the side. As I walked into the place, it looked just like anybody else's house anywhere. Nothing that rustic, spectacular or weird.

"There really *is* a still out back," he said, reading my mind. "My dad made moonshine. We make ethanol to power the generator."

"Same recipe, of course."

"Of course."

"Have a seat, Trey. Anything to drink?" I shook my head

"How did you figure it out?"

I handed him the picture. A broad smile crossed his face, then darkness. He dropped into the chair next to me.

"God those were days. We were invincible and the world was going to be perfect thanks to us. What was that—20, almost 25 years ago? How does this tie in with your girl?"

"I don't know, Max, maybe it doesn't. But you have a piece of the resort and the pageant, right? The van from Kaiser was used to move her. And Tom Chesney was shot last night. Now that all can be coincidence, or..."

"Or there's some kind of link between these things? Isn't that a bit of a reach?"

"Well, when you've got nothing else, it's worth a shot. I also have a favor to ask."

"A favor? What if I'm the bad guy? I kidnapped your girl, shot Tom, *et cetera*?"

"Then it could be you'd say no."

He laughed.

"OK, what's the favor?"

"Nina's sister, Carla, is in the hospital over in Knoxville."

"The girl they tried to kill last night? I heard."

"Can you arrange to have her brought here to the resort as soon as she's able to travel?"

"Sure, Trey, anything she needs."

"Good. Now, what do you know about Mark Brunson?"

"He's family… well, sort of."

He paused to watch my jaw hit the ground.

"Mark is my stepfather's illegitimate son. About 9 years ago my stepbrother, George, found out about him and got in touch. He was in hotel management, and I was thinking about moving my company here, so we developed the resort here together."

"Did you know he was in a money bind?"

"I heard his wife was taking him to the cleaners. Met her a couple of times, no real opinion. He hasn't asked for any personal help, but I did put up the ransom money if that's what you were wondering."

I was a little surprised. Brunson said he raised his own money. Maybe the plan was to fleece Kaiser after all. Or maybe Brunson just didn't want anybody knowing he couldn't raise the ransom. No matter what the truth might be, I was going to be more likely to get it from Brunson.

"So tell me about the guys in the picture. I've already met Tom Chesney."

"The other two? Both dead. Vin was murdered in a robbery. A year or two later, Mitch blew his brains out. Those three really made all this happen, I was just along for the ride.

"We were grad students at MIT when Mitch came up with this digital switching unit. We tinkered with it for a while and realized we were on to something. Instead of selling it to Hewlett or IBM, we decided to make the thing ourselves. We formed our own company. My stepfather, Harry Maitland, put up most of the money, so they put my name on it. Mitch was the electronic genius, Tom the businessman, and Vinnie was the salesman. We set up a partnership and K&S Systems was born. My stepfather handled the legal stuff. Mama kept the books for a while. George worked around the office; he was just a kid then. It was a real family company."

"You four were equal partners?" I asked.

"Mitch and I had 35 per cent apiece. Tom and Vinnie each got 12-13 per cent. The last fraction was doled out to various family members and friends. I know it seems a little uneven, but it was my money and Mitch's patent."

I nodded.

"The partnership called for the stock to come back to the remaining shareholders unless they had children. So after Vinnie and then Mitch died, George and I got all of their shares, and we decided to reorganize as Kaiser Electronics."

"How did Chesney lose out?"

"He sold his shares to Harry after a few years to invest in another electronics venture. Damn thing sank like a lead boat. I gave him a small piece of the new company, Kaiser Electronics, but it was a real shame. He could have used that money after his son got sick."

"I'm surprised he didn't feel cheated—hold a grudge."

"Against who? It was just a bad investment. We've stayed friends all this time. It was just bad luck."

He looked narrowly at me.

"You think he's involved in this! He was shot, for god's sake."

"Sure. But he could have been double-crossed by his accomplices. He was shot in the back at close range. Maybe he knew who was behind him."

"I think you're crazy. If Tom wanted to get revenge, even though I don't know how he could figure it could be my fault, he's had 20 years worth of opportunities."

"You're probably right, Max. We're still fishing for possible here, not likely. There's a definite link between our kidnappers and Kaiser Electronics."

"You're that certain?"

I nodded. "Not sure I can prove it, though." I explained about the mileage logs.

He nodded.

"I hear you're delivering the ransom tonight."

"That's the word."

"Good luck."

I thanked him, but I was really hoping I wasn't going to need it.
As I walked back toward the main trail I heard a rustle through the woods to my right. I turned quick, but missed it. I stood for a moment watching. Then just as I turned away again, I saw a movement and flash of pale color. Maybe the Widow Maitland running around the woods. She should have brushed up on her stalking technique. Pink makes lousy camouflage.

Chapter 25

Lee was still at the Cafe when I got back from Max's.

"Your new girlfriend had to go to work," she said. "Collecting the ransom, I suppose."

Nancy brought over a coffee mug and a full pot. I nodded, she poured.

"Where did you get these files? They seem awfully complete. You must have an amazing source."

"He's nosy enough," I answered.

"You want to share him with me? I could use somebody like this. Maybe he can get me out of this stupid job."

"Not enjoying your work?"

"I'm just so tired of fashion shows, beauty contests… I don't mind doing an occasional fluff story, but I was a political journalist. I want to do a lot more serious stuff. I can't stand all this… Do you know what "Barnyard Bingo" is?"

"Got me there."

"They fence off a small piece of ground, then divide it into a bunch of squares. Then they get a cow or horse or some other barnyard animal…"

"Oh, yeah, I've seen that at the county fair. People bet on the square the animal 'deposits' on."

"Exactly. I was working at a station in Helena, Montana last summer, and they sent me out to cover it at the State Fair. I had spent most of the 2 years covering the State House, but you know, you go where they want you. Anyway, I was doing a walk through the corral while I wrapped up the report when I stepped on the…"

"Fertilizer?"

"…and fell flat on my butt. It was one of the most embarrassing things ever."

"Are you kidding, you just described the perfect metaphor for life."

"Every now and then you step into shit?"

"Well, don't you?"

She grinned.

"Oh, I'm not still embarrassed, I don't think. It just represents a specific sort of news story—one without any real educational value or significance. Just entertainment, or a look at human silliness. Fluff. Because of that story, I end up doing this crap."

"But if they hired you based on your little pratfall, what did you expect?"

"I didn't know! I was talking to CNN about a *serious* news job. I mean, political reporting, hard news. I have a journalism degree from Missouri, 2 years as a local State House reporter. I wanted to work on Capitol Hill."

"So what happened?"

"I was putting together a demo tape—you know some of my better interviews and all that kind of stuff. Eric, my photographer and ex-boyfriend, threw in the Barnyard Bingo stuff at the end of the tape. I told him to take it off, but he faked the edit or something.

"When I got to CNN they started sending me out on some fluff pieces, but I figured they were just, you know, checking me out. Seeing if I was versatile. After a couple of weeks, I raised the question with my bosses. They said this was the stuff they thought I was best at and I was stuck with it. Then a couple of months ago they sent me to 'Fashion' and my life has been hell ever since. Whenever I tell them I want to do more serious stuff, they keep telling me how good I am at this crap."

"Maybe you shouldn't keep being so good at it?"

"You don't understand. Being a reporter is all I ever wanted to be. I can't screw up—I have to do my best."

"I'm just saying, if you want to stop doing Barnyard Bingo, don't keep doing it. You're an intelligent and talented woman, don't make yourself a doormat. Find a place that will let you do your real story. Hell, you got a hard news story right here. Make 'em notice you."

She shook her head sadly.

"As of first thing this morning, I'm not on this story anymore. They sent another reporter—a 'real one'—to follow you around. I get to cover the pageant and that's it."

I shook my head. She was in real pain over this thing.

"These do not sound like people you should be working for, Lee."

"But it's CNN, it's a great stepping stone in my career."

"If you want to do Barnyard Bingo," I said. "Why are you here if there's no story for you?"

"Curiosity, I guess."

"I don't think it's just curiosity, it's defiance. This is *your* story and no desk jockey in Atlanta is going to kick you off it."

She shrugged, but began worrying her lower lip.

"You have to think of your career the same way. Either you take command or…"

"More Barnyard Bingo."

"Exactly," I said. "Of course I don't have a job so…"

We both laughed. She reached across the table and grasped my hand.

"Thanks for listening. I was feeling sorry for myself."

"No problem."

Sue Nansen was counting bills when I got to the police station. The tall, skinny agent was placing it carefully into a black attaché case. Longstreet handed me a copy of the ransom note. It, of course, mentioned me by name and said I was supposed to go to the baseball game and wait for further instructions.

"So who's playing," I asked Longstreet.

"Asheville, how the hell should I know?" the Chief grumbled.

"Just wondering. A guy I went to high school with got drafted by the pros. He's at Macon or Columbus… somewhere down here. I just wondered if he was going to be playing."

"I wouldn't think you'd have a lot of time for old home week."

"Probably right."

Hatch showed up a few minutes later with backpack and a note encased in plastic. He was wearing rubber gloves and holding it gingerly.

"Someone left this at the front desk of the hotel." He said.

"Did you see who left it?" Agent Nansen asked.

Hatch shook his head.

"I thought you guys had video surveillance? Who's watching the monitors up there, Ray Charles?" Longstreet sniped.

"Hey! I don't tell you how to eat donuts, Deputy Dawg."

"If we could cool the testosterone just for a moment," Sue Nansen said. "Any traces or evidence?"

"Well, nobody's touched it without gloves—at least not since our desk person spotted it. And before you ask, the Williams girl was down here."

"Well, let's see what we've got," she said.

Made more sense to use the backpack. A guy walking around the ballpark with a briefcase was bound to draw attention. A fellow my age with a backpack looked like what I just was—a college student.

To no one's great surprise, the pack itself turned up no traces or prints. The bag, possibly the factory wrapping, had several sets of fingerprints, none of which would prove useful until we had a suspect. I was of course, relieved but not really surprised to learn my prints were not on it.

Finally, we were packed and ready.

"Agent Nansen? I was thinking about what you said this morning. About all that extra paperwork? I think I might have a bright idea."

She frowned initially but then the light dawned. I was a little surprised to find we were on the same wavelength. It was probably nothing, but it seemed a silly thing not to take precautions against.

A quick stop at Wal-Mart for a light windbreaker-style jacket, and we were off and running. I rode shotgun, with my eyes closed and relaxed as we cruised to the highway. I did have one question for Sue Nansen in the back seat.

"Does Ferguson strike you as a chronic screw-up?"

"What do you mean, chronic?" she asked

"He's been kind of a one man wrecking crew. Lot of stuff happening around him. None of it seems very helpful."

"Maybe he's just trying to show off. Show the rest of us up. The thing with Chesney was probably bad luck. The thing with you? Well, you're just a pain in the ass."

"G'wan with your flattery."

"To answer your question: No, he wouldn't be a State investigator if he was a serious screw-up. You're not thinking…"

"Go on, say it."

"There's no way *I'm* saying it," she said. You've got an accusation, let's hear it."

"Hey, even I'm probably not *thinking* it… yet."

Chapter 26

Long before one of the Vanderbilts decided to build a summer home on eight thousand acres of Carolina real estate, the Asheville region was a well known and used vacation spot. *Biltmore,* and the estates thereof, made the area even more popular. Not only is it an important vacation spot, but it also has a strong literary history. Carl Sandberg lived nearby. North Carolina's most famous writer, Asheville's Thomas Wolfe takes his final rest along with William S Porter (O Henry). The fun-loving, the fashionable, and the fabulous all come to Asheville.

McCormick Field, home park for the Asheville Tourists (who'd have guessed) sat south and east of downtown. Built in 1924, the charm of the old time minor league park endured through the modern repairs and renovation. I walked up to the box office and introduced myself. Sure enough, there was a ticket waiting with an envelope. Inside was another envelope:

Do not open until 5th inning

I slipped it into the pocket of my jacket.

It was Church Day at the ball park, the announcer said. In keeping with the spirit of the occasion, I chose Coca-Cola over my usual beer at the park. I struck up a conversation with the woman behind me in the concession line.

"I'm in Section E," I said.

"I'm in 'I', out in right field."

"I've heard that about you."

Sue Nansen smiled.

"I hear these guys are at their best in the fifth inning."

"I'll keep that in mind."

I got my large Coke, she got her popcorn

"Well, enjoy the game," she said

"You, too."

They managed to put me in the middle of the group from Asheville United Methodist Church. I don't think they were expecting a dose of religious diversity (I was raised Baptist) in the middle of their baseball outing. As the stranger in their midst, I was the center of attention. They were polite, sometimes overly so, but mostly curious.

I was hiking the Appalachian Trail, but hiked in to catch the ball game and meet up with a childhood friend going to school at the college (UNC Asheville). He left me the ticket. As the game went on, we all relaxed and enjoyed it. I was second team All-State in high school, so I was giving a few pointers to some of my neighbors helping them see some of the nuances of the game.

The Tourists, farm team for the Colorado Rockies, had a lefty pitcher named Crawford you should look forward to seeing at a Major League Park. His secret weapon—a side-arm curve ball, was only fun to watch from the sidelines. Their opponent, the Augusta Green Jackets, bravely put on their helmets and resolutely dug in, but the kid was just plain un-hittable. He had nine strikeouts in the first four innings, mowing down the side in the 1st and 4th, one weak roller and two sad pop-ups (one foul) had him perfect into the 5th inning.

The note said I was to leave at the end of the inning. Walk north toward the Thomas Wolfe house, following the map. Someone would meet me with instructions to find Nina. I was to leave the money at my seat. The kidnappers apparently had a lot of faith in the Methodists. A bag full of money would tempt anybody.

I didn't like this idea at all. It wasn't a matter of trusting 'my' congregation, or completing the drop, so much as not being able to make sure Nina was going to be freed. This vague, 'head north and you'll be met' plan stunk of a wild goose chase. The kidnappers would get their money, and I wouldn't get Nina.

I admit the game also crossed my mind. No-hit baseball games are almost as rare as snow in July, but a perfect game—to not even have anyone reach base—is an exceptional experience even for a hard-core baseball fan.

Fortunately, an errant throw from Third, resulted in a man on first and the end of el perfecto. I'd seen a no-hitter up in Toledo a couple of years ago. I could leave that. If the 5th had been perfect, I might have been tempted to hope the kidnapper(s) were baseball fans.

As the Home 5th ended, I got up as if heading for the bathroom. As I walked back down the ramp, I wondered how long it would take folks to get curious about my disappearance.

It was 8:30 and daylight was beginning to wane. I set out north toward downtown. Car traffic was pretty light, but the street was deserted. After walking a couple of blocks, I looked back and saw a jogger approaching. The woman had her shoulder-length blonde hair tied back, a dark tunic and red shorts. Over the next block, she caught and passed me. Nice legs, for a cop. After passing me, "The jogger" began to slow to a walk, stop and stretch. I picked up my walking pace, so she never got more than a couple of blocks ahead of me.

We went through the heart of town, passing within easy reach of the police station and city hall, and on toward the childhood home of Thomas Wolfe, closed for repairs after fire damage.

Just past the Wolfe house, right where Central Street passes under I-240, there was a car on the opposite side of the road that flashed its lights. I crossed to that side and approached the door.

As I reached for the handle, a pistol swung out the window and fired.

I could see the muzzle flashes as the bullets slammed into my chest, knocking me backward. The echoes of the gunfire rang in my ears as I slammed back into the wall, my head smacking the concrete. As I slumped to the ground, stunned. I heard gunfire in the distance and the car peeling away.

I could feel the blood soaking into the back of my shirt as I began to loose consciousness. The last thing I saw was Sue Nansen's face, but the last thing I thought was about how they just put holes in my brand new Wal-Mart jacket.

Chapter 27

I woke on a hospital bed. Looking up at the same face. I went to sit up.

"Hey, hey, take it easy," Nansen said.

I saw, or rather, felt her point. Body armor might stop a bullet from wreaking havoc or killing you, but it does not prevent you from absorbing some of the force of impact. The bullets that would have gone straight through you become sledgehammers bruising your chest and ribs.

Not moving, I would have to deal with dull, throbbing pains, like I had in my right arm. Moving (and breathing) left a screaming trail of pain in the center of my chest and down my left side. The left upper side felt bruised, regardless.

Of course, I tried to sit up just as all the pain circuitry got back to full power. I was proud I didn't start crying, or screaming. Since I was already hurting, I finished sitting up (barely).

"You took a pretty good pounding out there. Slow down, rest. Give yourself a day or two."

A day or two? With Nina in danger?

I tried to ease my feet off the bed, slowly.

"You should stay in bed, Trey. Doctor thinks you may have cracked ribs. Not to mention a slight concussion."

I had had cracked ribs before. I took a deep breath. "Yep, sure feels like it."

Cracked ribs are the worst. You can put a splint or a cast on a broken arm or leg, keep it still until it heals. Those ribs are aggravated every time you inhale. Try not breathing for a few weeks.

I looked at my bandaged left arm. "Got me in the arm too, huh?

"Creased," he said. "It bled some, but no serious damage. Doesn't even require a sling."

I nodded.

"What happened with the ransom?"

"Hadn't moved yet. They were still playing last time I called in, the 11th inning."

Missed a good game, I guess. "It was a set up, wasn't it? This wasn't about getting the money."

She blew out heavily. Her eyes rolled while she considered how events played out.

"No. I think they really wanted to kill you."

That bulletproof vest was just a silly joke between us up until the first bullet hit. We weren't being clever or clairvoyant—just paranoid. That jacket sat in the room like an elephant daring either of us to say anything.

"I must be on to something."

"Like..."

Like, how the hell would *I* know? "How about this, they *think* I must be on to something"

I looked around the room for my clothes. I was still wearing my pants, of course. The bulletproof vest was intact, but a bit conspicuous, the jacket, as I already mentioned, had holes, and my shirt was bloodstained.

"What am I going to wear for a shirt?"

"Oh. Don't worry, I'll find you something by morning."

"Morning, hell, I'm leaving tonight.

"What? You're not going anywhere; they're going to keep you overnight for observation."

"They can observe my ass leaving." I grumbled.

"I'm posting a guard, to keep you here. You're not leaving."

"Then he'll have to shoot me, and I have a bulletproof vest."

"I'm dead serious, Trey. You might have a concussion."

I stood up, slowly. She might have been right, but I still wasn't staying. I was certainly a bit woozy, but I'd had my bell rung before. I grabbed the ventilated jacket. A fashion no-no, but it wasn't as damp as my shirt.

I was calculating to best way to get to my shoes. With my equilibrium a little off, bending over might pitch me head first to the deck. Squatting, on the other hand was guaranteed to add those cracked ribs to the mix. While I was still calculating, the rest of the gang arrived. Doctor, Nurse, and the local cop all to tell me I couldn't leave.

"I'm still leaving," I said. "I don't think you can hold me here unless you arrest me. Even then I'd probably be moved to the jail."

The cop shrugged, the doctor frowned.

"I know, Doc. Discharged against medical advice. Any chance I can get some kind of shirt or something? My clothes are a bit bloody and I do have an image to maintain."

He chuckled. "I'll see what I can do."

I turned to the cop. "I suppose the local police have a few questions as well?"

The local police was Sergeant Michael Ramos. A pleasure to see diversity reach the wilds of North Carolina.

"Special Agent Nansen has given me most of the particulars of the shooting, but I had a couple of questions only you can answer."

"Shoot," I answered. He read my face for a moment, then slowly smiled at the joke.

"Did you see anybody in the car?"

I shook my head. "Tinted windows. Between that and the shadows under the bridge, I can't say I saw anything useful—except the gun."

"What can you tell me about the gun?"

"It wasn't a revolver. It wasn't Army Colt .45. Nine millimeter, I assume?"

"That's our guess," Sue Nansen said.

"You seem certain about the Colt. You a gun buff?"

"My dad's an Air Force officer. The Colt ACP was the standard sidearm for years."

He nodded.

"How many people know what happened to me?" I asked.

Ramos blinked twice. "This is kind of a small town in some ways. You can't keep a shooting like this a secret."

"No, I was just thinking about the end result. Somebody thinks they killed me. Maybe they shouldn't be disappointed."

The cop and the Fed shrugged in unison.

"You might have a point," Nansen said.

Ramos agreed to keep that little 'victim survived' element a mystery to the press. A couple of more cursory questions, and I was ready to go—in spite of objections.

"I won't drive you anywhere, you'll be stuck here in Asheville." Sue Nansen made one last attempt to get me to stay.

"I'll tell your buddy Ferguson I want to confess. He'll be here in a heartbeat."

Her eyes narrowed. I winked at her. She faked a smile.

My cell phone rang. I must have flipped it on without thinking. Since I was dead, I handed the phone to Nansen. She answered, then handed the phone to me without comment.

The voice was weak and scratchy, but it was the most beautiful sound I had heard in years.

"Who answered the phone?" Carla asked.

"Secretary," I answered. She knew better than to ask me questions like that. "You doing OK?"

"I'm fine, Trey. How's the search going?"

So Pop or AJ filled her in. Glad I didn't have to do it. I wonder how she was taking it.

"All dead ends so far."

"Don't give up hope."

"Oh, I'm not." It was Nina. We both knew I'd never give up.

The few seconds seemed like years.

"The reason I called was to let you know that Pop is on his way to see you. We've got something you should know about Nina and I. Might not have anything to do with what happened to her, but it's family stuff. You need to know anyway."

"I know some of it. I got your e-mail."

"How did you get e-mail there?"

"Your boyfriend Cavanaugh broke into my e-mail. He was nice enough to mail me a copy."

"Brian Cavanaugh? I'm going to kill him."

"No. *I'm* killing him. You're my lawyer."

I changed the subject. "As soon as you're feeling up to it, I've made arrangements for you to be at Crystal Mountain. Call Kaiser Electronics, and they'll send the helicopter for you."

"How did you ever arrange that?"

"You know me, friends wherever I go."

"I love you."

"I thought that was me, loving you. Glad you're doing OK."

Chapter 28

We returned to Pineville well before Pop did, and met with him at the train station. I filled him in on my night's adventures.

"My god, Trey," he said. "You are sure you are all right?"

"I'm a little bruised, but I'm doing OK, Pop."

The ransom money had been turned in by my Methodist friends. Nobody even seemed to have snuck a peek. Was the whole thing a plot to kill me, or did something happen to the kidnappers?

AJ stayed in Knoxville with Carla, who was probably going to be OK to travel in a day or two.

Pop hemmed and hawed around what he came to talk about.

Finally, I broke the ice for him. "I've seen Carla's birth certificate."

"Lying to the girls was never my intention. I just couldn't talk to them about it...especially after Leilani died. They were the only family I had.

"I met Lani on Venice Beach. I was in grad school at UCLA, she was getting over the death of her husband. I looked at her and just couldn't breathe. She was so beautiful—you remember." I nodded. "To this day, I wonder where or how I found the courage to go over there. We talked for a minute or two and I was amazed to find her looking me over. Part of me knew she was thinking 'what a geek,' but I kept hoping against hope. Finally, I managed to get her to agree to a date Friday night, probably a campus movie or a free concert or something.

"I was so excited, I turned around and started across the bike path without looking, crashing into a huge guy on a bike. When I sat up, she was laughing so hard she could barely breathe. I was completely humiliated. No way did I have a chance now.

"'I'm going to have to stay with you,' she said. 'I wouldn't want you to injure yourself.' She had such a wonderful way about her and she was so..."

I smiled, nodding. Lani had a power you just couldn't explain or forget. The girls have it, too. That's why I'm out on the streets getting shot at.

"…I was completely in love with her almost before I got to know her. She was so down to earth, I always felt comfortable with her. In time, I managed not to be completely intimidated by her beauty.

"At first, she refused to marry me. She used every possible excuse. Told me she didn't love me. I didn't believe her. Finally, she told me she was pregnant with her late husband's child. I didn't care. It was too soon, she said. I told her if she wouldn't get married it didn't matter, I wasn't living the rest of my life without her.

"Somewhere during her resistance, she explained about her 1st daughter as well. Carla, or Keilani, as they called her, was living with Lani's aunt on the Big Island. After Nina was born, I talked Leilani into raising the girls together."

"Carla and Nina had the same father?"

He shrugged. "She didn't say, I had always assumed her husband fathered both. She said he was her childhood sweetheart, so I figured she went from him to me."

"Do you remember her husband's name?"

"I've been wracking my brain ever since Carla asked. She wanted to believe he was still alive. She had a feeling somebody was looking for her while she was looking for him. But he's dead."

"Dead? You're certain?"

He nodded. "Lani was. She said it was a suicide. He blew his head off. His name was Mark, maybe Mickey. I don't think I ever knew his last name."

I found myself speculating about faked suicide.

"Why were the cops so sure it wasn't murder? Because Murder is something big. Something Lani would probably have mentioned, right."

"Suzuki." He said

"What? What kind of Suzuki?"

"That was the guy's name, Matt Suzuki."

"Could it have been Mitchell Sugai?"

Pop frowned. "OK, if you say so. It might have been that. You have to remember I only heard the name a couple of times. Who's Mitchell Sugai?"

Sue Nansen looked at me, blinking puzzled incomprehension.

"He was a partner in K&S Enterprises, a precursor of Kaiser Electronics. He committed suicide. It makes sense."

Nansen smiled broadly. "So money is the motive after all. Somebody at the pageant, maybe Mark Brunson, does a thorough background check, realizes Nina is worth a few bucks, and sets this kidnapping up."

"But Nina did not know she was worth any money," Pop reminded her. "Neither did any of the rest of us—how did they expect us to come up with the money?"

"The motive keeps leading us back to Max Kaiser," I pointed out. "Everything seems to have some relationship to him."

"You think he kidnapped Nina?" Nansen asked.

"Then volunteered to put up the ransom? I don't think so."

"Nobody picked up the ransom, remember? Maybe he thought you knew too much. I mean he's got the most to gain—she might be the heir to a large chunk of his empire. He'd have *carte blanche* access to Kaiser vehicles, Crystal Mountain resort… If nothing else, it's certainly worth questioning him. If we had any idea where to find him."

Well, I knew where to find him and I had plenty of questions of my own. As far as his involvement in Nina's kidnapping, I still had serious doubts. When we talked he had been very upfront about the details of his partnerships and seemed genuinely sad about Nina's father. I had some doubts about Max as a killer, but I knew it was a possibility. The real concern had to be that if this was about eliminating an heir to the throne, she was no longer a kidnapping victim. She was already dead. One look into Agent Nansen's eyes, and I knew she had reached the same conclusion. The attempt on Carla's life made it seem even more likely. He'd have to kill them both.

Nina was still alive. I don't know how I knew, but I knew. Even if I was just being pig-headed, finding Nina alive was something I could keep working at. Finding a dead woman wasn't. There was another answer. They had to be.

The question became what should I do. I was posing as a dead man, hoping the would-be killers will give themselves away, so I couldn't keep wandering around answering questions. Even standing watch over Carla would risk exposure. I needed a place to hide out and I still needed answers.

"I want you to let this go, Trey," Pop said. "I know you love Nina, but there comes a time we have to leave this to the professionals. You could have been killed tonight."

"I'm OK Pop," I said emphatically. "Listen, I'm not out here taking unnecessary chances, I'm just doing what has to be done."

"I understand that, Trey, but the authorities are trained for these kinds of risks. What good would it do for us if you get yourself killed? We all want Nina back, but whatever happens, our family is better off together. And you *are* family."

"But that's the point, Pop. These people have got Nina, tried to kill Carla, and 'killed' me. If we don't get these guys and pretty damn soon, they might succeed in killing us all. As far as the authorities go, With all due respect to our FBI friend, we have not seen priority nor competence from them."

"Just be careful, that's all I ask."

"Sure, you take good care of Carla, huh?"

"Of course."

I opened the car door and hopped out. I had to disappear before morning, and where better than with the invisible Max Kaiser and his alter ego.

"Hey," Sue Nansen asked. "Where are you going?"

"If you don't know, you can't tell." I held up my phone. "If you need me, call."

The steps up the face of the mountain were kind of tricky in the dark, but I made it up the hill in reasonable time. I moved, slowly and surely, along the path. I expected to stumble, fumble, and crash into trees. A good moon helped a little, but I was amazed at how well I managed to get around in the darkness.

Finding the path to Lonnie's was a lot more difficult. Eventually, I had to take off my shoes and feel around. There's something distinctive about the feel of astroturf. The woods were denser, the path narrower. I stumbled over a root or two, but I found my way to the house.

He was barely coherent when he answered the door. Disoriented, maybe surprised, but not a man face to face with a ghost.

"Do you have any idea what time it is?" He finally grumbled.

"We need to talk. It's a family matter."

"Yours or mine?"

"Both. I know why they kidnapped Nina. She's Mitchell Sugai's daughter."

I had expected a look of shock, assumed he might turn pale, knew he might grow weak in the knees, but I was genuinely surprised when he fainted.

Chapter 29

Max had about 5 inches or so on me, but we weighed about the same. My battered chest cried in protest as I hefted and dragged him to a nearby chair. His pulse and breathing were steady, so I knew he would come around in a couple of minutes.

I snooped around his place a little. As you would assume, his office/computer room was a modern-day marvel. With all that gear, he could out-hack Cavanaugh. He also had an excellent library, a workout room and fully appointed kitchen. Upstairs, I had to assume, was all bedrooms.

When I got back, Max was sitting back up.

"Mitch had a daughter? You're sure?"

"As sure as possible considering he and his wife are both dead."

"His wife, Leilani? Your girl is Lani's daughter? But Mitch and Lani were only married a few months."

I nodded.

He smiled. "I guess it only takes a few minutes to start the process, doesn't it? But that means she was pregnant when Mitch killed himself." He began to pace the room. "I wish I would have known. We would have done anything to help Lani. She was a wonderful lady and I really loved her.

He stopped and frowned. "Why didn't she come to me? Mitch was my best... sometimes my only friend. I could have helped. I would have treated Nina like my own daughter. They would both have been well taken care of."

"Nina was well taken care of," I said, pointedly, "until a couple of days ago."

He winced. "I didn't... I wasn't... being critical. I just wish I could have been a part of your Nina's life. Mitch was my best friend, I would have been glad to she was OK."

I could see pain on his face. "I wanted desperately to help Mitch, you know? I don't know what was wrong with him, but he kept getting worse. He was accusing people of drugging him, stealing his notes, trying to kill him. Lani did her best, but whatever demons were torturing him kept getting worse. When he really started going off the deep end, he started to put her in danger. Then, the afternoon of December 21st, he tore up our offices—then went home and blew his brains out. Merry Christmas, huh?

"Lani just disappeared. She didn't even stay for the funeral. We never saw her again. David Patton, our Security Chief, was a private investigator in those days. He spent a good chunk of time searching for her, but I guess we were looking in the wrong places. I thought she would go back to Hawaii, but she didn't."

He hung his head.

"She went to California," I said. Nina was born in June, if you wanted to check the math."

"Oh, I don't doubt you. Your girl will get everything her father would have had from the company."

"Which is?"

"Well, She'll get half the patent income, plus stock."

"Where are you getting the stock from?"

"What difference does it make?"

"Somebody loses if Nina gets her inheritance."

"Sure, we'll each have to take a reduced percentage in order for her to get her share."

"The question becomes, who can't afford the loss?"

"Wait a minute, I thought this was about ransom. The half a million you delivered?"

"Nobody collected the ransom, it's all a blind. The ransom drop was an attempt to kill me. Somebody is trying to keep Nina from getting her inheritance, but what I don't understand is why they haven't..."

"Killed her already? I think I know. She's only 20, right?"

"21 next week. Why?"

"The partnership agreement provides only for children to inherit —my stepfather's idea. Like I told you before; without children, shares are proportionally divided among the other partners. What I didn't mention was the trust clause. If there is a child, but it doesn't make it till age 21, those shares become part of a charitable foundation in his or her name."

"But when she hits 21, she's just another adult partner and it all goes back to you guys, right?"

"Exactly. They have to keep her alive until her birthday."
"Who are they Max? Who is waiting to kill Nina?"
"I don't know! Honest! My brother, George, had most of the rest of the stock, but he's recently sold off a good chunk of his shares to about 20 minor shareholders. Plus some to Mark, and some to his dad."
"Harry Maitland? I thought your mother..."
"'Widow' Maitland? Mama divorced him when she decided to come back here from New York. She called herself 'widow' cause she figured she'd do better at finding another husband. Harland Maitland is alive and well and living in New York."
"Does your mother have any shares?"
Lonnie shook his head.
"Wouldn't even take any as part of the divorce settlement," He said, shaking his head emphatically. "I have to tell you, Trey, my mother is not very well. I don't know if you heard any rumors, but the only reason she's not being... cared for, is because there's really nothing she can do to harm others out here."
I could sympathize. My mother was a drunk-turned-speed freak that I really never could deal with, so I don't.
"You said Brunson has a chunk, how big?"
"Seven-eight percent maybe. About four after Nina gets her share."
"Maybe down to two after his wife gets her piece."
"Oh, good point. That might be enough motive. I guess of the significant shareholders, Mark would probably be the most desperate."
He stood up. "How about some coffee?"
"Sure," I answered. "I think we also need to know who else might benefit. Can you get me a list of the minor shareholders?"
"Sure, I can even get the original lists for K&S. They're all on my computer. I can crank them out while the coffee's brewing."
I nodded as he left the room. I relaxed and closed my eyes.

It was morning when I opened my eyes again. Lonnie was holding a civil war era rifled musket, the .54 caliber bore looking like a tunnel.
"How's that for an old, country, antique," he said cheerily.
I cocked my head, as I looked at the weapon.

"I keep it in my office. It has all the stuff with it, powder cartridges, percussion caps, the works."

"Ever shoot it."

"Hell, no. It would probably blow up in my face. I wouldn't try that gun if my life depended on it."

I looked down in my lap and saw the computer printouts.

"Did you still want coffee, Trey?"

"Yeah, what time is it?"

"About 7:30. You were sleeping so good, I just didn't want to wake you up."

It only took a quick glance to see at least one name you wouldn't expect to see on the list. I reached for my cell phone.

"Hey Nansen, did you know your boyfriend Ferguson owned stock in Kaiser Electronics?"

"Come to the Police station," she answered. "There have been other developments. Your mother's here… in jail."

Chapter 30

For some people, Mom in jail would be a disaster, the ultimate embarrassment. For me, the only surprise was that Ruby Jean Farris was in North Carolina. When I was little, I knew she drank. By Junior High, I began to realize she was an alcoholic. After several truly half-assed attempts to dry out, she decided to try another, chemical solution. Alcohol was a depressant, she figured, so she would moderate its effect with amphetamines. Speed improved her high, and even better (or worse) had her losing weight.

Having always claimed her children ruined her figure, her newfound weight loss made it easy for her to ignore the dangers of her new regimen. She began popping more and more pills. Lo and behold, the high was better with the pills than the booze.

She also had more than her share of run-ins with the law, but between charming her way out of some, (After all, James Farris was Montgomery County's Sheriff for almost 20 years) and those tearful 'last chances' at rehab she begged for, she never really had a reasonable dose of consequences.

I went meandering down the hill, wondering what she had gotten herself into this time.

The twig snapping behind me was a surprise.

"Lonnie?" I asked without looking back.

"Whatever it is that's going on," he answered, "Max Kaiser seems to be in the middle of it. I have to deal with this thing."

"Your call." I said.

My call was to Brian Cavanaugh. I gave him the list of shareholders to run down.

"You want me to send the stuff by dogsled this time." He said sarcastically.

I looked at Max. "No, you can send it to my e-mail now—while we're on the subject, Cavanaugh, you go poking around in my e-mail again, there won't be enough of you left for dog *food*."

"Ooh, something personal in there?"
"Like you don't know."
"Hey, that Brunson guy you asked me about?"
"What about him?"
"Did you know he's married to Sugar Cain?"
"Sugar Cain?"
"One of the world's most talented porn actresses. Do you have any idea how many awards she's won?"
"I had no idea there *were* awards."
"Oh, yeah, they have awards in all kinds of categories."
"I don't care." I surely did not want a list of categories.
"I'd be glad to do a complete run-down on *her* for you. The usual —background, financial profile… I can even get you streaming video."
"Send me streaming video and I'll break your fingers."
"Okay, Okay. Just trying to help. It's just… well…"
"What now?"
"Well, if you meet her...would you get me an autograph?"
"Good by, Cavanaugh."

Consternation and confusion reigned at the police station. Lee Holt burst from the assembled news vultures and practically tackled me.
"You're alive!" she said with a tear or two on the run. We heard you were killed last night in Asheville."
"Rumors of my demise and all that. Although I was slightly injured… so if I could just get you to loosen… your… grip."
She jumped back. "Sorry, just a bit excited."
"He has that effect." Max said, grinning.
Lee looked him over carefully. "I've seen you before, haven't I?"
"Lee Holt, CNN, I'd like you to meet Lonnie…"
"McCoy."
As they exchanged pleasantries, we were becoming the center of attention, so I broke for the door, telling Lee to meet us at the Cafe after we finished in the cop shop. My former state cop shadow, Lowery, in uniform at the door, held out a hand toward Lonnie.
"Hold it… " he started.
"He's with me," I said.
He hesitated, then waved us in.

"While you were out there getting Hughes killed," Ferguson was crowing, "I was busy finding the truth. Brunson and the dead girl were behind the kidnapping for the first ransom which he apparently double-dipped from both his business and that poor sucker Kaiser."

That explained the discrepancy over the first ransom. But I did think it surprising Ferguson put two and two together like that. Besides, if the kidnapping was for ransom, where was Nina now?

"He kills the broad so he doesn't have to split the money, then drives down to Asheville and pumps four into Hughes."

I was about 18 inches behind him by then, and couldn't resist the cue.

"Boo!"

Sue Nansen, Longstreet, and Chris Daniels all tried to describe the look of horror on Ferguson's face when he heard my voice. I didn't see that face, but I saw the effect of such a sudden shock and a very guilty conscience.

He spun around and faced me. "You're supposed to be dead."

I smiled a little half-smile and raised an eyebrow. "Miss me?"

"Couldn't have," he muttered loud enough for me to hear.

I was looking at his face and I knew. And he knew I knew. He was our gunman.

"The way your hand was shaking," I taunted. "You couldn't have hit a barn from the inside."

"You couldn't have seen me! It all happened too fast!"

He reached for his gun, then realized the game was up. He collapsed into a chair.

"I had to do it," he muttered. "I was in too deep."

"HE shot you?" Sue Nansen asked.

"You heard him."

"But why?" Longstreet asked. "I knew you two didn't get along, but…"

I shook my head. "He was in the kidnappers' pocket all along. Just a little fish following orders."

I asked Ferguson about his co-conspirators. Who called for my shooting? Who kidnapped Nina? Unfortunately, he was recovering from his shock. He wanted a deal. He wanted his lawyer. We sent him off to the cell he was so eager to put me in a couple of days earlier.

After he left, we compared notes for a while on how Ferguson had confused and obstructed the investigation almost from the beginning. I reminded them that he was also on the scene when Tom Chesney was shot, and might have been the guy who shot him.

We all did agree that it was unlikely that he was the mastermind of the scheme. Most likely, just a hired gun.

"Okay, so who's the big fish?" Nansen asked.

"Mark Brunson," I said. "He was getting cleaned and pressed on his divorce."

"I don't know, my money's on Kaiser," she said.

I smiled at her. "I'm sorry, I should introduce my friend here. Special Agent Susan Nansen…"

"Maximillian Napoleon Kaiser, at your service." He even bowed slightly.

Her eyes widened. The police chief's jaw dropped momentarily, then he roared with laughter. "I can't believe it!" he said with tears streaming down his cheeks, "'Weird Lonnie' is the millionaire electronics genius who practically owns the town."

Max smiled at him. "I must admit, even I'm sometimes amused by the irony. Trey tells me that Nina is the daughter of my former business partner. He thinks that heritage is what is putting her in danger."

"I do have some questions," Nansen said, "for the both of you. But first, I suppose you want to know about your mother, Trey?"

Not really. "Something to do with Drugs, I suppose?"

"Murder. She says she killed the woman in your hotel room."

"There's a dead woman in my hotel room?"

"Yeah, I forgot you wouldn't know anything about that yet." She handed me a photo of the deceased.

"She's the phony nurse that tried to kill Carla."

"I noticed she fit the description, so I sent a copy to Knoxville. What makes you so sure it's her?"

"That busted nose is a dead giveaway. Carla popped her a good one as she tried to poison her. Note the beautiful matched shiners."

"You sound like a proud father."

"We took karate together as kids. After her accident. Master Cho would be very proud. Definitely murder?"

"Absolutely."

"But you aren't convinced Ruby Jean did it?"

Nansen frowned at me. "She confessed to the shooting."

"You think she's assuming I killed her, right? Why aren't you assuming the same thing?"

"We don't think the girl was killed in your room. There wasn't enough blood. Besides we're pretty sure you never came back to the resort at all last night. Either way, her version of the story doesn't jibe with the facts."

"But she's sticking to it?"

"Adamantly. Maybe you can talk to her."

She'd be less of a pain in the ass if I left her in jail.

Then again, a good son couldn't really leave his own mother in jail. Besides, I knew from experience she wouldn't learn from it.

"When the hell did she show up anyway?"

"She apparently got in last night." She showed me the xeroxed airline ticket.

"After the girl was killed, right?"

"The ME thinks so, but we still have to wait for the official word. She might have been killed before you were last night."

"Tell Ferguson it was the same gun. It'll give him incentive to cooperate."

"Good idea."

I steeled myself. "I guess it's time to talk to Mom."

Chapter 31

She hadn't been in custody long enough, I was guessing. Her blood shot eyes and sniffles told me she was still lit. When she first started on speed, she passed off the physical symptoms—short, quick, breathing, runny nose, red eyes—as an allergy, but it wouldn't take bright kids like my sister and I long to quickly realize that was a crock.

She was starting to lose steam, though. Her body was starting to sag a little. The guts always fade out before the head. I had seen the whole show before.

It was why I think she used the stuff. Ruby Jean always had to be the center of attention. The more outrageous her behavior, the better. Drugs were a source of her outrageousness. She needed them to disregard the consequences, to make her unaware of us—to free her from caring what anyone thought.

"Mikey! Ooh, how's Mama's Baby." She made a huge show of hugs and kisses, which I accepted without enthusiasm.

"Good morning, Mother."

"Good morning, Mother," she mimicked in a low falsetto. "Aren't you glad to see me, Baby? I know you're mad at your Mama, gettin' herself in all this trouble, but that's no reason to be an old grump."

Old grump, my ass. It doesn't take a lot of trips to jails, emergency rooms, and rehab centers to ruin your relationship with anybody—even your mother.

"Nobody's buying your little story, Ruby Jean. You'll be out in a little while."

"What! What have you been telling them?" She jumped to her feet. "You can't believe what he's been telling you. He's lying!" She exclaimed to the bored officer in the corner. "I killed her."

"Strangled her?"

"No, no, I shot her baby. Don't try to confuse Mama."

"You didn't read the medical report. She wasn't shot until after she was dead. All of it done before you landed in Charlotte."

"How do you know when I…" Suddenly, her eyes rolled back in her head, she began to shake, then crumpled to the floor.

The cop jumped to his feet.

"She crashed," I said, calmly, "You might want to call for medical help." I laid a finger along her jugular vein. Her pulse was flying, over double her normal rate, I guessed. She was breathing fast as well.

The officer left the room, quickly replaced by Nansen and Chief Longstreet.

"She's probably going to be OK," I explained. "But I figure you'll want a doctor to check her out."

"You seem awfully calm, Trey," Sue said.

"Considering it's my mother? I've been picking her up off the floor since I was a kid."

The cops looked at each other, but had the decency not to comment.

Max poked his head in the door.

"Hey, did you want to pick up your girlfriend?"

My eyebrows probably reached the top of my head, as I turned toward him.

"Oh, I'm sorry. Not Nina, Carla. She called for the chopper, and I thought you might want to wing over there and pick her up in person."

I looked at Ruby Jean's hand twitching on the floor.

"Good idea, not much I can do here."

"Trey Hughes, meet Jim Rhodes."

"What's up, brother." The Pilot reminded me of my dad. He was a man about my size, with a military bearing and a lightning quick smile. Probably ex-Air Force. I wondered if he knew my dad. Not as impossible as it sounds. Pilots are a fairly close-knit bunch, and Black pilots are still a bit of a rarity.

We were flying from the parking lot at the train station. As we walked over, Max pointed out the van near the station.

"Courtesy of Catholic Charities in Atlanta," he explained. "They're still making do with their old one while they wait for the new *pair* I ordered for them. We had to have one for little Brad Chesney."

"How's his dad?" I don't know why I didn't ask last night when we were at the same hospital.

"Still stable, but no sign of recovering consciousness."

"Doesn't look good does it?"

Max shook his head. "But his family is going to be taken care of. I'll make sure of it."

I took the co-pilot's position while Max dropped into the back. The most dangerous moments of any flight are takeoffs and landings, so of course that's when our pilot struck up a conversation.

"Ever been up in one of these?" He asked as the bird rose and sideslipped quickly away from the face of the mountain.

"Yeah, and I've been to a few amusement parks, too," I answered as he nonchalantly tail whipped in a half-circle. "I've even played RIO in an F-15, so you don't have to go easy on my account."

He chuckled heartily, as we accelerated forward.

"Rhodey doesn't get a lot of chances to open her up," Max said, grinning. "Most of the folks he shuttles are a bit sensitive..."

"Little ol' ladies," he grumbled. "So how'd you get to hitch a ride in a 15?"

"My dad's career Air Force."

"Hughes… not Mike Hughes?"

"Yeah."

Rhodey flashed the full set of teeth. "Trey Hughes... I remember you! You couldn't have been more than 11, 12 years old. We were down in San Antone flying maneuvers. You probably wouldn't remember."

"I remember the heat."

"Yeah. It *was* pretty fugly down there."

I did not remember him specifically, but I remembered how the black officers and their families had a big cookout the one weekend. We went to a park: swam, played softball, and the usual picnic stuff. It was a great time. Kind of like a family reunion.

"So you weren't interested in following in your Dad's footsteps, huh?"

"Nope."

Jim Rhodes took one look at AJ. "Sorry, we'll never get off the ground with you on board." He deadpanned.

AJ faked a laugh, and handed Carla to me in the cabin.

Rhodey clapped him on the back. "Sorry," he said. "Just had to do that,"

I strapped her onto the center of the bench seat along the rear bulkhead.

"Hey, you," I said lovingly.

She reached up and kissed me. "My hero. I hear you saved my life."

I shook my head. "You saved your own life, kid. All I did was chase her."

I strapped myself in the seat to her left. She wrapped her arms around me and snuggled. My sore ribs might have grumbled a little, but I wasn't about to complain.

"This is all my fault," she said. "I was so caught up in my search for the truth, I never thought about the trouble it could cause me, or Nina."

The turbine started to whine, so we put on our head phones on.

"It wasn't your fault, Carl. Sooner or later they had to go after Nina just because she *might* get curious."

I didn't want to ask, knowing it was probably salt in the wound. But I did, anyway.

"How did you find this stuff out anyway? That Pop wasn't your birth father and all that."

She glared angrily, for a moment, then softened. "Dr. Fennally over at Case. He was starting a research project getting DNA tests for death row felons in Ohio. I helped a little during my last semester."

I nodded. Several prominent Law Schools have developed projects investigating death row convictions to see if new DNA evidence can conclusive prove the innocence (or guilt) of convicted inmates.

"Anyway, we were doing DNA, but I was reading up on other serology stuff including blood typing. You know I knew my type, so I found out Mom's then I looked at Dad… Tom's and realized he couldn't be… he wasn't…"

"He couldn't be your biological father."

"Exactly. So I started digging into the records trying to find out who I am."

"Then you found your birth certificate."

She snuggled up against me again. That headset started digging into my sore arm.

"Which made things worse than ever. Now I'll never know who I am."

As much as I sympathized, we had been together too long to have her doubting herself. We were a family, and I was not going to let her get away with backing out of it on a pretense.

"Got to be tough, having to find yourself… Maybe you can ask Ruby Jean for a few pointers. She's in town, still finding out who she is."

"Hey! You leave your crazy mother out of this."

"Hey, you stop feeling sorry for yourself. I know you feel like the world's turned upside down on you, but we've known each other a long time. You've always known who you were before."

"But everything's changed."

"You've been through changes before."

"That was before I found out I don't have a father."

"He's the same father you always had, Kitten."

It was Pop's nickname for her. I knew it would get a rise out of her. She shot up to full height.

"Kitten my ass, you son of a…"

"Now, that's the Carla I know and love," I interrupted proudly. The guys chuckled over the headsets, reminding us we weren't exactly having a private conversation. She glared at me for a while.

"Can you turn these things off," she asked. "I'm getting a real annoying noise."

After she flipped off her intercom Rhodes turned to me.

"Boy, you got to have brass ones the size of chandeliers."

"Don't worry," AJ rumbled. "She'll cut 'em off for him.'

I laughed. The only way I was really in the doghouse was if she was starting to buy all that 'this changes everything' business she was spouting earlier. If that was the case, I might as well start the 'New' Carla off on the right foot.

We flew directly to the top of the mountain. Carla slapped at my hand when I reached over to help her out.

"Oh no you don't. I hate you," she said, softly. "AJ, would you help a lady to her chair."

He grinned at me as he bowed low. "But of course, m'lady."

"M'lady?"

"You wouldn't know how a *gentleman* would act," She said with an evil grin.

"That's OK," I said, matching her expression. "Alex is better at heavy lifting."

It was the old Carla that made the casual, but unmistakable hand gesture.

"Inform Mr. Hughes," she said to AJ. "I'm no longer interested in anything he has to say."

"Hey, just a couple of reminders before you never speak to me again. First, you made me promise years ago that if I ever caught you feeling sorry for yourself I was supposed to kick you in the ass, right? The second thing is, you do know who your family is. Even after the 'new' Carla learned the truth you called Pop. He just didn't get back to you before you decided to get pissed and feel sorry for yourself."

"Hey!" She squawked.

"Hey yourself. And even after you got mad at everybody, you still e-mailed Alex. You still need your family. More importantly, you still have your family."

"He lied to me."

"Of course he did. Pop was scared. He thought if you didn't think he was your 'real' father, you wouldn't need him anymore."

"That's crazy."

"Is it? Where do we stand right now? How are you two getting along?"

I saw her brows knit together. She was struggling with the truth, but she was getting there.

She angrily spun her chair and began rolling away.

"Don't go away mad."

Her finger gesture was much more emphatic this time.

Chapter 32

"You stood me up," Lee said, without anger. I had gone to have a drink at the resort bar and ran into her. I had forgotten we were supposed to meet her at the Cafe.

"Sorry about that. Family business."

"I heard. A Lot has happened around here, too."

"Like what?"

"You have to buy me lunch."

"No way. I've seen you eat."

"Very funny."

Well she didn't insist on *Chez* rip-off across the square, but she wouldn't go for pizza and neither of us wanted to go down the hill. We ended up at the resort's restaurant. *The Mountain Grille* combined casual elegance with authentic Tex-Mex cuisine. Said so on the menu.

"Did you know your Mom's in the hospital?" Lee asked. "It's her heartbeat. Sue Nansen said the doctor thought it might be serious."

"You two on speaking terms now?"

"We ran into each other at the Cafe," she said, hinting a smile. "She also said you and your mom didn't seem particularly close."

"I can't help Ruby Jean… and I won't keep watching her get worse. Don't worry, I'll check up on her later."

"There's also a federal warrant on Mark Brunson for... fraud?"

I nodded. "He stole the ransom money from his company."

"Wait, I thought the ransom was recovered?"

I explained how he conned money out of his own company while Max provided the cash in the bag for the ransom drop.

"He realized people watching would think the money was safe until after he had gone."

"So he kidnapped Nina to put the scam in action?"

"Or he saw the potential for the scam when he saw the first phony ransom note."

"So, there never was a ransom?"

"Only as a smoke screen."

"But if he didn't kidnap her, who did?"

Who indeed. If he was the kidnapper, you think he'd have found a way to get the larger of the two ransoms, wouldn't he?

"They ID the dead woman, yet?"

"Haven't heard anything. They're still looking for a suspect. The murder was apparently done while you were still with Brunhilda, so you're off the hook. One of the security guys got knocked out, which kind of rules out your mom."

I knew Sue Nansen was holding something back. They just seemed too certain Ruby Jean was innocent.

Our cheerful little blond waitress arrived with our food. Lee had picked the grilled chicken salad, I went for grilled tuna. We were both disappointed. The lettuce and salad veggies lay miserably on the plate anticipating last rites. The chicken didn't look much better. Fortunately, (or, unfortunately) they had covered the mess almost completely with some sort of lumpy-looking ranch dressing. My tuna was barely warmed with a sauce almost devoid of, well, taste. *Almost* fried potatoes on the side.

"This is awful," she said after a couple of bites.

I dropped my fork as well. "The worst part is, it isn't cheap either."

"Do you suppose the Pineville Cafe would deliver?"

I shrugged. If not, it would be worth the trip downhill.

We complained to the Manager, Sherri, who was very apologetic. "I'm dreadfully sorry," she said, "but the kitchen has been total chaos since this morning when our *sous* chef quit."

"I don't know," I said stabbing the fish to make sure it was dead. "It's possible *Sous* had the right idea." I offered her a forkful. "Care to try?"

She declined, and agreed to eat (sorry, couldn't resist) the check. When we got up to leave I dropped a reasonable gratuity on the table.

"What the hell are you doing, Trey?"

"Tip… for the waitress."

"But the food was lousy!"

"Wasn't her fault. She didn't cook it, she just delivered it."

Lee walked away, shaking her head and muttering.

I looked around the restaurant. There were only a few people, but I felt sorry for them. The more I thought about that tuna, the madder I got. Finally, I decided to *sous* the chef myself.

He was one of those perpetually angry little guys in his mid 50's. You know, the kind that always wanted to be big and intimidating, but ended up about a foot short of that 6-5 he man. He was reading a magazine at the counter, half-leaning on a knife stuck point first in the cutting board. A smoking saucepan behind him holding the charred remains of something neglected.

"What do you want?" He asked in an unconvincing French accent.

"I decided to have lunch after all," I said. "But rather than have you poison me, I decided to get my own."

He waved the knife with a drunken hand. "How dare you!" he bellowed. "Come back here complaining about Andre? You get out, you…"

"You keep waving that knife around," I answered. "Somebody's going to lose a finger."

He swung the blade under my nose. I grabbed his wrist and slammed his hand on the counter. The knife bounced to the floor with a clatter.

"It's not me," I explained, "who's in danger of losing a finger."

"You cannot treat me like this," he complained. "I am *Cordon Bleu*!"

"You keep waving knives you're going to be *Cordon* broke."

He glared for a moment, then stalked off in a huff.

"I wondered what happened to you," Lee said from behind me.

"I decided to cook you lunch," I said, grinning.

Sherri dashed in, red-faced and completely breathless. "What are you doing?" she howled, "We have customers out here! Andre just walked out! We have no chef. What am I supposed to do now?"

"First, your chef was hardly worth thinking about. Second, what you need here isn't a chef, but a cook. Tell you what, I'll fill in for a while, while you see if you can find your friend *Sous* who quit earlier."

"Sue?"

"Your other chef? With knothead gone, she'd probably come back."

"Well I suppose I could call Angela… but I can't have you people back here."

I had already started into the refrigerator, planning dishes as I went. Cooking was an easy thing for me. With Ruby Jean usually out of commission, my sister Marsha and I learned to cook at a young age. On the weekends, Dad and I fired up the barbecue grill out back. Cooking became a retreat for me. A place to relax and think when I needed to.

"Of course you can, I'm cooking."

"I'll call security."

I began chopping spinach leaves. The lettuce was beyond hope, but the cabbages looked pretty good. Shred a few carrots, boil some eggs—I was on my way to what Marsh used to call Popeye salad.

"Fine. Tell Hatch I said howdy. If he wants lunch, it's probably going to be a while. The customers come first."

"What… you can't just take over…"

The little blond waitress stepped in.

"The natives are becoming restless. What do I do?"

"Tell the folks your chef got sick, but you have a special chef taking over, but it'll take a little bit and they might not get exactly what's on the menu. Apologize, buy a round of drinks, knock 50% off the bill, and see who's up for the adventure."

She snapped a mock salute and bounced back into the dining room.

"Hold it!" Sherri sputtered. "You can't just come in and take over our kitchen."

"Had me fooled," Lee answered, nibbling a carrot stick.

"You don't really have anybody else. It's me or nobody."

"But we… I don't know… can you cook?"

I began slicing zucchini. "I can't be any worse than Cordon Bleu, who just left."

I sliced 3 jalapenos in half and flipped them backhand into the pot of bean soup bubbling on the stove behind me. I began to peel onions.

"We don't have… you're not insured."

"I'm also not on the payroll…anything else?"

She walked off, shaking her head. It was going to take somebody with more horsepower to run me off, she decided.

"I can't believe you're actually taking over a restaurant," Lee said. I can't even believe you can *cook.* You're a regular Renaissance Man."

"Michelangelo's *David?*"

She laughed. "You might have the… attitude, anyway."

I began to spoon mustard into a bowl about half full of honey. "See if you can find a couple of lemons over there, huh?"

"So I guess you won't be fixing me lunch after all?"

"Sure, we'll just eat as we go."

"We?"

I chopped the top off a bunch of carrots.

"You just changed your name," I told her.

"To what?"

"*Sous.*"

Chapter 33

"I can't cook!" Lee almost backed into the stove.

"Don't panic. I'll tell you what to do."

"Do I have to?"

"Of course not. But you might want to expand your expertise. Go from fashion reporting to food."

She flipped me off. "Lot of that going around," I commented.

I sampled our chef's pathetic version of a barbecue sauce. It needed more....everything.

"Hold your hand like this," I demonstrated a cupped palm.

I poured about a teaspoon of salt into her hand.

"That's your measure. Pour that into the pot. Then, give me two measures of that cayenne pepper and 1 of the chili powder. Then stir slowly for a minute or so. And whatever you do, don't touch your face."

"That doesn't seem very precise. Wouldn't a measuring spoon be better?"

"Do you carry a spoon with you at all times?"

She looked at me strangely. "No"

"When was the last time you left home without your hand?"

She chuckled in spite of herself. "You're the chef."

"I'm a cook. The chef was the reason the food was lousy."

Lee was a quick study in the kitchen. She peeled carrots and chopped parsley, cored apples and pears, squeezed lemons and oranges and fetched in the refrigerator. She stirred and flipped and tended the oven. An excellent second pair of hands.

I made chicken with grilled vegetables, Pork chops with grilled apples and pears—both with the Tex-Mex barbeque sauce, broiled steak with roasted potatoes and homemade steak sauce (on the side), and grilled tuna with a *spicy* dill sauce. Honey-sweetened Corn muffins with raisins to finish.

The restaurant patrons taken care of, I turned to feeding us. Lee got the chicken with vegetables. Since I knew Carla hadn't had lunch, I fixed a pair of chops with a Polynesian sauce made from a pineapple I found, with rice and grilled vegetables (her favorite), a Kansas City Strip with the potatoes for AJ, Cajun style blackened chops for Pop. I had chicken, Polynesian style with potatoes.

Tina, our waitress, brought back compliments from the guests. Sherri came back with Security.

"Somehow I knew it was you," Hatch said. "They told me some lunatic was taking over the grille, and you seem to be the most dangerous guy on the premises. Your girl friend disappears, Brunson vanishes and we find a dead girl in your room. Why not poison some of the resort patrons."

"I guess you don't want lunch, then," I said grinning back.

"Sorry, I had pizza across the square."

"Your loss," Lee said around a mouthful of food.

"Any word on the dead girl?"

"Got a hit from New Orleans police. Our deceased is one Evangeline Broussard, still hunting for next of kin or a current address. You sure you've never seen her before?"

"She was the phony nurse that tried to kill Carla."

"Phony nurse? Nobody told me anything about a phony nurse. When was this?"

I was filling him in on the incident when my phone rang. I handed it to Lee. When I finished, she handed it back. "Your sister, Marsha," Lee said with a giggle. I answered carefully

"Who the hell is Sue?"

"A friend," I said, chucking. "Hey, Marsh, how's 'Chelle doing?"

Marsha named her daughter Michelle, but won't say if she was named after dad or me.

"What did you do to Carla?"

Calling Marsha was a pretty drastic act for Carla. Maybe I was a bit too hard on her.

"What? I just made her lunch." I tried to sound innocent.

"Peace offering." She knows me annoyingly well.

"We had a little argument." I told her the story as we knew it.

"So you yelled at her?"

"She was feeling sorry for herself. It isn't allowed. We have a deal."

"And you couldn't allow her even a little moment of self-pity?"

"No! Damn it, Marsh, she's been feeling sorry for herself since *January*. When Nina got kidnapped I needed her—but she was off hiding because she 'wasn't sure who she was'. I still need her and Pop to see if we can figure out how to find Nina. She can do her crying after we get her back… on second thought, forget that! She doesn't get a chance to reject us just because she didn't know her genetic background. None of us get to pick the family we get, so she can just get over it."

"You really are pissed aren't you?"

More like scared. In some ways the girls were the only family I had. With Dad in Europe, and Marsh in Houston—both with new families of their own—Nina and Carla were the only family I had left. With Lani gone and Pop in Arizona, they probably thought the same of me. We depended on each other. Now Nina was missing, and Carla was trying to bail out, not because she didn't care, but because she felt like the world had done her wrong. We had always fought and faced things together, now suddenly; we all had become unnecessary and redundant to her. Carla had always been my anchor and support. I would be out there during Spring practice or Summer workouts and I would be hurting and wanting to quit, but I kept thinking about how she fought her way, through the pain, without complaint. I'd lower my head and work harder and harder because I had to be strong like my hero.

"She cut me out, Marsh. She shouldn't have done that."

We both paused for a long time.

"You two will work it out. You guys are inseparable."

"I know. That's why these things hurt so much."

"Take care, little brother."

"Love ya, Sis. Kiss Michelle for me."

"What about Tom?"

"Oh sure, Like you'd need an *excuse* to kiss him."

Angela, the former *sous* chef, finally arrived to take over the kitchen. She was a square woman, not just because she was stocky, but also because she was barely tall enough to see over the stove. As I suspected, she knew somebody to work with. He was probably 12, about 6’5. With a full meal and wet from the shower might have come within 10 pounds of her.

She checked the sauces and salad dressing, sampled the corn muffins.

“Very nice,” she said. “Where did you study?”

“Chaminade High School, Dayton.” They offered an after-school cooking program. Carla dared me. Of course, I won the award certificate. Guess who set off the fire alarm?

She narrowed her eyes for a moment.

“This is really very good. Have you ever considered becoming a chef?”

“Well… not recently.”

“A pity,” She shrugged and set to work preparing for the dinner rush.

We walked out to the square.

“I must admit I’m very impressed,” Lee said.

I gave her an ‘aw shucks’ smile. “Maybe a bit more than just a dumb jock?”

“I never thought of you as… OK, maybe just a little.” She smiled at me. “Any other hidden talents?”

I smiled back slowly. “Several, but hidden is a relative term.”

“Mr. Modesty.”

“Hey, there are things I don’t do well, too.”

“Like what?”

“He can’t dance a lick,” came the voice from behind me.

“No rhythm,” another voice responded.

“You also don’t want to hear him sing,” Carla said, grinning. “He swims like a rock, snores, he’s only an average poker player…”

“Who asked you, Matilda?”

I tried to sound gruff, but I just couldn’t stop grinning. MY Carla was back.

Chapter 34

Max had moved us into his permanent suite at the resort. It was huge, fancy and high tech. In the main salon, the coffee table lid opened to flip up a pair of flat computer monitors. The keyboards and an inkjet printer were built into one of the end tables.

The same computer networked to all the bedrooms and even the bathroom.

The Master bathroom was an awesome display of Italian marble complete with Jacuzzi. The kitchen, although smaller than the restaurant's, was actually better equipped. The bedrooms were not big on free space, with the beds, only slightly smaller than some former Soviet republics, taking up most of the acreage.

My room was closest to the door.

"The only room without a waterbed," Carla explained. "Nina told me you hated them."

Nina's waterbed was one of those old-fashioned high motion types. The motion tended to keep me awake. I know for a fact that I'm OK on some of these controlled wave beds.

"Where's Pop?"

"His room's on the other side."

"No, I meant where is he?"

Carla shrugged. "He wasn't here when we got here."

"Maybe he went sightseeing?" Lee suggested.

"With Nina missing?" Carla asked.

"It's just a matter of finding Brunson, right, Trey?" Lee asked. "I mean we figured out the kidnapping, we just have to get him and he'll lead us to her."

"Seems that way doesn't it?" I said.

"What do you mean, 'seems that way'?" Carla asked. "You don't think it's this Brunson, do you?"

It was only a feeling, but I was pretty sure he was only guilty of scamming the ransom money. "I'm not going to be sure of anything until we find Sis. I know what we have points to Brunson, but it's possible we're overlooking something."

"Like what?" Lee asked.

"If we knew what," AJ said softly, "we wouldn't be overlooking it."

Lee looked up at him, frowning. Then she smiled, watching him until he shifted uncomfortably.

"So what next? Where do we search?" Carla asked.

"Well, we already have Pineville covered." I explained about our search team in town. "I suppose we can go through what we have and see if we find anything."

Carla had taken the corner of the sofa nearest the printer and had begun sorting through the stuff Cavanaugh sent a couple of days ago. I resettled her there while Lee sat on the chair to our left. I swung her legs across my lap and massaged them, just like always. I handed her the list of shareholders. For about the next few minutes the only sound you could hear was the shuffling of paper

"Marsh said I had my head up my ass," Carla said.

"Such language," I teased, "and from an English professor."

"She was right, you know."

"Could you wait while I get a tape recorder?"

"Ha! That's almost funny." She punched my arm.

"We were both a little..."

"Yeah. Sorry about what I said, I guess I was just..."

"Scared. I know."

"I needed you and you weren't there. I never thought about how I was the one who made sure you wouldn't be there for me. I blamed you anyway. Then you caught me feeling sorry for myself."

"It's OK, you're allowed," I said, grinning.

"My ass," she said, grinning back, "what I needed was what I got, and you know it."

She snuggled against me and sighed.

"Maybe I just needed a good meal," she said, smiling up at me. "The lunch was great! Just like mama used to make. And it was very thoughtful."

"I figured you could use an edible bite after that hospital food."

I could feel her shudder. "That stuff just doesn't have any taste."

"Well, that's because they don't want you hanging around just for the blue plate special."

"Maybe that's where the restaurant found their 'chef'," Lee joked. "But they found a better one in Trey."

"Stop it, I'm blushing."

"How can you tell?" AJ said, heading toward the kitchen. "Anybody want a beer?"

"Sure," I said.

"You know without some idea what to look for, this is a total wild goose chase. What should we be looking for? Brunson?" Lee asked.

"I guess. See if we can find anything that might indicate where he's running to."

I gave a brief history of Kaiser Electronics, then explained my theory behind the kidnapping.

"Look for anybody else who might be in financial trouble if Nina gets her fair share of the company. Also keep your eyes open for anything that doesn't look sound or feel right."

"Aren't you overlooking the best suspect of all?"

"Max Kaiser. I know."

"Well?"

"It's not Max. Someone might have done it for him, but I just don't think he's involved enough to care. He might have the most to lose, but I think he'd be the least affected."

Carla looked skeptically at me, but she knew me well enough to not challenge me. I knew her well enough to know she wasn't going to blindly take my word for it. I'd suspect him myself if I didn't know him. Maybe I knew him too well.

I went back to the papers. And found an interesting fact.

"Call up my e-mail," I told Carla. "See if Cavanaugh sent me any more information on Woodland, Bancroft, and Maitland."

"Woodland, Bancroft is a major corporate law firm," Lee said. "They're on retainer for several Fortune 500 companies."

We all stared at her.

"I dated a lawyer. What can I say? Corporate lawyers have wet dreams about partnerships at Woodland, Bancroft."

"She's right, they're very prestigious. Dr. Fennally wanted me to interview with them," Carla said, "but that's just not my kind of law."

"Wall Street?"

"Absolutely."

"How much would they offer a fresh out of law school lawyer?"

"I don't know, maybe six figures."

"Twenty years ago, Brunson made 115 thousand from Woodland, Bancroft."

"He's a lawyer?"

"Nope. Dropped out of Bronx Technical High at 17. Why would you suppose they'd pay a high school dropout more in 1985 than a lawyer in 2005?"

"Blackmail."

"That would be my guess."

Max said nobody in the family knew about Brunson until about 9 years ago, but here was proof that at least Old man Maitland knew eleven years earlier.

"Who's Sugar?" Carla asked.

"Oh, print that stuff. She's Brunson's wife."

"There's a picture…"

Cavanaugh. On the bright side, he hadn't sent video. Knowing I was already going to kill him for reading my e-mail, he could have figured he had nothing to lose.

"OK, here we are," Carla said, pulling the first sheet off the printer. "Sugar Cain… Stage name?"

"You think?"

"Born, Evangeline Broussard…"

"…New Orleans, Louisiana," I finished.

"The dead girl in your room!" Lee said excitedly.

"Makes sense, I guess. With their assets tied up, both Brunsons needed the phony ransom," Carla said

"So Brunson killed her?" AJ asked

"He's certainly going to vault to the top of the suspect list," I said.

"So your Mom has to be off the hook for sure," Lee said.

Carla sat up, eyes blazing.

"You mean that psychotic…"

"I told you this morning she was here, didn't I?"

"I heard him," AJ said.

"I didn't think you meant *here,* here. Did you at least warn Dad?"

I shook my head. "She's in the hospital over in Asheville. Another OD."

She shook her head angrily, but said nothing.

"What else did your guy send on Brunson's wife?" Lee asked.

"She's a big time Porn star," AJ said, nonchalantly. Lee stared at him like he'd turned orange or something.

“What?” He asked.

“I had no idea you were a connoisseur, Alex,” Carla said.

He smiled broadly. “Just heard the name before,” he said.

“Here you go,” Carla said. “Brunson and his wife were partners in an Adult Movie company called MoHo Productions.”

“MoHo?”

“According to these numbers a very successful enterprise,” Carla said. The thing is, He bailed out a couple of years ago… but that doesn't make sense. This company looks like a license to print money. Why would he bail?”

“Jealousy?” AJ suggested.

“Crystal Mountain,” Lee said. “I did my homework before I came here. The original plans called for this resort to be more kids and family oriented—the ‘Disneyland of the Appalachians’. Can you imagine what would have happened if people found out one of the men behind America's newest family resort was producing porno movies? Would have been bad for business. Later, the resort profile changed, but it was too late by then, I suppose.”

I nodded. “So the wife gets her own money making venture, then surprise, surprise, decides to get rid of her husband. After all, she was probably worth seven figures by the time the deal was done. Plus she puts in a claim to half of his fortune… apparently he wasn't big enough for a pre-nup in those days. It’s like the old joke, ‘what’s yours is mine and what's mine is… still mine’.”

"But wouldn’t he have gotten half of her company when they divorced?" Lee asked.

"Nope. It’s a voluntarily divested asset,” Carla explained. He gave up all claim while still married. Probably signed papers to that effect."

"Do you suppose it's just coincidence," AJ, asked grinning, "she bailed out on her marriage right after she gained complete control of her own company?"

“No.” I said, without hesitation.

“Sucker.” He said.

“Sucker twice. I'm willing to bet he put up all the cash for the venture in the first place.”

“Makes sense,” Lee said. “He’d have the money, she would have the business contacts.”

“Plus sweat equity,” I said, trying not to smile. “I assume she performed in many of the features as well. Cavanaugh claims she’s an award winning actress.”

"But the question is: Did she do all her own stunt work?" AJ asked.

"Too late to find out now."

“You guys are sick,” Lee said.

“This is news?” Carla laughed.

“The question is: Could Brunson inherit her share now that she’s dead?”

“Not if he’s implicated in her death,” Carla said.

Chapter 35

Carla's phone rang.

"Hi Dad. Where are you? Oh, we're fine. We're up on the mountain… Sure, good hunting. We'll talk tonight."

She caught me smiling and stuck out her tongue.

"Dad is searching down in Pineville with Tom and Walter. He wants us to join them for dinner."

"I thought they'd been all over the town already," AJ said.

"Sure, but there's no harm in double-checking."

"They even had her in town for a while didn't they? Isn't that where you found her ring?" Lee said.

"What ring?" Carla asked. "What are you talking about?"

"Her High School ring. She managed to leave her ring in an abandoned building down in Pineville."

"I don't remember Nina wearing a ring," AJ said.

"Alex is right," Carla said. "She doesn't usually wear jewelry."

They were right. Nina wouldn't normally wear any ring, let alone that one. Desperate for a clue, I hadn't been very skeptical about it. Maybe she managed to grab the ring while she was being taken, but it was doubtful she would happened to be wearing it when she was captured. On the other hand, it might have been a plant by the bad guys. A classic red herring. I was so excited to find any trace of her, I never thought at all about the possibility of it being a false clue.

Come to think of it, even though I figured out how they got her down the hill, we never did answer the question of how they got to her in the first place. She wouldn't just open the door for anybody, and, given half a chance, would have wrecked the place before they could get her bundled out of there.

"You didn't think of that did you?" Carla said, reading my mind.

"No. You're probably right. Then again she's been acting a little strangely."

"You mean you two still haven't resolved your… situation?"

That little... Nina had been begging me all along not to tell Carla we'd been romantically involved. I'd been struggling since the beginning with my natural inclination to be honest with her. The whole time, Nina just didn't want me to know she'd already spilled the beans. All that hell she was putting me through for wanting to tell Carla—when she already knew.

I would have given her the benefit of the doubt—assume Carla found out herself, she's a bright girl—but I knew them both too well. Nina didn't want me to come along or spend a lot of time with me for fear of telling on herself. Carla, as we all know, has a real problem taking 'no' for an answer. Eventually, Nina told her sister the truth, but wouldn't admit that to me. That's why she'd been so furious at me for the last few months—guilt.

AJ, in my line of sight, held his hands out defensively (wasn't me). Caught in a little guilt by association.

"Assuming facts not in evidence," I said without smiling. Two could play this game.

We played staredown for a moment. Then I reached for my cell phone and called Sue Nansen.

I explained I wanted Carla to get a look at Nina's room, sealed since her disappearance. Should have been the first thing. Nobody read Nina better than her sister. Agent Nansen agreed, as long as she was there.

We had a little time to kill, so we went back to the files.

"Does it say anywhere who Brunson sold his interest in his wife's company to?" I asked.

"Wouldn't he have just sold it to her?" Lee asked. I just shrugged. It was possible he hadn't.

"C&M Industries," AJ said.

"Just a hunch," I explained to Lee. "I suspect 'Sugar' would need a business partner—emphasis on business."

"That's pretty sexist," Carla said. "Just because she's a woman she needs a man to help her with her business?" She shook her head in mock disappointment.

"No, actually, it just fit the pattern of her last partnership," I said. "I figured she was more the people person."

"Better at stroking the clients?" Lee said.

"Something like that."

"She'd need somebody to make the nuts and bolts business decisions." Lee said, giggling.

"C&M owns a piece of Kaiser, too," AJ said, checking that list.

I pulled up the e-mail on C&M Industries. Surprisingly, Cavanaugh didn't have much on them. A holding company for a holding company. Privately owned.

"Here's something," Carla said. "Brunson and Broussard's Partnership agreement. A strange survivor clause."

"Strange how?"

"A provision for children, but even though they weren't married to each other at the time, no mention of spouses. Shares revert to the other partners."

"Sounds like the same clause as Max Kaiser's original venture, K&S Enterprises."

"So much for Brunson's motive for killing his wife," Lee said.

"Well, there's still keeping all his own assets." AJ pointed out.

A knock on the door announced the arrival of Sue Nansen.

Instead of the FBI, when I opened the door a uniformed security officer barred her way.

"Mr. Hatcher said I was supposed to make sure it was OK before letting anyone into the suite," he said over his shoulder.

I said the magic word and he stepped aside.

"You mean those fancy Federal credentials couldn't get you past a rent-a-cop?" I joked

"I didn't show him."

"Makes sense. No need hunting rabbits with a cannon."

"I'm an idiot," I told Carla as we got to Nina's room.

"I know that. Care to be specific?"

"You'll see."

The door opened.

"Nothing's been moved," Agent Nansen said.

"They cleaned this room," Carla said. "Nina was never this neat."

She was right. I realized I had been looking for *anything*. A message, a sign. It never crossed my mind that the REAL sign would be nothing. The room had no sign of the usual Nina.

No clothes on the floor, items almost mathematically spaced on the dresser. Not a thing out of place. None of us were this fanatical, not even my dad, the Major.

"Clothes in the closet? Suitcase closed. This is *all* wrong," Carla said. "Somebody cleaned this room."

"Why would they clean the room?"

"Because her usual housekeeping would have left the police thinking there was a struggle."

I checked the vanity case on the dresser. Nina's watch, bracelet and a couple of necklaces were all there to be accounted for. I was surprised by the ring I did find. It was a woman's gold band with a diagonal pattern.

"Hey Carl, did you know Sis was carrying this around?"

Her jaw dropped. "No. I had no idea."

"What is it?" Sue asked.

"Their Mom's wedding band. As far as I can tell, the only thing missing is the ring we found at the Laundromat."

Hatch appeared in the doorway. "Hey, guys."

"Thanks for the beefed-up security," I said sarcastically. "If any one really wanted to get us what difference would Barney Fife there make?"

"He might holler before he gets clobbered. I thought Ms. Gustafsson might find the sight of a uniform reassuring."

Click. "Maybe she did," I said, answering a totally different question.

Opening the door for Security. A uniformed guard gets a pass from most people. They don't necessarily notice the subtlety of badges and insignia, nor do they generally confirm identity. A person unaware of any threat would pay even less attention. Nina would have answered the door for a uniformed Security Guard.

"How many uniformed guys do you have, Hatch?"

"We all have uniforms. But we generally dress between 12 and 16 over the 3 shifts. More if we have a trade show or convention. They did a jewelry show back in March. We all worked overtime—and unlike my guys, I don't get overtime."

"Straight salary?"

"Well, I'm supposed to get time off—you know, comp time. Or as I call it 'con' time—because you can't take it for any good days like New Years Day or a day around Thanksgiving. The company won't allow it. Then they're always screwing you on the hours. They won't do hour for hour, they want a 2 for 1 sort of thing and since they get to keep track…"

"So, you don't get that many days?"

"Actually, I still get plenty, but any day I seem to want, there always seems to be something. The last day I tried to take off was the day Nina disappeared."

"What? You were here, I saw you."

"They called me when they realized it was going to be a situation. Dave Patton didn't want to get too involved with things without bringing me on board."

"Patton works with you?"

"Well, we have kind of a mutual cooperation thing. We kind of act as consultants to each other—decide whether to ruin the other guys vacation, day off, whatever. Some deal between the resort and Kaiser."

Lee grabbed my left arm. "Listen, Trey, I wanted to buy you dinner, but there's something I really have to check out. Raincheck?"

"Sure." I was surprised she was making a deal out of missing dinner. What she was up to? Did she find a lead? She hadn't received any phone calls. I hoped she wasn't headed for trouble.

"Don't worry, Dad," she said, as if reading my mind, "I have a bodyguard in case I'm out too late."

She glanced over at AJ, who smiled broadly. I obviously missed something.

"Have fun, kids." I waved my hand in blessing.

"Looks like you missed your big chance," Carla said.

Chapter 36

Dinner was at the Cafe. Carla and I, Pop, and our friend Walter. Tom was staking out the abandoned laundromat—just in case.

I explained about the phony security ruse to get Nina to open her door.

"Makes sense," Carla said. "Do you think it was one of the regular security guys?"

"Maybe," I said. "But it could have been anybody. Kaiser's security people wear almost identical uniforms, and they're also commercially available. All they would need was an opportunity, and Hatch's day off made that work."

"Seems kind of risky."

"No, I do not think so," Pop said. "With the chief of security gone, the phony could claim to be newly hired or additional security for the beauty pageant. Even if they were skeptical, they probably would not have checked him out with Hatcher until he returned."

"You said that lard-head Patton filled in for the guy on the mountain?" Walter asked. "Maybe your bad guy was Kaiser security."

"What makes you say that, Walter?"

"Well, they have a reputation around town as bully-boys. Everything from stomping the kids and local blacks to… rumor has it, a protection racket."

"Protection racket?"

"Over in new town. Pineville's a dry town, but there are a couple of places, you know, on the sly. The local police are still a little thin, so they don't bother unless there's a complaint or a disturbance. Plus, quiet as it's kept, most of Kaiser's boys are auxiliary Sheriff's deputies. The word is, most of these places are paying a healthy fee to Kaiser Security to avoid legal hassles and prevent disturbances. One place was practically destroyed in a riot before the Pineville cops got to it. Several of the brawlers on both side were recognized as Kaiser Cops."

"Maybe we should talk with Patton." Carla said

"There's a roadhouse just on the edge of town," Walter said. "*Nate's*. Cops leave it alone because it's right on the county border, a jurisdictional dispute. I served with Nate in 'Nam. I know he isn't paying. There have been incidents out there."

"Where trouble goes Patton might not be far behind, huh?"

"Exactly."

"Let's go." Carla said.

"Slow your roll, toots," I said. "If we know there might be trouble we should probably get some legal back-up."

"Carla shouldn't go anyway," Pop said. "It might be dangerous."

I certainly wanted to duck under the table before the explosion, but Carla surprised me.

"I can take care of myself," she said, too calmly.

"It's a pretty rough place, but I don't think they'd hurt a…" Walter caught himself. "Pretty young lady."

"In a wheelchair, you mean?" She patted his arm

"What do you think, Trey?" Pop said.

"If we don't take her along," I said. "They'll catch her hot-wiring a cop car or something." I learned the hard way that telling Carla she couldn't was just throwing gasoline on a fire.

It was easy to talk Sue Nansen into joining us, solving our back-up problem. We waited until about 10:30, figuring the hell-raisers would look for as big an audience as possible. Should have come at ten. The *battle royale* was already in full swing. Towering over the other combatants was AJ and an older black fellow—Nate, I presumed. They probably could handle these guys a couple at a time, but it looked like they were outnumbered. Most of the non-combatants were jostling each other out the door, but some were forted under tables and hugging the walls.

I jumped out of the car and elbowed my way into the melee. The first person to grab me was just a drunk. I tossed him aside. The next guy was sober, so I kicked him in the knee. Other folks joined in as I fought my way toward AJ. The knot of combatants moved toward me, brawlers peeling off to face the new challenge. I caught a glimpse of Sue Nansen, swinging a leg from one of the busted chairs lying around like a police baton. Nate also had a short piece of lumber to help him out. AJ relied on his own huge mitts—his hand quickness honed by years of top collegiate football. Me? I combined the Karate I learned as a kid with an unquestioned willingness to fight dirty.

As I got to AJ at the line of scrimmage, I saw a fellow picking himself up from the deck behind him, a knife blade flashing as drew it from his boot. I caught his wrist just as he went to stab him in the back, and levered his arm against my right forearm. He screamed into my ear as the bone snapped. The elbow I threw back into his head quieted him a bit.

Hidden between the twin towers, Lee was swinging a makeshift club like Hank Aaron at the plate.

"What kept you?" AJ rumbled over the chaos.

"I'm sorry, Ollie," I answered as I began to hear sirens over the din of battle.

Our adversaries were persistent, at least. By the time we managed to wade through most of the brawlers, a few of the first round losers were up for a second wave. Tangled with one tall, wiry sort of fellow, I caught a glimpse of a familiar face. I tried to duck as Jason Thompson, the little guy from the incident at Kaiser's gate, swung his stick at me, but he managed to tag me pretty good.

I fell to one knee, feeling a bit woozy. He raised his stick again, but was tagged with a heavy scotch bottle in the hands of Lee Holt. He swayed a bit before AJ airmailed him with a left. He hit the deck as flat as a professional wrestler. Before anyone else took a swing, gunshots rang out from the doorway. I glanced over and saw Chief Longstreet grinning while several uniforms dove into the scrimmage.

It was a multi-jurisdictional action. Pineville Cops, a State trooper, and a couple of County Deputies all stepped in, sorting us out: Kaiser security thugs, a couple of whom I recognized from the incident at the gate, including my friend, Thompson, who tagged me with the club, local toughs, who may or may not have been hired for the purpose, drunks, just enjoying the opportunity for a fight, and of course, bar patrons, defending themselves, or helping out the out numbered bar staff.

"Hey, Trey," Lee said, pointing. "Isn't that your friend the chef?"

Our good friend the *Cordon Bleu* chef was the fellow who tried to stab AJ in the back. I hadn't really noticed his face when I disarmed him (almost literally).

"The good news is," I joked, "he won't be able to cook for a while with that arm."

In a time-honored southern tradition, the strangers in town, AJ and I, were the only ones arbitrarily handcuffed. I was going to have a pretty good-sized egg on the back of my head. AJ a slight cut over his left eye. Lee was sporting an ugly bruise along her jawbone. Nate looked unmarked, until I noticed a knife wound in his leg.

The grand prize winner among the good guys was our FBI representative. Somebody dropped one right on the bullseye. You could already see the matched set of shiners under both eyes that universally indicated a broken nose. It was a square hit, so her nose wasn't bent, but it was certainly going to swell. Blood trickling down her upper lip, she was hunched over a mirror inspecting the damage.

"Good thing you got those government issued shades," I said.

"Take those cuffs off," the Police Chief ordered the Deputy standing between us.

"You're not in town," he drawled. "You can't give orders. We're waiting for the Sheriff."

A small man in a Grey sport coat stepped up flashing a badge. "This is part of an ongoing State investigation. I *can* give orders. Turn them loose."

AJ and I grinned at the deputy as he unlatched us.

"Mark Chandler, I'm the new state investigator," he said. "You must be Hughes? They told me you'd be where the trouble is."

"They replaced Ferguson?" I pretended to sound shocked.

"Attempted murder's a killer on your resume. He's been amazingly cooperative. Of course, cooperation is the only thing that will keep a needle out of his arm."

"Makes sense."

"Ferguson tells us he was taking orders from the head of Kaiser Security, a fellow named David Patton. We're assuming Patton got his orders from Brunson."

"But how does Brunson link up with Kaiser Security?"

"According to Ferguson, Brunson was masterminding a takeover of Kaiser."

Then again, you can't trust Ferguson as far as you can throw a bus. It didn't make a lot of sense, a man in Brunson's financial shape trying to take over Kaiser.

"Patton also murdered Brunson's wife according to Ferguson," Chandler said.

"How do we know it wasn't Ferguson?"

"Guess we don't. We'll grab Patton and see what he's got to say."

I shrugged, and surveyed the room. No sign of him.

"Got a man down," one of the Pineville cops said, looking under a table.

Chandler and I walked over and looked at the victim. Flat on his back, feet pointing out, it wasn't likely he had ducked under the table during the festivities. He was obviously dead. A long boning-type knife stuck out of his chest. No longer red-faced and sputtering like the last time I saw him.

"Don't tell me…"

Who else? "David Patton," I confirmed.

"Shit."

"Won't get much out of him now," Longstreet said.

Chapter 37

"Somebody is definitely covering his tracks," Carla said, wheeling in behind me. "First, Brunson's wife, now Patton."

"Don't forget Tom Chesney. No witnesses. Somebody feels us closing in, and wants to make sure nobody is around to testify against them."

"Who, Brunson?" Chandler asked.

"Maybe. Just answer one question. Was there any place they could have dumped the body of Evangeline Broussard that could have pointed more directly at Brunson?"

"Thumbing his nose at us, that's what that is," Sue Nansen's broken nose gave her voice a honking quality.

"You might want to ice that nose before it swells." She had packed it with cotton to stop the blood, but she hadn't thought of the ice. Wait until she hears about the brace.

"I'm just saying the placement of the corpse almost screams Brunson's name. Which means either he's really psychotic…"

"Or somebody wants us to think it's him," Chandler said.

"Hey, you're quick for a State cop."

His blue eyes stared at me for a moment, realizing I might have been damning with faint praise, considering the only other State cop I knew was in Pineville jail.

"But if it wasn't Brunson, who did it?" Sue asked.

"Max Kaiser," Lee joined in. "I know he's a friend of yours, Trey, but almost everything that's happened has some tie to Kaiser Electronics."

"Sure, but Max is a recluse by nature," I argued. "Hard to believe he would suddenly take such an active role within his own company. Besides, I got the impression Tom Chesney was the only person he really trusted over there."

"What about Karl Werner?" Lee said. "He was here until just before the fight started. He met with that dead guy and one other fellow."

"What other fellow?" Chandler asked

Lee shrugged. "We were following Werner, hoping he would lead us to Max Kaiser. We didn't recognize either of the other guys."

"Could it have been Max Kaiser?"

"Apparently not. Alex knows Kaiser, it wasn't him."

Chandler eyed Alex, who was helping a paramedic load Nate onto a gurney.

"Hell of a recluse," he said. "Everybody seems to have met the infamous Max Kaiser but me."

"What you get for wandering in late," I joked.

He threw up a crooked smile. Unlike my old buddy Ferguson, the new guy seemed to be hiding a genuine sense of humor behind his gruff exterior.

"Next to Max, who has the biggest chunk of Kaiser?" Carla asked.

"Five or six different entities—C&M Industries, Woodland-Bancroft, George Maitland, Brunson… Wait a minute! Who doesn't fit here?"

"What do you mean, who doesn't fit?"

"Woodland Bancroft is a multibillion dollar law firm, right?"

"Sure, and Max's stepfather, Harry Maitland, is a senior partner. What's your point?"

"Why would they still want stock in Kaiser Electronics? Certainly the golden goose for a Corporate Law firm would be in handling legal affairs for Kaiser, particularly in light of recent Microsoft and Cisco cases."

"Well, it might be questionable ethics, but I sincerely doubt they could sanction them for it unless one of the other shareholders would object. Most of them appear to be family," Carla said.

"Maybe that's the 'M' in C&M. If the Maitlands and Brunson hold that significant a block of the company, wouldn't they want a man involved in the day-to-day operations? Somebody like Karl Werner?"

"OK, if Werner and Patton were here to meet the third guy," Chandler wondered, "Who was he?"

"Well, it obviously wasn't the older Maitland, and let's just try the idea that Brunson is long gone. Who's left?"

"George Maitland!" Carla said.

"George Maitland."

That would explain why AJ and Lee didn't recognize him. He could be the guy willing to do the kidnapping and killing to come out ahead. I never thought Brunson had the nerve, and Max didn't seem greedy enough. Maitland, *et al*, had a chunk of Kaiser big enough to kill for. An answer without elements I didn't like, or facts I didn't believe. All I had to do now is figure out a way to prove it.

"What makes you so sure it's him?" Chandler asked.

I shrugged. I wasn't sure, but I didn't see any other suspects in this deal.

"Last I heard, George Maitland was a successful lawyer in New Orleans. Why would he want to risk it all by kidnapping your girlfriend?" Longstreet asked.

"You know Maitland?" Carla asked.

He nodded. "He was a senior in High School when I was a sophomore. He grew up in New Yawk, as he used to say, until the end of his junior year. Max must have been in grad school or already in business because I don't remember ever meeting him."

"If he's from New Orleans," I said. "What do you suppose the odds are he knew the late Mrs. Brunson?"

"You figure he killed Patton in revenge?" Chandler asked.

"More likely to cover his tracks." Carla was stealing my lines again.

"It's also quite possible he didn't actually use the knife himself. There are a few other fellows who might have been willing to do the job for a small fee."

I indicated our little *Cordon Bleu* chef. "That little guy there has a tendency to play with knives," I said. "He might know what happened."

"We're going to run them all in and see what we can sort out," Longstreet said.

"Don't forget Karl Werner," Lee reminded. "If they're tying up loose ends, he might be next."

"Shouldn't we also be looking for Max?" Carla asked.

"I for one would like to speak to Max Kaiser." Chandler added.

Suddenly, every one was looking at me. I did know where Max might be, but should I tell the others? If George Maitland was running Max's company for him, Max might be willing to cover for him. Protecting family was something I could certainly understand. On the other hand, brothers have been known to kill each other.

"Where would Maitland be staying?" I wondered aloud. "I doubt he checked into Crystal Mountain—under his own name, anyway." It was a rhetorical question.

He'd stay with family. Max would have no problem putting up his half-brother while he spent a few days in the old home town, and Lonnie's mountain retreat was the ideal place to hide out while you're up to nefarious deeds.

"Maybe we should sort out this mess," Sue Nansen said. "Mark Brunson is still our prime suspect isn't he? We need to find him before we start looking for anybody else."

The other cops agreed. Chandler wanted us to come in and help sort out tonight's Pier 6 brawl, but as the other agencies felt it was unnecessary, he chose not to press the issue. Not like we were leaving town.

I did have a plan for me, tomorrow, but it required a little help from the authorities. Ditching Carla (and the others) might be a bit tricky. I 'nonchalantly' suggested to Sue that she should invite our friend Max in for a chat tomorrow morning. While they kept him occupied, I was planning to search his place for signs of George Maitland.

Our ride had disappeared. I looked at Carla, who was as surprised as I was.

"They must have seen somebody sneaking off," she said.

Pop also, we found, had his cell phone off.

"Not much we can do until or unless they call in, huh?" I said.

"Can I kill them both?" She said.

"Only if nothing happens to them first."

Pop and Walter might have found something to keep them occupied for the rest of the night, but I was going to bed. We hitched a ride back into town with Lee and AJ. It took some arguing and whining (on both sides) before Carla would agree to go up the mountain.

"Do you know where they are?" I finally argued.

"Well… no."

"Is there any way of knowing where they are?"

She puffed in frustration. "I suppose not."

"Well, I'm going up. Let me know if anything happens."

“You wouldn’t leave me,” she said, knowingly.

She was right, but I wasn’t going to say it.

“Oh, all right!” She finally agreed. “But you’ll stay with me tonight, huh? In case they need us?”

“Sure, kid.”

Chapter 38

Getting up was going to be extremely tricky. In addition to the obvious question of how to get out of a waterbed without disturbing your sleeping partner, Carla was actually resting on my left arm. It would have been so much easier with Nina, who a nuclear blast *might* waken. I could have rolled her onto the floor and back and she would most likely never notice. Hell, some mornings Nina didn't remember things she said and did AFTER waking up. Carla was a much lighter sleeper, and since we weren't used to sharing a bed, she was a lot more likely to be disturbed.

Sneaking out of bed was really underhanded, considering how freaked out she was. Not hearing from Pop and Walter had her really bent out of shape. I held her through her restless night until she finally fell asleep. Still, it was going to be a lot easier than hiding or ditching her later. Besides, the early morning escape would help me avoid the thing I hated most—lying to her. Like most women, she loved to hold a grudge and she was certainly never going to forgive me for this stunt, but lying was something that always tortured ME. Even if other people never forgive you, you have to find a way to forgive yourself.

The arm had to come first. I started slowly, inch by inch. I was almost out when she started murmuring. I froze, as always in the most uncomfortable position possible and listened. It was only a couple of minutes before her breathing evened out. I wondered if she dreamed about me, too—ego, I guess. I shifted a little at a time, pausing occasionally. The worst part was standing up at the side of the bed. Even a 'waveless' bed will react to about 230 (still, I hope) pounds being suddenly removed. If I shifted too quickly, she'd wake up, and it was impossible to camouflage what I was trying to do if she caught me in no man's land.

It was about 5:15 by the time I slipped out of Carla's room to start across the living room toward my room. I knew AJ was an early riser, so I might have only a few minutes to get dressed and slip out without notice. In the pre-dawn light, I considered my phone on the table. But why give people extra opportunity to yell at you? While I had stopped to think, AJ's door swung open and a wedge of light fell into the room.

I froze where I stood, watching Lee cross the room to the bathroom. I suppressed a laugh. AJ's t-shirt was so huge, she almost had to worry about walking on the tail. She looked like a little girl frightened by a nightmare, drawn toward the comfort of her parents' bed. She crossed without turning back or noticing me.

I was just Mr. Sneaky Pete this morning, I thought, as I stood in the woods near the trail to Lonnie's cabin. I was uphill from the trail, on the opposite side of the road just close enough to see him emerge as he went down the hill. It seemed like days, but it was only about 9 o'clock when I saw him break cover heading downhill. I stayed for a extra couple of minutes, closed my eyes, maybe even nodded a bit—it had been an early morning.

Working my way through the woods parallel to the main trail, I kept my eyes and ears open. When I got to the clearing at Max's cabin. I became a statue again.

I felt guilty. Not just for sneaking around behind Max, but behind Carla as well. I knew she would never be able to navigate this terrain, and that all telling her about it would have done is give her a chance to make me feel worse, but the truth is, I wanted her with me. She had a better eye for detail, She was as smart as I was (probably smarter), tougher than I would ever be, and knew Nina better than Nina. There were times I'd almost be willing to swear they were the same person.

A lot of the times I caught hell from her, it was completely unfair. I hadn't done what I was accused of, usually some kind of misinterpretation of my words or behavior. I would either take it or fight back, depending on my mood, and the best way to get her goat. Eventually, she'd feel guilty and we'd make peace. This time I knew damn well I deserved whatever trouble I was going to be in.

As I suspected, Lonnie didn't bother to lock his doors. I searched the house top to bottom. No one had lived here except the owner. The guest rooms were… dusty, the other rooms also had no sign of human presence. I suppose George could have slept on the sofa, but if he did, he had neither breakfast nor coffee, judging by the dishes.

Since I had Max's computer system at my disposal, I checked my e-mail for new stuff from Cavanaugh. Two items of interest he sent were Evangeline Broussard's birth certificate and the partnership behind C&M industries. It was no surprise there were only two principle shareholders, Bruce Coleman and George Maitland.

If George didn't stay with Lonnie, maybe he was staying with the 'Widow'? Her place was somewhere further back in the woods. What the hey? It wasn't like I had a lot of other things to do.

I sat on my heels at the edge of another clearing, looking for signs of life. The old cabin was probably over a quarter mile past Lonnie's. There was a clearing off to the side that I assumed they used for Max's copter.

Nothing seemed to be moving, so I eased into the clearing and began to circle the cabin slowly. Off to the far side of the building was an honest-to-god outhouse, famed in song and story. It even had the little crescent moon cut into the door. Seemed like a pretty good spot, downhill—and hopefully downwind.

I went in the back door. No particular reason, just change of pace. No reason to lock up out here at all. I checked the kitchen. The counter and sink showed more than a couple of dishes. A trio of cups sat on the table, each holding dregs of coffee, two black, one cream. They might have been fresh from this morning, but where were the drinkers? I had a good vantage point on the only path out of here, how do you suppose they could get out without me noticing?

I checked the two bedrooms, number one, neat and tidy, the other much more lived in. Nina's room (or mine).

Stepping into the main room, an item on the glass and wood coffee table caught my eye. The table itself didn't make sense. It was definitely big city chic (a decade or so back, anyway). It was as out of place as one of those wagon wheel based tables would be on Park Avenue. The pink hat in the center of it looked every bit as ridiculous as it always did.

Suddenly I knew what Nina's ring meant, and why nobody cared about ransom. I also had to begin to wonder if Max Kaiser might be involved after all.

I remembered a cop picking that hat up when it fell off the woman's head that Saturday in Dayton. It was Nina's bike she hit, too drunk to realize the wrong girl was on it. I always knew it was never just an accident, no matter how often people told me it was. Now I finally knew why.

As Mitch Sugai's rightful heir, Nina was worth half of K&S and subsequently, Kaiser Electronics. With the other partners either sold out or dead, Max and George had the whole thing. Killing Nina was the only way to keep it. The original plan 10 years ago was to kill her and make it look like an accident. Maybe she figured out she had hit Carla instead, maybe not. Either way, she couldn't just keep trying. So they started watching us, realizing we really didn't know anything. It was only when Carla started searching for the girls' past that we became a danger again.

Not just Nina this time. It wasn't just her existence that was threatening; we were in danger of finding proof. They meant to have us all dead no matter what.

Nina was the bait to get the rest of us here, for them to kill us. Evangeline, Vince diRosa's daughter, had to be killed as well. When Brunson married her, she may or may not have known about her potential stake in the company, but when she filed for divorce, she definitely became a liability. First they drew her into the conspiracy to kill Nina and Carla, then silenced her.

Nina must have seen the "widow" and palmed the ring. 'Crash', the inscription, was meant to be a clue, a warning. I was just too fatheaded to understand it.

I stared at that hat, unable to shake myself from that day 10 years ago.

Shaking my head for about the 19th time, I finally had a gear clang into place. If she was still alive, Nina would almost have to be right here in the area. I had been over Max's pretty thoroughly, but I wondered if he had any secret rooms or a cellar or someplace else to hide her. It seemed given that Max was now a part of this thing. It certainly seemed likely he would know something about his mother plotting for almost a dozen years to murder people.

As I stepped forward toward the door, I heard a rushing whistle of air, then the back of my head exploded in stars and pain. I don't even remember hitting the floor.

Chapter 39

I felt like a whole flock of idiots, letting somebody sneak up and knock me out like that. When I came to, I was bound hand and foot. My head throbbed, the room was swaying, my mouth was dry as a bone, and I smelled smoke.

Smoke? I didn't feel the heat, yet, but the most obvious answer was certainly fire. My eyes were adjusting to light, but I was definitely seeing smoke.

I had pitched headlong into that glass table and probably looked like I'd lost an argument with a Ginsu salesman. The room was filling up with smoke, and the only thing saving me was probably the fact that I was face down on the floor.

The glass. The edge of one of the shards I was lying on would make a good weapon to cut my bonds. Sure enough, the light cotton clothesline parted pretty quickly. It just felt like it was taking years. I also sliced my left thumb pretty good, shifting the glass shard to cut the cord binding my feet.

By the time I got my feet free, I was having trouble breathing, even on the ground. The room was shifting around on me, but I couldn't tell you if that was from the smoke inhalation, or the thump on the head. The nearest exit wasn't the door but the window. I peeled off the sweatshirt jacket I was wearing and wrapped it around my right arm. I smashed through the window with my forearm, then used my covered hand to remove the fragments.

The flames of the fire were mostly on the outside of the cabin. I sucked in a good breath from outdoors before I felt strong enough to dive out the window past the flames. I barrel-rolled down the hill toward the outhouse, making sure I hadn't picked up any fire. Fortunately, I also hadn't picked up any major chunks of glass.

I sat coughing in the dirt, watching the flames and smoke spiraling up over the trees. I reached for my pocket, then remembered I had left my phone behind so Carla couldn't yell at me.

I kept coughing while I inventoried my damage. For a guy who busted more than his share of glass, I was relatively unscathed. A few scratches, but only a handful of significant cuts. I couldn't actually see my face, but I wasn't dripping a lot of blood anyway. A good sign. I felt the spot on my head where he tagged me. If folks were going to insist on cracking me on the head, I would really appreciate it if they could pick separate spots. I could feel the blood seeping into my hair.

More covering tracks? Would they burn the cabin to the ground, just to eliminate me or was there something else? Either way, I was behind enemy lines without any means of communication. It was certainly time to move.

I was just reaching the edge of the clearing when I came face-to-face with a 9mm pistol. Behind the pistol was an arm, behind the arm was, apparently, George Maitland. I thought for a second about the bulletproof vest I wore the other day, back in my room. A useless souvenir. Why didn't I think of *that* when I was sneaking around getting dressed?

"You should be in there," he said in a strange voice.

"Too hot in there, George. Besides I always wanted to meet you and your mother."

He shook his head. "Mama says 'no witnesses'."

"That why you killed Evangeline?"

"Sugar? I loved Sugar, but she had to die. She couldn't be trusted anymore."

"I thought she was married to Mark?"

"Sugar has sugar for everybody. Didn't you know that?"

The gun seemed less certain than at the beginning. His eyes were glazed over, as if drugged.

"I heard that. Tell me about Sugar's dad."

"Mama said he was going to be trouble. We had to have Karl running things not Vince. Vince had to go. Blood everywhere."

His face dripped tears. I got a couple of steps before he straightened up. His eyes snapped into focus. "Mama wanted us to get rid of Sugar, but I couldn't."

"Where is your mother?"

Bad question. He straightened out his arm, new resolve behind the gun.

"No witnesses," he giggled. "You should be in *there*."

"I had to find Nina."

"Little sister. She's safe… In the safe place." He giggled again. He had to be on something.

"Why do you want my little sister?"

"Keep her in the safe place until SHE gets here."

Waiting for mama to return.

"Where is it? Where's the safe place?"

He smiled. "Darkness. The safe place is under the moon, in the dark."

The gun began to sag. Maybe I could… Nope. The gun snapped back into position as soon as I shifted my weight. He was like a bad watchdog, not wanting to attack, but trained to anyway. The gun wavered again.

"You don't want to do this, do you George? Killing people just to get more money."

"It isn't fair," he said in a strange falsetto. "The Chinese gets money, the other strangers get money, but what about Georgie?"

Mitch Sugai was only part Japanese, but I wouldn't gain much by correcting him.

"Put the pills in the drink. If Lonnie doesn't make a place for Georgie, Mama will."

"You gave the pills to Mitch Sugai?"

He kept staring into space for a second. "He got real crazy, then went away for good."

"Then you killed Vince."

The gun swung back in position.

"The knife. It had to be a knife. Steal his money and his watch. I didn't want to do it. All that blood." He looked at his empty hand. "Mama made it better, she cleaned up and gave me medicine."

Mama seems to have been giving Georgie medicine for years. He pretty far gone by now.

"I don't think you want to do any more killing, George."

He shook his head slowly.

"Mama said," he said emphatically. "No witnesses. You should be there."

He stepped closer. Point blank range. The gun shook violently.

"No Witnesses," he screamed.

The explosion was deafening.

Chapter 40

George smiled at me for a moment, then slumped to the ground. His shattered gun arm hung, practically amputated by the .54 caliber bullet. I ripped the shirt from his back, tying it like a tourniquet above the wound. I barely looked up as the tall figure of Max Kaiser came from the woods, his muzzle-loader held at arms length, like a poisonous snake.

"I thought you said that gun didn't fire, Max."

"I lied," he said, tonelessly.

He stared down at his half-brother as if frozen, barrel pointed unconsciously at him. I couldn't imagine what it cost him to take that shot.

"Call for help," I said emphatically.

After I jolted him back, he spoke into his cell phone for a couple of moments.

"Chopper will be here pretty soon," He said

"Good," I said, "he's bleeding like nobody's business. He's going to be in shock pretty soon."

"I'm sorry, Trey," he finally said.

"Sorry? Sorry for what, you saved my life."

He looked at me as if pained.

"I think maybe I knew about this, you know, subconsciously. George and Karl Werner were always as thick as thieves, and I should have realized some of these things they did while they were happening, but after Vince was killed I just never..." Tears rolled down his cheeks. "George wanted to be more involved in running the new company. He and Karl seemed to be doing great, and hell, it wasn't like I ever wanted to be a suit. Then Mitch died, and I guess I bailed out completely. Tommy felt kind of uneasy, but nobody... we didn't know that he would resort to kidnapping and murder. George and Mark must have planned this kidnapping right under my nose. I always knew he was a bit neurotic, but I never saw him as a psychopathic killer."

Max, your Mom's the psychopathic killer. I just couldn't tell him the truth. George Maitland was a psychological snake pit of drugs and self-loathing used as an instrument by his mother. They killed his partners, and it was always possible they could get around to him too.

"I hate to tell you this, Max, but I don't think he was working with Mark Brunson." It was as much as I could bring myself to say.

"We'll find out soon enough, the feds are flying Mark back from the Bahamas."

Well, at least he was alive. The rest of the witnesses had all been silenced.

"Shame about your Mom's cabin," I said, watching the smoke billow into the sky.

"It's no big deal. She can stay with me when she gets back."

"Oh, where is she?"

"She was supposed to be in Charlotte with George. He was supposed to be meeting with his business partner Bruce..."

"Bruce Coleman." I remembered that third cup in the kitchen. It was more likely Coleman was here than she was there.

"You know him?"

"Not personally." How could Max's entire family establish a conspiracy of greed and murder right under his nose without him knowing?

"If George is here, do you think he left my Mom stranded in Charlotte?"

"I wouldn't worry much, yet. I'm sure she's OK."

"Let's go ahead and move him into the clearing," he said. "Rhodey will be here in no time."

I was still keeping pressure on his arm, trying to make sure he didn't bleed out.

"There's a hole in my arm," George explained.

"We're taking you to the hospital," I told him. "You'll feel better soon."

His eyes focused briefly.

"You were supposed to burn," he said, "in there."

"I heard. No witnesses. Not like Nina, who's safe."

"Safe," he giggled again. "In the safe. Just past the moon."

"He's on something," Max said. "If anybody's over the moon, it's him."

We supported him as we walked him back to toward the landing area. George was mostly silent as we moved.

"Carla's dad and Walter were found out on the Cherokee reservation this morning," Max said. "They went off the road and wrecked last night. Tribal police say it was a blown tire."

Carla's going to kill me. "Were they hurt?"

"Shaken not stirred. They were mostly pissed because the car they were following got away. They couldn't call because Tom's phone was dead."

"No idea who it might have been?"

"Probably Karl Werner. Maybe somebody hired to kill Patton. Not even a very good description of the car. Dark and sort of big."

"All cats look gray in the dark, I guess."

We heard the thump of the helicopter rotor as we entered the area. George sat quietly with us at the edge of the clearing, mumbling and singing to himself.

"I'm staying," I told Max. "I think Nina's here somewhere."

"You need to come and get checked out. You're a bit scratched up there."

"I'll be OK. She's got to be around here somewhere. You have any caves up here?"

"Trey, there's nothing up here. No caves, nothing. The only shelter left in this area is my cabin."

"I don't know, Max, maybe George and the others built something—a lean-to or a shed, maybe they set up a tent. I'm just convinced she's here."

"Trey, you can't depend on George! He's not even sure which planet he's on."

As if on cue, George began singing to himself. The words were inaudible but the tune rang a bell.

"Pink Floyd," Max said in answer to my raised eyebrow.

I nodded. "See you on the dark side of the moon."

"There's first aid stuff back at my place," he said. "You should clean those cuts and scratches before they get infected or something. Don't worry about the water, it's clean. We tied in to the resort systems. Indoor plumbing and everything."

I nodded.

"I'll call Hatch and the feds. They can come help you search."

"So much for Max the recluse."

"It's OK. I should probably have killed him years ago. You can get a little goofy up here."

The copter rattled down in the clearing. Max helped George into the bird then boarded himself. Glad to finally have a reason to really open it up, Rhodes really zipped out of the clearing, the wind from the rotors almost knocked me flat. He was barely clear of the trees when he cranked it over and dove full tilt down the hill. He swooped down the hill racing toward Asheville as if his tail was on fire.

My face was in pretty good shape, nicks and scratches, but only one significant cut on my right cheek. My arms had a pretty good collection of minor cuts and scrapes, but only a couple of deep ones. The worst cuts were my thumb, which needed a good tight wrap to control the bleeding, and my right forearm, one that was definitely going to need some stitches. I had to wrap it pretty heavily, too. A little soap and water, peroxide, and a few band-aids and I was ready to rock.

Max was probably right. I wasn't that chopped up, but if I had gone slogging around the woods searching for Nina without cleaning and bandaging those cuts, I would have probably picked up a flesh-eating bacteria or something.

Good thing the cabins had running water...

Safe in a safe place, George said. The darkness beyond the moon. Could it really be that easy?

Chapter 41

I used to run 400 meters in High School, but I shattered my best time by a good chunk on my way to that outhouse. My nose and lungs were burning from all the smoke I had breathed in earlier, but I had the rest of my life to cough.

I had to be right. If the cabins have running water there was certainly no need for an outhouse. I pulled the handle, but the door didn't open. I pushed on the entire frame, thinking perhaps the building was hinged to fall over. After trying to knock it over from each side, I began looking for an ax or hatchet to chop my way in.

Maybe there's a latch. When I twisted the handle instead of just pulling, the door unlatched and swung outward.

It still looked like an outdoor john. The bench along the back wall had the proper hole with a flip-up seat. Along the side to my left, a remnant roll of toilet paper hung in the holder on the wall, the modern replacement for the Sears and Roebuck catalog. The right hand corner had a vent pipe running up from the bench. Standing by, ready for use.

I scratched my unshaven chin. Everything looked just like it was supposed to. The cigar was a cigar, Dr. Freud… except…

No odor. Even with an outside vent, an outhouse in use would still have… ambience, wouldn't it? If its use was ceremonial, or decorative, why the sophisticated latch? This had to be what I was looking for, George's safe place. The question was how to open the safe.

I went to work at the bench. Maybe the top lifted… nope. I checked inside the bowl and found an electrical switch, but it had no noticeable effect. I checked the kick board in front of the bench, again without success. *The floor. It had to be.* It wasn't budging, though. I scrabbled at the boards, beat on it with my fists. I needed an axe. I walked around the smoldering cabin. No sign of any tools. I also noticed the downed electrical wire between the cabin and john.

Maybe the thing opened electronically. I decided to take one more look before hiking back to Max's. I knew he had to have an axe for firewood.

It was a little iron ring right at the front left corner. I pulled it and heard a barely audible click. I opened the door and lifted the heavy floor. The bottom was metal—steel, probably. A set of narrow treads led underground.

The nearest flashlight was a quarter-mile away, but how big a bunker could you build under an outhouse without anybody noticing? I found a prop for the floor/lid, then eased carefully down the dark stairs. Holding my left hand in front of my face, I found the ceiling to be low. I eased my feet slowly in front of me as if I was blind. A concrete wall faced me at the bottom of the steps. Using the corner as a guide, I followed the wall until I hit a metal filing cabinet. I made a right turn and felt along that wall. In spite of the hint of light and feeling my way, I crashed into the cot and fell onto a definite human form.

Nina.

She didn't move as I shifted back to my feet. Unconscious, I really hoped.

I had to get her out and take my chances. I felt my way down her arms. Her hands were tied. Me without a knife, of course. I slipped my hands through her armpits and began dragging her toward the steps as best I could. Heading backwards, to protect her, I crashed into the stair riser. As I worked my way along the steps I could feel her heart fluttering, but she didn't seem to be breathing.

I dragged her out and started mouth-to mouth.

"C'mon sis! I been through way too much for you to die on me now."

I re-checked her pulse. It was weak, I thought. I kept breathing for her even as I heard the helicopter in the distance.

"You die on me princess, and I'll never forgive you." I grumbled, swore and prayed with the same sentence.

I smacked her face gently. "Come on baby girl, Wake up."

She moved.

Just my imagination. No, this time she really did move. I saw her chest rise. She was going to be OK.

She woke quickly, rolling her head languidly. Her eyes opened, lighting up the world again.

"Trey," she groaned.

All I was doing was crying.

"How ya doing, babe," I finally creaked.

Her eyes fixed me as I took her into my arms

"Hello, Trey."

"Hello, darlin',"

"Trey?"

"Yeah?"

"Do you plan on untying me anytime soon?"

"I don't know. I like the idea of knowing you can't get away from me for a while."

I wanted to sing, scream—something! I felt like I was going to explode, but I was so full I couldn't find a way to express any emotions. After I untied her, we kept holding each other.

"I knew you'd find me," she said.

"That makes one of us," I said.

"Geez, get a room," AJ rumbled from behind me. I was so focused on Nina, I never heard the chopper land nor his approach.

He lifted Nina one-handed, as if a small child, and wrapped her in a huge bear hug.

"Hey," I joked. "Find your own girl."

They both chuckled at each other.

"Glad you're OK, Angel."

"Hey there, Big Bear."

"Where's the rest of the gang, AJ?" I asked. "Did you hijack the copter?"

"They should be along in a couple of minutes. They went to Kaiser's house to set up a command post. They were thinking you might be back there. I saw the smoke and knew you would be here."

"Hey, I didn't start that fire."

"No, but the most likely place to find you is at the scene of the latest disaster."

"How's Carla?" Nina asked.

He glared angrily at me. "She's down in Pineville with her dad. He was in a car accident last night."

"Papa? Is he OK?" Nina asked.

"Bruised ribs and a bump on his head. He's OK. Carla, on the other hand, was really freaked out because she had no idea where you were, Trey."

"I know. I should have brought my cell phone."

“She woke up from a nightmare to find you gone, then finds out her dad was almost killed.”

On top of Nina’s disappearance and her current identity crisis. Just what I needed—more guilt. On the plus side, finding Nina might buy a little forgiveness.

“You could have left a note,” AJ said. “Let us know you were on the trail.”

“I thought it was a wild goose chase,” I lied. “Besides, you guys would have tagged along and I was still trying to protect Max’s privacy.”

“In other words, you don’t trust Lee or I?”

“No. I trust all you guys, but you remember the old saying about three men keeping a secret only if two are dead.”

“Who’s Lee?” Nina asked.

“Alex has a new girlfriend,” I said.

I could swear AJ blushed. As if you could actually see it.

“We should get angel here to the hospital. Get her checked out. Your face is bleeding, too.”

“Don’t change the subject,” Nina said. “Tell me about this Lee.”

“We should go to town first so Carla and Pop can see she’s OK.”

“C’mon guys, who’s Lee?” She was hopping from foot to foot like a little kid in line for the toilet.

“You’re right,” AJ said. “We should head for the copter.”

As we started up the trail, we met up with Lee.

“What, you couldn’t wait for the press?”

“So much for being a hero in the new millennium,” I said.

“So this is Nina? I can see what all the fuss was about. That State cop is going to be furious… he’s really beginning to think we’re excluding him.”

“Well, he can have first crack at searching the outhouse for evidence,” I said.

“Outhouse? Oh, he’ll love that. All that muckraking.”

“No, not like that, it’s a phony, there’s a bomb shelter under the outhouse. Apparently they kept files down there.”

Just then Sue Nansen came into view on the trail.

“You two are a sight for sore eyes,” Sue said.

“You should know Susan.” Finally finding an emotional safety valve, I began laughing uncontrollably.

Chapter 42

"If he's hysterical, can I slap him?" Nina said, raising an eyebrow toward me.

"I think you're in line behind Carla," Lee said, glaring at me.

"Nina, meet special agent Sue Nansen, she of the sore eyes."

"Glad to see you're safe and sound, Ms. Gustafsson," she said, trying not to smile.

I kept grinning at her.

"What?" she finally demanded.

"So let's see 'em."

They had taped the bridge of her nose, and she was still wearing her Ray-bans, but from close range you could still see the dark circles working under her eyes.

She stared daggers at me, but with an angry flourish she whipped off the shades.

"Must have been one hell of a party," Nina joked.

"Wasn't bad," I answered.

To her credit, she hadn't made some lame and futile attempt to hide the damage with makeup.

"I see you've been burning evidence," Sue said.

"Hey! Ain't you heard of smoke signals? The evidence wasn't in the house, anyway, it's in the crescent moon hotel."

"Crescent Moon…"

"The outhouse."

Her upper lip curled. She was assuming it was a working 'house. Who was I to argue with the FBI?

"Well… maybe I'll let the state guy root through that."

"Good idea. You guys are going to need flashlights. It's just a bit dark in there."

"I would guess so."

"Let me know if you find anything."

"Where do you think you're going?

“We’re going to take Nina into Pineville, then on to the hospital to have her checked out. Me too.” I pointed to my arm, which was starting to seep blood through the bandages.

“Yeah, OK, but Trey? No more disappearing acts, huh?”

“Nope. We’re all going to stay pretty close from now on.”

“You got that right.” Nina slipped an arm around my waist as she snuggled next to me.

“Don’t worry Mom,” AJ rumbled, “we’ll be home in time for supper.”

“Get out of here, you comedians.”

The sound of the slap echoed off the building behind me.

“I got that on tape,” Jay said cheerfully, “in case you want a copy.”

“I’ll take one,” Nina said, grinning.

In the short time it took to get to the bottom of the hill, Lee had found her wayward cameraman and got him there in time to shoot the happy reunion. It was all laughter and tears of joy until I got into range of Carla’s open right hand.

It wasn’t the blow that hurt nearly as much as the pain on her face.

“You abandoned me!”

Not much I could say to answer that.

“Do you have any idea how badly you scared me? I was already worried about Dad, then I wake up to find you’d disappeared without a trace, without a hint… After I told you how frightened I was.”

She had a point. Sneaking out was the easy way, and I was going to pay for it.

“Nobody knew where you were. We thought you had been kidnapped or killed. Maybe that you had a head injury from last night’s fight and was wandering around confused and lost. We were all frantic.”

I started to speak, but I really didn’t know how to answer her.

She cut me off, anyway. “I know you, you’re going to try to smile and pat me on the back and say ‘sorry’ and expect things to go on like always. All’s well that ends well, right? What you did was unforgivable! The end did not justify the means. I’m glad you found Nina, but…”

"You couldn't go where I was going, Carla. Rather than spending half the morning arguing that with you, I needed to just get the job done."

"The least you could have done was tell Alex. HE could have gone with you. You could have gotten yourself killed and we would still have no idea where to find Nina."

AJ, hearing his name took a step closer.

"She's right," he said. "I could have watched your back."

"If I had told you, AJ, you would have wanted to go with me. I needed you to stay with Carla."

"You never asked me to do that, either."

"Didn't have to."

He nodded.

"Wait a minute! You still think I'm some little girl who needs a baby-sitter? I'm a grown woman…"

"Who can't have it both ways, toots. Either you needed someone with you, or you could take care of yourself."

Talk about lighting a fuse. She spun, then charged at me. I side-stepped her. For a couple of minutes we were bull and matador. She grazed me twice, but no damage done. The last time, she caught Nina a good shot. I swung her back to her feet.

"You should know better, kid." I smiled at her. "Stay out of this."

Carla had stopped rolling at me, but was beginning to sniff angry tears.

"You're not getting of the hook that way! I had a right to know what you were doing. You of all people know how I feel. I won't let you treat me like I'm helpless."

"I have *never* treated you like you're helpless. I just knew you couldn't go with me this time."

"Since when do you get to decide my limitations?"

"Oh, grow up! There might be a Santa Claus, Virginia, but life still has a few deep dark secrets. The biggest one is, we *all* have limitations. You don't have any more right to feel sorry for yourself about yours than any of the rest of us."

We faced each other silently for a few moments.

"You are *such* an asshole!"

"Like I said, limitations." I gave her my best smile.

She still glared at me, but said nothing. She was going to stay mad at me for a while.

"If you two are ready for a cease fire," Nina said, "We should probably get Trey to the hospital."

Blood was soaking through on my bandaged right arm.

Carla's eyes softened a little.

"You're bleeding. You should have said something," she grumbled.

We weren't going to all fit in the helicopter. Alex offered to drive Pop, who was always a white-knuckle flier. We decided Walter should go as well, since our two car wreck victims hadn't been properly checked out. Lee was going to stay behind—she had work to do.

"CNN with the news scoop, huh?"

"Quit this morning. Jay owns the tape, I have the story. We're going to sell it to the highest bidder."

"Excellent. No more 'bingo'?"

"Exactly."

"Good luck, lady," I said, kissing her on the cheek.

"Hey," AJ joked. "Kiss your own girl."

"Fat chance," Nina said, giggling as she took my arm.

"I'll ride with Dad," Carla said.

"I'd love to ride in the 'copter," Walter said.

He hadn't been in one since '70, he explained.

"Be fun to have nobody shooting at me up there."

"That probably jinxed it," Nina said.

As we climbed aboard, Nina turned back to me.

"You two fight dirty."

There's an understatement.

"I promised her…"

"That doesn't mean draw blood, Trey. What's going on with you two? I'm used to you guys arguing, but I've never seen her that furious, or you that vicious."

"It's… complicated, Nina. You have to ask *her*. I can't explain it."

"Can't, or won't?'

"Both," I said, flatly

She started to press, but decided not to. Smart girl.

"There's one question bothering me since before you disappeared," I said.

"Hm."

"Whatever made you decide to enter a beauty contest, anyway?"

Chapter 43

Nina smiled at me.

"It's your fault, you know."

I was completely blindsided by that.

"OK, I'll bite. How is any of this my fault? As I remember it, I was the last one in on this thing."

She searched my face with those beautiful eyes. "I just wanted you to notice me."

"When did I ever not notice you?"

"You never paid any attention to me! Back when I started high school, you were the big stud Quarterback. Every girl in school wanted to go out with you. I never had a chance. Then you went on to college and it got even worse."

"What are you talking about? I always spent time with you and Carla."

She shook her head.

"Oh, come on. That's not what I mean and you know it. You had to spend time with us that way, we were like family. To you, I was always this gawky tomboy—Carla's little sister. I saw the girls you went out with. They were all perfect hair and perfect makeup and big chests, always wearing the perfectly coordinated outfit. I thought if I could be more like one of them, you would spend more time with me. I thought you would love me."

"Nina, I do love you. Always did."

"No, no, nothing like that girl Lindy, or Tiffany, or Shirelle. I was your kid sister. You used to come to my basketball and volleyball games, most of the time with your latest. Then after the game, you'd kiss me on the cheek, pat me on the head, then run off to have real fun. It was cruel."

I knew Nina had a thing for me back in those days, but she was, after all, a freshman. Carla and I thought it was important that she had her own friends, developed her own presence. It never occurred to me she thought we were ignoring her.

"It was never anything like that. Those girls were just girls… I never had any serious feelings for any of the girls I dated in High School. We were just out having fun. You guys, you and Carla. You were the only girls who ever mattered."

"Sure. That's why you went to that fashion show with Beth Robinson."

During her first year at Western, Nina and the girls from her Basketball team were asked to put on a fashion show for charity. I was asked to escort one of her teammates. I had always assumed it was Nina's idea.

"The fashion show people called me. What was I supposed to do?"

"But why Beth and not me?"

I shrugged. "I didn't know I had a choice. They called and told me I was escorting Beth. It would have been a lot more fun with you. Is that why you two quit being friends?"

"I thought you liked her better than me."

"Did you ever see me go anywhere or do anything with Beth?"

"No."

"On the other hand, I remember the fellow you were with… didn't you two go out several times?"

"That's hardly the same thing. Jason and I were friends… it was never serious."

"As opposed to Beth and I?"

"OK, maybe the whole thing was a little irrational."

"A little?"

She smiled. "I guess maybe more than a little. It made sense when I was doing it."

"Is that why you *quit the team*? You thought you had to change for me?"

She snuggled against me. "Silly, huh? I guess I'm still that insecure 13-year old."

"You listen, girl. I love you. Whoever you are, whatever you do. Before you ever do anything stupid again for my benefit, check with me first?"

"I promise."

"Trey?"

"Hm?"

"Who won the pageant?"

"It's tonight."

"Why didn't you say so? I can't go to the hospital. I still have a chance. I have to get dressed."

I stared at her, mouth open in shock, until I saw the corner of her lip twitch.

"Very funny. You have an awful lot of faith," I said, chuckling, "that I'm not willing to wring your neck."

I closed my eyes, it had been a tough morning.

"You and Carla? You'll make peace, right?"

"Unless she thinks I shouldn't have gone to that fashion show with Beth Robinson, either."

She slugged my arm; she also giggled.

"You're an asshole."

"I've heard that.

Turns out I could have loaned myself out as a dressmakers' dummy. Five stitches in my thumb, an even dozen in my forearm and twenty down my left leg. Never even felt that one. Nina was a bit dehydrated, and had an interesting combination of sedatives and psychotropic drug residue in her system.

"You're going to need a few back here," the doctor reminded from behind my head. "You were hit in the head?"

"Yeah."

"Lose consciousness?"

"I prefer the term misplaced."

"We're going to have to…"

"Hold it. I'll put up with the stitches, but I'm not staying overnight for observation."

"You might have a concussion. You need to stay here."

"We had this conversation a couple of days ago. I'm not staying."

"You were…" he peered around at me. "Oh, yes, the man with the bulletproof vest. I didn't place you."

"And you're worried about *my* head?"

"This is the second time in a couple of days. You're more likely to have trouble. Do you at least have someone who can keep an eye on you?"

"I think so. I also have plans not to get hit in the head again. I was thinking about wearing a helmet."

"Can I at least take a precautionary X-ray, you might have a skull fracture"

"I don't have a skull fracture, but you can take your X-ray."

"You won't find anything." Nina had arrived to check on me.

"They say *I'm* OK," she said, cheerily.

"*They* need their eyes checked," the doctor answered. "You look a lot better than OK."

I didn't have to look to know she was preening.

"Thanks, Dr…"

"Ross, Donald Ross."

"After the ordeal I've been through, I could use a boost in ego." She said.

"And a larger hat," I shot back.

"Stitches? I sure hope they *don't hurt*." Dripping sarcasm.

The doctor reached for the xylocaine needle.

"What's that for?" she asked.

"Numbing the area."

"Hardly worth the effort. His head's been numb for years."

Max arrived as the nurse was covering the stitches with a bandage.

"George is going to keep his arm, but he's going to lose some motor control. You did a good job of first aid, they said."

I shrugged.

"He's going to be hospitalized for quite a while… Apparently he's been on some kind of witch's brew of drugs for years. It might be a long time before he can stand trial. If ever."

He noticed Nina in the corner.

"Hey, you must be Nina. Welcome back!"

"Nina, Max Kaiser." I did the honors.

"*The* Max...."

"Yep. But my friends call me Lonnie. We have a lot to talk about, the three of us."

"I thought Carla should fill her in," I suggested. "She should be here fairly soon."

Max nodded. Nina looked confused.

"George said Mama was behind the kidnapping. He didn't make a lot of sense, but I think I believe him....but you already suspected, didn't you?"

I just nodded. "You wouldn't have believed me if I told you."

He shook his head. "You didn't really trust me, either."

"I just couldn't assume either way."

"How could I have let this happen? How could I not have noticed?"

"You said yourself, you never wanted to be a suit. They all gave you the freedom you wanted, so you didn't want to ask a whole lot of questions. When the time came, you did the right thing. Saved my life."

"Guess so. But my own family! I just can't believe it."

"They made their own choices, Max. You can't be responsible for everybody else."

"Then why do I still feel guilty?"

"We all feel guilty, Max."

Chapter 44

They had patched me up, and I was waiting for the others when a fellow in his 30's came up to me. He looked vaguely familiar.

"Hello, Trey, I'm Brad Carlyle. I'm your… I'm married to your mother."

That's where I'd seen him. I knew Ruby Jean had a new husband. Third victim (the Major was number one), this one didn't seem much older than my sister. I offered him a hand to shake, but said nothing.

"Look, I know you and your mother don't get along…" he gave me a chance to jump in, "and I'm really not trying… I just thought you should know she's going in for surgery tomorrow."

"Surgery?"

There's a complication. It's difficult enough to stick to principles when your mother is a drunk and a junkie, but knowing she's going in for major surgery…

"Her heart has become too erratic, the doctors say. They have to install a pacemaker."

All those amphetamines had come home to roost, I guess.

"She's going to have to kick the habit for sure this time. Look, I just thought you should know. I'm not trying to pressure you into anything."

He didn't have to. She was still my mother wasn't she? "What time tomorrow?"

"Eleven."

"Thanks for telling me."

"Sure."

He looked at me carefully, thinking I might give a hint of how I was reacting to the news. I wondered myself.

"It's a pretty serious thing," he added. "Just thought you should know."

"Right." I answered.

Still nothing. No anger, no fear. No idea what to do or say next.

He walked off toward the door.

"Tell her I said 'good luck', anyway." I heard my voice say in the distance. Now there's a pathetic message. *Good luck? Good grief!*

He turned and raised a hand in acknowledgement. I sat down in a chair and closed my eyes. Just a little rest.

Only one person tries to wake me up by blowing in my ear. I thought I'd have a little fun with her.

"Very funny, AJ," I said, without opening my eyes.

I heard a sharp intake of air as the others laughed.

"Got her to stop didn't it?"

"You should see the look on her face." Max said.

"Serves her right," I said, opening my eyes. "She only does that because she knows it annoys me."

Nina was pouting. "It's romantic."

I patted her knee. "Of course it is my dear. But you shouldn't start the car unless you plan on driving it."

"Where are the guys?" Pop asked as Nina blushed.

"AJ and Walter went in search of food." Carla said.

"You didn't go with them?" Nina asked incredulously.

"Wasn't hungry." Actually, I was asleep.

"Guilt," Carla said.

I smiled enigmatically.

"Well, I'm plenty hungry," Nina said. "Let's go find those guys."

It was a good thing we had dinner in Asheville, because they needed crowd control for us when we landed back in town. The press, its appetite whetted by Lee's story, was desperate for fresh pictures and sound. Max and Nina stepped up and began the impromptu press conference while Walter and I got Carla into her chair. She didn't say anything to me, but she didn't slap me again either.

I pushed her chair to a position next to her sister, then backed out of camera range, taking a position next to the police chief.

"We've got it covered now," Longstreet said. "APBs on both Pearl Maitland and Karl Werner."

"What about George Maitland's partner, Billy Collins, Bruce Coleman, or whomever," I asked.

"We'll add him to the list."

"What about Max?"

"Oh, we have a few questions for him, but the records we found don't implicate him. There's a file on you about a foot thick. How can a High School and College football star get a 'C' in Phys Ed?"

"Easier than you'd think," I said, laughing. It was a personal thing between the teacher and me. He'd have flunked me if he could have.

"They seem to know everything the three of you did for the last 10 years. Must have cost them a fortune."

"Anything else interesting."

"Yeah, Mitch Sugai's journals and work notes."

"We'll probably never get them for that murder."

"I thought it was a suicide?"

I shook my head. "They were feeding him hallucinogenic drugs, but I don't think we'll ever be able to prove it."

The pack of reporters shifted toward me. I gave them the 'aw shucks' expression.

Yes, I'm glad to have her back.... It was no big deal, I was just following a hunch... Oh, a nick or two—no real damage....No I don't think it will ruin my professional reputation....You'd have to ask Ms. Gustafsson....

As the reporters fanned out for other sound bites, and the crowd thinned, I could see Dinah Washington across the street. I walked over to see her.

"I see you found her, praise Jesus."

"Yes, ma'am. It probably won't be long before I'll want to throw her back."

She shook her head, grinning.

"I'm going to end up working for you pretty soon, won't I, all the car rentals I owe you for."

"Oh, no, all your bills with me are taken care of."

"Oh, no, Miz Dinah. You have a right to make some money here."

"It's not me. Although I would. Mr. Tom Chesney, bless his soul, said Kaiser Electronics was paying your bill. I been praying for him and his family ever since he got shot. That poor little boy. I sure hope somebody's taking care of him."

I looked back at Max.

"I think he's got a guardian angel."

She followed my gaze.

"That Lonnie boy was always doing for others, even when he didn't have nothing himself. I think the Lord took special interest in him since the devil got his mama. She always was trouble, especially for that Collins man."

"Collins?"

"Pearl McCoy wasn't more than a girl of fifteen when she ended up in a family way as they used to say. She claimed it was a local teacher named Collins. Later a blood test showed the father was a boy went off to the army and later got himself killed in Vietnam, Jimmy Kaiser."

"But the damage was done for Collins?"

"It wasn't just an accusation; he had been with the girl. He didn't know himself until after the blood tests. He lost his teaching job. They still had morals clauses in those days."

Bad enough to be accused of fooling around with an underage girl without actually being guilty of it. Even without proof of paternity, the inability to deny such a thing would probably be the end of a teaching career.

"Any idea what happened to him?"

"Well, his wife left him. He moved to Asheville—think he had a brother or something there—but he wasn't there for long. We heard he eventually killed himself."

Longstreet escorted Carla and Nina across to join us.

"C'mon Trey, we have to go up and talk with the cops," Nina said. "And I'm not going anywhere without you."

"A bodyguard's work is never done," I answered.

"I'm serious, Trey. I want you with me. No sneaking off playing cop. I want you to promise."

"Promise."

We walked across the road to the station.

"If you hadn't wandered off the last time, they wouldn't have got me."

I laughed. "The last thing you said to me was: '…get the hell out of here. I need some rest'.

"You should have known better than to believe me."

"You have a point."

"Some security guy knocked on my door saying you were hurt. When I opened it there was a big guy with a gun and the crazy lady.

They let me grab some clothes, so when I got a chance I palmed the ring."

"Carla figured out the clue, days later."

"It was obvious, Trey."

"Apparently not to me."

"Well, it's over anyway I guess."

"All over but the shouting," Carla said.

She was a sure bet for some of the shouting.

Chapter 45

I couldn't look Hatch in the eye. We were face to face across the same conference table in that pine room at the resort. I kept thinking about Ferguson, who kept threatening me with jail and fighting the urge to laugh. I suspect Hatch was reminded of the same thing.

Nina was the one on the spot, but Chandler spent most of his effort scowling at me. She wouldn't talk without me in the room, and he really hated the idea of me being here without his approval.

"They didn't really say much to me," she was saying. "They fed me, let me shower sometimes. But most of the time I spent down in the vault alone. The crazy lady did keep asking me one question. She wanted to know if Trey and my mother were close."

"You mean his mother, don't you?"

"No, I thought the same thing. She started screaming at me. She wanted to know about my mother, Leilani."

Chandler stared at me. Like I knew.

"She really hated you, Trey. Her voice would go up about 2 octaves every time she mentioned you."

"I have that effect on women."

Nina rolled her eyes. Hatch laughed.

"That's the only time I remember any of us being mentioned."

"Are you sure you don't know who the third man is?"

Along with Pearl Maitland, Nina saw three other guys while in captivity. George and Patton were the kidnappers at her door, and they guarded her most of the time, but the third guy she only saw once. He didn't seem to match any of the players we knew, nor was he a known felon.

"No. I told you I didn't recognize him."

"Didn't they mention his name or call him something?"

"She never addressed him by name. They talked about a lot of people, but nothing that would make me link a name to him."

"He has to be somebody we know," he grumbled. "Let's go over it again."

"Look, I woke up. He and the crazy lady were talking."

"Pearl Maitland?"

Nina shrugged. "Whatever her name is. They talked for another minute or so, then he left."

"And you didn't hear anything they said?"

"No, I didn't hear anything they said." I could hear her teeth grinding.

"Listen, maybe we should call it a night…" I tried to interject.

"Hey, you're only here as a courtesy. You can leave any time," he snapped.

"Am I under arrest?" Nina asked, way too calmly.

"No of course not…"

"Then we're both leaving."

She headed toward the door. Not wanting to ruin her dramatic announcement, I stood, winked at Hatch and followed her out.

Carla was waiting when we got to the room.

"Max says you can take the helicopter in the morning if you wanted to go to the hospital." She paused expectantly for a moment. "Marsh called, too."

"Hospital?" Nina asked.

"His mother's having surgery. He's going to be with her."

"Trey, you can't let yourself be dragged back in to your mother's chaotic life."

"I never said I was going," I tried to protest.

Carla smiled knowingly at me. "He's going. If that psychotic bitch died and he wasn't there, he'd torture himself for life."

The really annoying thing was that she was right. I would go, get myself emotionally knotted up again.

"*I* won't go," Carla said emphatically. Ruby Jean actually tried to stab the girls when we were kids—messed up, of course. Carla never forgave her. I'm not sure I did either.

"I wouldn't ask either of you. Hell, I don't know if *I'm* going."

"I'll go with you," Nina said.

My cell phone rang. Nina grabbed it. "Mr. Hughes' mobile phone, how may I direct your call?… Well, hello Brian… Oh, I'm just fine thanks. Trey was really heroic... Oh, of course Brian, I'm sure you were a valuable source of information. You saved my life, too...Yes, he's right here," she handed me the phone. "Brian Cavanaugh."

Oh, great. "Cavanaugh?"

"You could have let me know. What am I supposed to do now? I have all these unanswered questions."

"Questions?"

"For example, Harry Maitland doesn't have a birth certificate."

"I don't care."

"He's a phony! Don't you think the cops might want to know?"

"They'll probably find out."

"Should I send it to them?"

"They won't be able to use it. It was obtained illegally."

"They could say it was an anonymous tip. I hear the FBI boss lady is kind of hot. Maybe I could help her out, break the ice."

"Still reading other people's e-mail?"

"Keeping an eye on the cops. Some guy named Chandler e-mailed his brother about her."

"That's invasion of privacy!"

"Sure it was. The state police are already monitoring his transactions, I just went along for the ride."

"Good-bye, Cavanaugh."

"Wait! What am I supposed to do with all this research?"

It was a truly evil laugh I left him with.

Chapter 46

"This isn't going to work," Nina said.

"Would you rather have one of the waterbeds?"

I was comfortable. In fact I was just about to fall asleep. Nina wasn't that big on talking in bed, but when she did it was always one of those last-all-night, pain in the ass kind of 'where can we go from here' jobs. She never worked from the quick answer and off to sleep subject list, it's got to be me and her, her and Carla, me and Carla or something even more complicated. I knew she wasn't talking about the bed, but I hoped if I was obtuse enough she'd let me sleep.

"I was talking about Carla," she said emphatically.

"We'll be OK, kid… honest. We might not be the same, but Carla and I will make peace."

"I don't know, you really hurt her this time."

"Makes us even."

"Oh, come on. You don't believe that."

"She cut us out, you know. We could have helped with all this insecurity jazz, and her hospitalization, but instead…"

"We cut *her* out, don't you see that? We were a couple. We spent all our emotional energy one each other. We left her to fend for herself."

"Bull," I said. "She could have come to either one of us at any time. She didn't know about us, remember?" *Gotcha!*

While we were on the subject of lies and deception, she had a pretty big one to answer to me on.

"I don't know, maybe she… sensed it. Anyway, she never really…" she caught me grinning. "All right, I did it! I told her about us, OK? You happy?" She began crying. One of those slow and steady, cry-all-night, kind of jags. Figuring she might be need it, I let her go for a while. She would have soaked my shirt—if I was wearing one.

"This is my fault. I came between you two."

"Oh, be serious," I joked. "You've always been in the way."

"No, I mean this new feud between you and Carla. It's because I came between you two. She's angry because she feels like you picked me over her."

"She said that?"

"Of course not. She might never say it out loud, but wouldn't she have confided in you, otherwise?"

"Lot of ego… you thinking it's all about you."

She smacked my chest with an open hand.

"We have always been able to trust one another because we knew we wouldn't take sides against on another," she said.

I raised both eyebrows. Those two have been ganging up on me since day two. I didn't meet Nina until the second day of school.

"Oh, You know what I mean. Never anything earth shattering. Then this thing comes along, and she doesn't know what to do. She couldn't very well ask you whether she should tell me, could she?"

"Why not?"

"You'd have had to tell *me*."

"No, I wouldn't."

"But you're in love with me… we can't have secrets between us."

"You mean like you told me when Carla learned about us?"

"That's different."

"Of course it is. How silly of me."

"Look, I'm not doing very good at this."

"Good. Can we have this conversation tomorrow?"

"No. We have to work this out."

"In the morning."

"We can't keep doing this to Carla."

"Carla? I think I've been missing something." I tried my best Groucho.

"You can't joke out of this."

"I'll keep trying."

She said nothing. I rolled to my back, ready to sleep.

I had almost got there, when she tried her next tack.

"Trey?"

"Hmm?"

"Do you ever feel guilty?"

"Not for long."

She smacked my chest again, hard. I don't think she realizes how much that stings. Then again…

"Be serious!"

"Then be specific. What do you want me to feel guilty about?"

"You and me. Did you ever feel guilty about us?"

"No."

"Never? Not even about Carla?"

"I felt guilty about not telling her, but I didn't have to... did I?"

"You're going to keep throwing that in my face aren't you?"

"Every chance I get."

She was quiet again, but this time I wasn't fooled. I waited patiently

"I did," she finally said.

"Felt guilty about us?"

"Carla said she was OK with it but..."

"When exactly did you tell her?"

"In the beginning."

It didn't make sense. If Carla knew all along, why would Nina suddenly have the guilts?

"Why would you feel guilty about us all of a sudden?" I rolled to my side facing her again, "Especially since Carla knew about us."

"I don't want to talk about that." She shifted uncomfortably. "I just wondered if you ever thought of Carla... you know, while we were together."

"You mean, did I think about her instead of you? Of course not, when I'm with you it was about us. When I'm with Carla it's about her and I."

"What about the three of us?"

"Then," I said, chuckling, "it's about you two. I never get a word in anyway."

"I can't date you anymore, Trey," she blurted.

Then the tears. I just let her run for a couple of minutes without interrupting. She sniffed and snuffled against my wet chest. I was really kind of confused. She had broken up with me last fall. No tears, no guilt.

"I don't know darlin'," I said. "You seem to be taking the news a lot worse than last time."

"I'm sorry, Trey."

"It's OK, kid."

"I made such a mess of things. With you. With Carla."

"Stop that. We tried it, it didn't work. You didn't ruin anything. We'll work it all out."

"Don't be so noble and forgiving. I don't deserve it."

"Hey! No regrets, huh? Beating yourself up won't solve anything. So the romance didn't work out—I still love you."

"After what I did…" She stopped.

"What is it you did that you're not telling me?"

The tears started again. No crying, no sobbing, but the full waterworks.

"Tell me."

She shook her wet face.

"We never did do any good hiding things. Why are you so intent on being miserable about this?"

"I can't tell you."

Fine with me. I was never a big fan of these late night, empty-out-your-soul conversations anyway. When I go to bed, the goal is to sleep. I have no problems with the usual sexual alternatives, but upright and dressed is my preferred motif for far reaching conversations.

"I cheated on you…well, sort of."

Cheated? Sort of? Cheated is like pregnant, dead, or married. No middle ground. I know some of these people apply that 'lust in your heart,' or 'emotional relationship' standard to cheating, but that's just silly. You never really choose how you feel, only what you do.

"Define sort of." Boy, I certainly *sounded* calm.

"Bryce Jordan."

"Nina!" I sat straight up.

Jordan was our *wunderkind* red-shirt freshman quarterback. Plenty of attitude, lots of skill, brains of a guava fruit. If he was half as good at anything as he thought he was, he'd be a pretty good guy to have around. This was pathetic. Even if she did cheat, she should have *did* better.

"It was a mistake. It was after the Cincinnati game, and you and I had split and I guess I was feeling a little vulnerable."

"Jordan? You should have felt stupid. I can't believe you took up with 'Junior'."

"I thought you liked Byrce?"

"I suppose in a twisted way, I do. It doesn't mean I'd let him date…"

"Your sister? That's what you were thinking, weren't you. I'm still your kid sister. Besides, this isn't about Bryce Jordan. This is about me." She latched onto my hand. "I will always love you Trey, but this relationship just doesn't fit me right now. I need to reach out, look around. Besides, you and Carla were always better at this than we were."

"Carla and I were never like this. I mean sure, we fooled around a little as kids…"

Well, I wasn't daft enough to believe just because we got back together for a couple of days every thing was going to be like it was, but I didn't expect another shot in the head either. Like her I wasn't taking it as well this time.

"So this was what?? One time for the old times? Or did you decide this after you ran out of fresh air in that shelter?"

"I just couldn't tell you… hurt you."

It was a tough thing, but I guess I did sort of know. Didn't hurt less though. On thing really did bug me a little.

"Jordan?"

"It was just that once. I mean, he's no Trey Hughes."

"Got that right."

She snuggled up against me. I guess she was ready to go to sleep.

"*Bryce* Jordan?"

She smacked my chest again.

"Hey! I should do that to you, so you know how it feels."

She covered up and rolled away, giggling.

I was drifting off, finally.

"Trey?" She breathed in my ear.

"Hmm."

"You sure you can forgive me? I mean we're going to be OK, right? Still friends?"

"Go to sleep, Nina" I grunted, "and quit asking stupid questions."

She kissed my neck. "I Love you."

"Yeah, yeah."

Chapter 47

Nina shook me in the morning.

"Figured you'd want an early start, since you're going to Asheville," she said.

"I never said I was going," I grumbled.

"Oh please. You couldn't live with yourself if you didn't. I'm even going with you."

It's early in the morning when I hate the women who know me too well the most. The fact that she was right made me even more aggravated about it. Besides, on this of all mornings she should know better than to be *that* cheerful.

"We can go downstairs and have breakfast," she said, happily.

Good. I knew just what to have to get even.

Fortifying myself with a big bowl of grits—just for Nina's benefit—eggs, and bacon, we rode Max's helicopter to Asheville.

"What about Carla?" Nina asked.

"She would never come. You know how she feels about my m… about Ruby Jean."

She clicked angrily. I was obviously answering the wrong question.

"I mean," she said, "maybe you and Carla should try again… you know, since we split up."

I said nothing.

"I remember you two used to be pretty close…"

"Hey! Just 'cause you quit a job doesn't mean you get to name your replacement. I have managed to find a woman or two without your help, you know."

"You sound angry."

No foolin'. I was going to get over having Nina leave me. I was even putting on a credible illusion of not being devastated by it, but I would be damned if I was going to let *her* tell me what to do about it.

I went back to saying nothing.

"You're not mad at me are you?"

She was sitting up front, with Rhodes. As she spoke, she turned back with a huge grin. I thumbed my nose at her. I sure wanted to be mad at her, but it was Nina… I'd never make it stick.

"You got two options, pest," I grumbled angrily. "Do the job yourself, or butt out."

"Just for that," she said, laughing, "I'm not going to show you what I brought for you."

"I thought you just said I wasn't getting any more of those kind of goodies."

"That's not what I'm talking about, fathead." She held up a canvas tote.

I felt myself hinting at a smile. "Just checking."

I was shocked to find my sister at the hospital. I had assumed she had heard, but, to be honest, I would never have flown in from Dayton.

"I guess I had to," Marsha explained.

I nodded. "Nina made me come."

"I did not!" She complained. "I just told him he'd never forgive himself."

"No coercion there," Marsha said.

"Certainly not when she actually *is* my conscience. You left my girl behind?"

"I had to travel fast to get here. I left her with her daddy."

"You go in to see her?"

"No." A shadow crossed her face. "I guess I couldn't. There's still time if you want to stick your head in."

I knew how she felt. It was OK, even important, to be there, but facing her was something completely different. Too much anger, too much pain.

"Fifth floor," she said as if I was going up to see her instead of staying in the surgical waiting room.

I realized Nina and I were walking down the hall together. "You don't have to come," I told her.

"Yeah, I know," she said, never breaking stride.

Ruby Jean looked old. Her face was drained of color, her eyes dull and lifeless. All those years, she never really looked like a 50-year old woman. It had always been kind of a Dorian Gray thing.

"Hello, Michael," she said, softly.

"Hey Mom,"

"Do I look that bad? It's been a long time since you called me Mom."

We smiled at each other. The first genuine smile we shared in a long time.

"They tell me your sister is here."

"I saw her."

"Is that her hovering in the doorway?"

"Nina," I said.

"Good, they found her." She waved toward the door. "Hey, baby."

I leaned over and kissed her forehead. Warm, but clammy.

"You rest, huh?" I said. "They'll come to get you in a little bit."

"Take care… Trey." I was surprised, she never called me Trey.

"She looked terrible," Nina said as we got on the elevator. "I mean I used to be scared to death of her. But she looks so…"

"Tired."

"Yeah. Just not scary at all."

Brad Carlyle met us at the elevator door.

"Look, I'm going to go downstairs, get something to eat. You want me to get something for you?"

We assured him we were OK. Then joined Marsh in the waiting room.

I really was OK for an hour or so...No, it was probably more like 15 minutes before I started to get a little jumpy. They watched me pace for a minute, then Nina reached into her little canvas bag.

"I know how you get freaked out in hospitals and you've been in quite a few lately. I thought you might need a diversion."

She pulled out a set of chessmen and a board. It startled me for a moment, because Nina wasn't a very good player. My sister was.

"Are you three going to conspire against me for the rest of my life?" I grumbled.

They shrugged at each other. "No reason not to," Nina said.

"C'mon little brother," Marsh said, beginning to set the board. "I'll even let you win a game or two."

"My ass." She could beat me, sure, but I didn't need any help from her.

My cell phone interrupted about an hour later.

"Trey? Oh, man, you're just not going to believe this! It's just so absolutely fucked up even I don't believe it…"

"Cavanaugh…"

"I mean I knew old man Maitland was hiding some thing but, oh geez..."

"Cavanaugh, could you for once in your life start with the fucking point?"

"They're brother and sister."

I really am just going to kill him one day.

"Who?"

"Harland Maitland, Esquire was born Harold Mason McCoy in Buncombe County NC. He's Pearl McCoy's older brother."

"Well, that might explain some of George's instability."

"Man, what kind of guy marries his sister?"

"I don't know." I'm not sure I care.

"I also found another pair of ringers, too. Karl Werner's real name is William Collins. His son William Jr., or Billy, is wanted by the DEA for trafficking Meth. He's got a truckload of aliases including Bruce Coleman—he's the 'C' in C&M Industries, Barry Carpenter, and Brad Carlyle, who owns a shipping company in Portland, Oregon."

"That makes him my mother's husband."

"No shit?"

Made sense. Ruby Jean married her connection. The fact that I was her son probably came as a big shock to him, but he was probably glad to use her as a distraction to me. I looked around the room.

"Has he come back?" I asked Nina.

"Your stepfather? No haven't seen him, why?"

"Just a long time to go for a sandwich."

It could be a coincidence. Collins is a fairly common name. I was probably getting a bit paranoid. On the other hand, it was clear that my new stepfather was a major drug trafficker, which was something I was going to have to deal with. But what were they up to? The surviving partner clause in those partnership agreements practically encouraged mayhem. Were they just after Nina, or was Max a target as well? Would they still be trying?

What if Ruby Jean's heart condition was helped along by something else? Something like maybe digitalis. As a long time amphetamine user, no one would suspect the use of something else to affect her heart. Was I here out of the way while Collins and Collins tried to take out Max? Or, were Collins *pere and fils* making a run for it? It was probably nothing, but...

"Got to go." I said to everybody as I hung up.

"Go! Go where?" Nina asked. Marsh echoed the sentiment in more colorful language.

"Back to Pineville."

"Why?"

"Cops. A few questions," I tried to sneak out.

"Liar." There are days I really hate Marsh.

"Look guys, it's probably nothing. I might even be back before she wakes up."

"I'll go with you," Nina said.

"No," I tried to sound casual. "You stay and keep Sis company."

I kissed them quick and headed out.

"Trey!" My sister called at my back.

I raised my hand in a wave. I had lied to them, but I left them safe anyway. They would be furious when they found out, of course. At this rate Ruby Jean was going to be the only person still talking to me.

Chapter 48

Jim Rhodes was lounging in the cafeteria. "Hey, what's up Youngblood?"

"We have to get back," I said flatly "Max might be in danger."

Even though he was older, he was in the cockpit firing up the rotors by the time I got to the helicopter. In no time, we were screaming along just above the reaching treetops running wide open. I flinched by reflex at a treetop I thought was too close.

"You OK, Trey?"

"Long as you don't hit anything."

I called the cops while we were on the way and had them fan out around town. I called to Hatch up at the resort to make sure Carla and AJ were safe. That left Max's house to me. If we were lucky, he'd just be surprised to see me.

"Why can't we land at the clearing? I can come with you"

"No. We'd lose the element of surprise. If we came thumping down into the clearing, they would be out and in ambush before we could get out of the 'copter. It might be slower, getting there by foot, but it'll also be quieter and sneakier."

"But, if these bad guys are there by now, we don't have time to waste."

"If they're already there we're probably going to be too late. All we can do is take our best shot."

"Guess you're the boss, but I should still come with you."

"We need you here at the bird. We might need a medical evac."

"Oh, come on! You're leaving me on the sidelines."

"Hey, you had to evac George, didn't you?"

"You're going in there alone? You're nuts, you know that?"

"Hell, Rhodey, I hope I am. I'm hoping this is just plain paranoid. If I'm wrong, Max and his loony mom are playing checkers or something and everything is copacetic. It's finding out I'm right that scares me."

He reached under his seat.

"Just in case, brother."

I reached out and took the offered Colt automatic and racked the slide.

"Here's hoping I don't need it."

The clearing he dropped into in the park never seemed big enough for the copter's rotors, but he fit it in anyway.

"You can get back out in a hurry, right?"

I looked at the trees and rock face around him and had my doubts. I guess I insulted him.

"You just hold up your end, sonny boy. Leave the flying to the grownups."

I went up the hill quickly, but not too quickly. If I went up too fast, I would have to stop and recover before I could do anything. By pacing myself I would be running on all cylinders when I got to the danger zone.

I was approaching the house through the woods when I saw a flash of white off to my right. As I got closer I recognized the uncombed shock of white hair and knew who it was attached to.

"Walter!" I hissed.

He didn't jump as high as I suspected he would. He turned warily. I waved toward him. He waved me forward. He was holding an assembly line twin of the Colt nestled in the small of my back.

As I approached, Walter whistled. A pretty good bird call.

"Hey, there son,"

"What are you two up to?"

"We were keeping an eye on Lonnie, in case Pearl showed up. Sure enough, about an hour ago, she shows up with Karl Werner. We've been keeping an eye on them ever since."

"How did you find this place?"

"We've been keeping an eye on Lonnie since he was a kid. You see Jimmy Kaiser was my older brother. He married Pearl before he shipped off to the army. They claimed a blood test proved he was the boy's father, but the test was rigged. He never knew. Hell, I never knew until the real father told me."

"Who's the real father?"

"I am."

Tom had snuck up on us while we were talking.

"My dad was a judge. I guess he didn't want his son involved in what was a pretty ugly scandal at the time. So he fixed it. After

Jimmy was killed, I wanted to come forward, but it would have gotten the judge in trouble, so I held my peace until the judge died."

"Lonnie doesn't know?"

They shook in unison. "We're all just old friends to him."

I nodded.

"I think he's in trouble," I said. "What would you say if I told you Karl Werner's real name was Collins?"

"Collins? You mean as in the teacher Pearl put through hell?"

"It's possible."

"Hey, we'd better get in there!"

"I have a plan to make sure nobody gets hurt. You guys move directly in front of the house, wait exactly 5 minutes, fire a shot, then call the police. After that, keep an eye out. If anybody else comes toward the house, fire another shot. Make sure you stay out of sight the whole time."

"What are you going to be doing?"

"I'll be watching the back," I said.

Walter smiled skeptically "Yeah, right."

The back door was, as usual, not locked. I eased quietly through the kitchen and flattened myself against the far wall. I crouched down to peer around the doorjamb. William Collins was standing near the front door, occasionally peering out the window. He held a Remington pump shotgun in his hands. He seemed to be uncomfortable and nervous about holding a gun—which made him more dangerous—likely to shoot in panic.

Max sat on the couch, all I could see was the back of his head. His mother must have been farther over. The important thing was that I had a clean shot to get to Collins.

The gunshot out front, as I assumed, focused his attention out there, but before I could get across the room, two more shots rang out. Speed and reflexes won out, as I slammed him to the ground, knocking the gun free before he could spin around. The impact put him on the deck 6-8 feet from where the gun hit. Before I could get back to my feet though, that crazy old woman pounced on me, gibbering like a baboon.

As I struggled with her, Collins was rolling toward the gun. Max, hands tied behind him, dove onto the weapon, blocking him. I was still trying to peel her off, when the door opened and Collins Jr. walked in. He pointed his gun toward Max, but before he could act, Pearl screamed into my ear. He swung the gun toward where we were struggling and fired three times. Her scream died as I assumed she was hit. I fell back with her landing on me, reaching for the gun at the small of my back. He was still looking at us, while his father continued to wrestle for the shotgun with Max. Because Lonnie was all arms and legs anyway, he was holding his own in spite of having his hands tied.

The guys out front fired a couple of rounds. Billy stepped back to shoot out the door. I prayed those fools out there had the sense to keep their heads down. William won the battle for the shotgun, and Billy turned back to Max. I now had the gun in my hand, but it was still stuck under Pearl. The reason he had stopped shooting this way was that he thought he had got us both. I saw no reason to correct their assumption by wriggling out from under her. Slow and easy does it.

"It's just too bad, Max," Billy said. "We would have just kept leeching off your company for years, but that crazy bitch over there…" he waved his pistol toward her, "just had to kill that girl. What a gangfuck! First of all, how tough can it be to kill a girl in a wheelchair? All she had to do was shoot her, or push her down some steps or something, but noooo… she had to do it fancy! The kidnapping goes off without a hitch, then George gets freaked out and that idiot Brunson tries to make a fast buck. Next thing we know, cops and feds are crawling up every orifice. Then these idiots try to kill all the witnesses and they fucked that too. Now, I got to run and I need all the assets I can get. With George out of commission, and you gone, Daddy here can use his power at Kaiser to bleed the place dry."

He shook his head sadly, then turned to look at us.

"Crazy bitch. I ought to shoot her again. Too bad about that boy, Trey," he chuckled. "Won me 10 large in that bowl game last winter. Sorry, sonny. You were just standing in the way of progress.

He turned back. "Well?" he asked his father.

The old man looked at Max, then shook his head sadly.

"Gutless," he said. "Never had the *cajones* for this kind of stuff, Max, he always drew the line when it came to killing. Going to have to do it myself, I guess."

He raised the gun to aim.

"I think not," I said.

He spun around to face me as I shot him. I shot again, and his gun dropped. He fired into the ground as he fell left toward the door. I kept the Colt trained on William Senior.

"Drop it."

He dropped the shotgun as I began easing out from under Pearl. I checked her pulse as I drew my cell phone and punched a button.

"Need you up here yesterday," I told Rhodes.

I didn't even listen to his response. William was untying Max.

"He was my son," He said, "I couldn't do it, but I couldn't stop him. I mean…"

He stopped because nobody was willing to listen. Max came over and joined me.

"Got to move. Grab the first aid kit, and we'll move her to the landing area."

She was bleeding pretty badly, but I was guessing she was going to make it. As soon as he could, Max was back and we began carrying her out. Tom and Walter came out of the woods to help. Rhodes, true to his word, had no trouble and almost beat us to the clearing. Max, Tom and I piled in, with Pearl on the deck, and screamed out toward Asheville.

"You saved my life," Max said as we did our best at first aid on his mother.

"I owed you one," I answered.

"Collins is gone," Agent Nansen said. "By the time your pal Walter got back to the cabin, he had already left."

"There's a shock." I had assumed that he would, but he wasn't that dangerous.

We were back in the surgical waiting room. Nina was furious because she didn't get to help. Marsh thought I took an irrational risk. I was going to get the icy glare, times two, for the rest of the day.

"Where is Walter?" Tom asked.

"He came with me. He's with Max down in the trauma unit. Looks like his mother might make it, thanks to you, but she's probably going to be paralyzed."

I didn't care, honest. I helped her because there was no way for me to do otherwise, but any sympathy for her was lost 10 years ago on that Dayton street. For her to be paralyzed would be poetic justice, her vultures come home to roost, but there's a lot of pain and misery and frustration that part of me really couldn't wish even on her. On the other hand, there was a little character in the back of my head dancing a little jig over her misfortune.

"Make sure we get a statement before you head back." She said to me.

"Head back?"

"Carla said you were leaving tonight?"

"I'm not. I guess she is."

"She said we. I just assumed it was you."

"Must be traveling with AJ. He's got his NFL mini-camp this weekend."

Nina tried to hide behind Susan. Apparently, Nina knew her plans as well, but Carla had no intention of saying good-bye to me.

"I might stay here," I said. "I hear the State cops are hiring. I could be the next Steve Ferguson."

Marsh's jaw dropped. Nina looked pained.

"Just don't think about joining the bureau," Susan said, chuckling, "or *I'll* shoot you."

When I laughed, Marsh realized I had been joking. She shook her fist.

"Seriously? Maybe Houston for a couple of days."

"You're always welcome," Marsh said.

"What about me?" Nina asked.

"Of course, you're welcome, too."

"No. I mean, where am I supposed to go?"

I smiled. "Open ended question."

"Ha, ha. What if I wanted to go somewhere?"

"You can go anywhere you want," I said. "You're going to end up pretty rich?

"Alone?"

I shrugged. "You fired your bodyguard."

She looked disappointed, almost panicked.

"Of course… you can always invite a guest. Where are we going?"

"Actually I want to stay here for a few days, relax. Keep me company?"

I smiled. We both knew the answer, but I could at least let her suffer.

"So what next for the FBI?"

"Back to Charlotte—organized crime, RICO cases… I've got a desk full. We'll keep looking for Collins, but he's probably already left the country. Going to be hard to prove conspiracy anyway."

"Dead men can't testify. Well, good luck." We shook hands. She took a step then came back and kissed me on the cheek.

Nina smiled at me. I winked at her.

"I just can't believe you saved the crazy woman's life," she said.

"He kind of had to," Marsh said, "She sort of saved his life."

It wasn't because she meant to, and I really don't think that was why.

"Actually, it surprised me, too. It's weird, I think I could have killed her… maybe still could… but I couldn't just let her die."

"Carla's never going to forgive you for this one."

Carla was the worst of us for holding a grudge, and there was no doubt she was justified on this one. Forgiveness was going to be difficult, if possible.

"Got to have faith," I said. Almost like I believed it. It was up to Carla, not me, to choose between love and war. Love was always my choice.

"She'll come around." I said, hopefully.

"You're expecting a lot from her," Marsh said.

"I know."

Chapter 49

Carla moved from the house in our old Dayton neighborhood to a downtown apartment with a balcony overlooking the Great Miami River. Since the building had an elevator, she insisted on a top floor apartment. AJ helped her move in at the end of July. One thing led to another, so I didn't get a chance to see it until early October.

She greeted me with a cheerful smile. "Hey, stranger."

"Hey, Ms. Lawyer, congratulations on your bar exam."

"How's your head?"

I had been knocked out during the game in Washington the previous Sunday. I really could have kept playing, but they benched me as a precaution. My team, the Carolina Panthers, had an off week, so I played up my head to get a couple of extra days to visit back in Dayton. I had been invited to the Panthers' training camp at the last minute, signed as a free agent, and earned a backup spot at linebacker. I was also on the kickoff team, which was where I got leveled Sunday.

"It's not that big a deal. I just got my bell rung."

"They said it was a concussion."

"No worse than that Penn State game a couple of years ago."

"Just remember: They might call it the 'Suicide squad' but that's a poor excuse for getting yourself killed."

"I do believe the little woman cares."

She responded with an invective that was neither lady, nor lawyerlike.

"Sis sends her love." I said, taking the easy chair.

"I still can't believe she quit school."

"Being a vice-president and major shareholder in an international corporation is a pretty big thing—and an education in and of itself, no? Besides, she didn't exactly quit. She's signed on at UNC-Asheville for the next semester. You could take an active role in the company yourself, you know. Kaiser is quickly working itself out of the clutches of Woodland, Bancroft. They could use a smart lawyer."

"Worried about your share?"

"Worried, hell. I'm still amazed Max gave me a percentage of the company."

"Well, you did save his life."

"I owed him one. He saved mine."

"I got an e-mail from Alex. He loves Seattle. Lee got a job at a station in Tacoma, said to tell you they promised her no 'bingo'. What does that mean?"

"That's between me and Lee."

"Oh, come on."

"Just means they promise to take her seriously."

"Do you think those two might be rushing things? Sharing an apartment?"

"I don't know. They seem to like each other. I suppose as long as they set good ground rules it should work out."

I was surprised how fast their relationship had progressed, too, but I choose to be optimistic.

"I think it's awfully risky."

"You're just not a romantic. You can pester them at Thanksgiving dinner, find out for yourself?"

Since I have a Sunday game scheduled in Charlotte Thanksgiving week, I nominated myself to host Thanksgiving dinner for the extended family.

"Did Dad tell you he's bringing a date?" she asked.

Oh, no you don't. "I'm going to try fixing a deep-fried turkey. They tell me they're pretty good."

She eyed me suspiciously.

"OK, Trey, What do you know?"

"About your dad? He's bringing a colleague for Thanksgiving, like you said."

"You rat! You've met her, haven't you?"

"I spoke to her briefly. She wanted to talk to me when Pop called to make sure it was OK."

"What's she like?"

"Well...She's a woman."

"Oh, you're funny."

"Thanksgiving. You'll meet her. Find out for yourself."

Before she could respond the door swung open. Katarina Weiss bounced into the apartment. She bounces everywhere. As far as I can tell, my stepsister is a creature of pure energy. Since I was playing football and on the road a lot, Carla agreed to host Kat while she finished high school here in the States.

She bounded into my lap and began hugging and kissing.

"Kit Kat!" I said, laughing.

"It is great to see you big brother."

"How's school?"

"It is a bore. I have made great friends, they invite me to go hang, but *Tante* Carla won't let me." She pouted miserably.

"Hey, I just want to make sure she knows her way around a little better before she goes running off to parties in the middle of the night."

"You must help, Trey—she is worse than Mama."

I get paid to take chances on the football field, but that's not dangerous. Refereeing a battle between any two women is suicidal.

"Hey, don't put me in the middle of this. You both have a bit of a point, but you two *roommates* get to work out your own rules. Maybe you should have a party here."

"What?" They almost chorused.

"Invite your friends here, Kat. Once Carla gets to know some of them, she might be inclined to let you go hang with them."

They both looked incredibly skeptical.

"I don't think I have time to plan a party," Carla said.

"You don't have to. It's Kat's party. She does the planning and the preparation, and the clean-up—you only help where and if you want to."

Both of them looked at me as if I'd grown a third eye.

I shrugged. They wanted my opinion, I gave it.

"Can I go to the football game tonight?"

"Soccer, you mean," Carla corrected looking at me. I smiled back.

"Sure. Do you have a ride?"

"Yes. Erica is going."

"Good. Call if you get stuck somewhere."

"Thanks, *Tante*."

She was dancing out of the room when she stopped.

"Did Papa tell you the good news?" Kat asked.

"No, what?"

"He is being promoted. He is now Lieutenant…"

"Lieutenant Colonel."

"Yes. He is very surprised."

"I'll bet. That's great! I'll have to call him."

As she left the room, Carla asked, "Why does she call me *Tante*?"

It was German for aunt. I suspected Kat used it as a friendly dig, implying not only a family relationship, but also a put down as old-fashioned or just plain old.

"Term of endearment," I answered.

"What does it mean?"

I held my hands out. "Ask her."

"That bad?"

"I can only tell you what, she's the one who can tell you why."

"Good news about your dad, huh?"

"Yeah."

"But I'm a bit surprised," she said. "What's the point of promoting the Major now, I thought he was retiring?"

"End of the year."

"Won't do him much good, then."

"Sure it will. His pension is based on his last rank. Pays to have friends, doesn't it?"

"You think Max is behind it?"

"Of course. Suddenly, the Carolina Panthers are willing to invite me to training camp, and the Major gets a promotion. Lee has no trouble getting work, and a Law school opening appears at the school AJ wants to attend. And as much as I hate to say it, I'm sure you're getting juicier offers than some of your fellow Case graduates. I'm not saying we don't deserve what we're getting, but if a word in the right ear can make things go more smoothly…"

"It's not very fair to everybody else, though, is it?" She swung herself onto the couch. "If we get jobs because of Max, we're not succeeding on our own merits."

I moved over next to her, swinging her legs across my lap.

"Did you think AJ was qualified for law school?"

"Sure."

"Do you think I've been playing OK?"

"You've been great."

"There you go. Max got the Panthers to take a look at me; they liked the way I performed, so they signed me. If I wasn't any good,

I'd be watching the games on TV. All we ever get are opportunities, C. What we do with them is up to us."

She shook her head. "They were opportunities we wouldn't have had without Max Kaiser."

"You don't want the chance, don't take it. But you also have to turn down any leads that would come from your Dr. Fennally, Me, AJ, Lee, or anybody else you know."

She slapped my hand, which was absently rubbing her feet. "Stop that. I'm still mad at you."

"It's not the same you know," she continued. "Max has influence only because he's rich. Dr. Fennally is a highly respected educator. He recommends people on their merit."

"So he's recommended you to people because he thinks you would be good at the job?"

"Exactly."

"But if Max thinks you would be good at the job, you don't want the job? Even if it's a job you want?"

"I just wouldn't know if I got the job because I was good or because I was connected to Max Kaiser."

"Who cares? They might hire you because you're a woman or because they like how you laugh at the managing partner's lousy jokes. They might hire you because they saw you on TV. Why they hire you is irrelevant. It's all about what you do when you get the opportunity. Take all the advantages you can get, kid, you deserve them all."

"I still feel like it's an unfair advantage."

"You can always join the family business. Or is it unethical to work for your sister?"

"Bite me."

I leaned over her, as if to kiss… or bite. "If you insist."

She shook her fist at me. "You do…"

"You said…" I mocked.

"I'm still mad at you. Besides, you're still in love with my sister."

She had me there.

"For all the good it does me. But then, I love you, too."

"You have no conscience at all do you?"

"*You* love Nina, why should I feel guilty?"

"You're going to have to decide, you can't be in love with us both."

Of course I could. It was the only insurmountable fact in my universe. I might be able to date only one of them, but I would love them both at least until I died. Loving them was easy, choosing between them....

"Sez you. We're all grown adults here. How we feel is one thing. What we do about it is a totally different question."

"You can't just trade us off whenever things become difficult, Trey."

"You can't just hide behind your sister, either. Whatever we do or don't do is our choice."

"Nina loves you."

"She also left me," I pointed out.

"She'll be back," she said.

"No. I don't think so."

"Bryce Jordan?" she teased.

"My ass. She will do better than Junior. She already has."

"You met him?"

"Rod. He's not bad for a good 'ol boy. You might meet him Thanksgiving"

"Trey?" She smiled at me.

"Yeah?"

"There is such a thing as *too* damned understanding. It's great that you two can still be friends," She slapped my hand, "but inviting him to Thanksgiving dinner... Will you stop playing with my feet… inviting him to Thanksgiving is just nuts."

She went on for another minute or so, but I had stopped listening. Since when was she annoyed by my rubbing her feet?

I ran a finger down the sole of her foot. Toes should curl in reflex. No reaction.

"What did you just do?"

"What?" I knew I had a guilty smile on my face.

"Never mind," she said angrily. "Just quit playing around. I'm still mad at you."

"Yes, dear." I said with sarcasm.

Something had just happened. Maybe she didn't want to talk about it yet, maybe she wasn't completely aware herself, but it seemed likely she was feeling something, a tickle, a buzz, a feather—*something*. Maybe it took four months for the little electrical nerve cells to start making the right connections. She wasn't sure what it was, but that could change. Maybe in time all the connections would be reconnected and things will be the way they used to be, maybe she'd only get some of it back. Maybe it was all a cruel joke, just enough to taunt and torture us with false hope.

The important thing was we could face the new changes the way we always did. We still hadn't sorted out the *last* set of changes, but we were together. It was a start.

3069267

Made in the USA